This is a work of fiction. All characters, organizations and events portrayed in this novel are either products of the author's imagination or used fictitiously.

SHADOWS OF THE KNIGHT

Previously published as Her Fierce Knight.

Cover Design by Erin Dameron-Hill

Copyright © 2016, Second Edition
Dusty Tome Publishing

ISBN: 978-1-7333887-8-8

Shadows
of the Knight

Realm of Honor

MICHELLE MILES

Chapter 1

Princess Laerwen emer'Aranhil Bloodfire stood on the dormant volcano and looked down into the ruin that was once her kingdom. Her gut clenched into a tight knot. The charred black earth still smoked from the recent fires. It still smelled of death. Homes had been burned to the ground. Some had stood centuries including that of the royal palace.

She had climbed this mountain numerous times as a child. She knew every handhold. Every foothold. Every nook and cranny. When things had gone to hell, the safest place for her—she knew—was here on the mountain. She'd paused halfway up to turn and watch the horror play out in front of her. Helpless, all she could do was wait for the sun to come up.

Now it had. The burning dawn revealed the loss of life and devastation.

Looking at the destruction below, one would expect such a result from a volcanic eruption. But the Hin'dar Rhule had not exploded in thousands of years. This destruction was not from the lava that had once flowed. This was from the bloody Fomorians, a race they thought long imprisoned in the Sorrow Lands.

Laerwen wore the voluminous skirt and blouse, both bejeweled with shimmering stones against the red and green silken material, that she'd worn to the previous night's ball. The matching sari was tossed over her shoulder, though she'd lost her veil somewhere in the fray. Glancing down at her attire, she seemed rather out of place in the aftermath of the attack. She jerked off the jewels on her head and flung them to the ground.

Hiram, her father's advisor, trudged up the hill with a slow careful pace. He wasn't as agile as he used to be and she was surprised he'd found her. His long cobalt tunic was smeared with a black streak of blood. The knees of his trousers had a mixture of blood and mud, as though he had knelt by someone's side who might have been dying. His black hair stood in tufts about his dirt-smudged face. It was clear he had been running his long fingers through the thick locks over and over. Worry lines wrinkled his brow and around his mouth. Seeing it etched on his face so prominently did nothing for her nerves.

He paused next to her, his chest heaving as he tried to catch his breath. They stood together to survey their ruined realm. He emitted a little gasp of horror and she knew it was the first he'd seen it from this vantage point. It looked far worse from this distance than on the ground in the midst of it. Tension emanated off him in waves. Tension and distress and sorrow.

"So many lost." He whispered the words, but she still heard.

"Aye." It was the only response she could force past the lump in her throat. She swallowed it hard, regaining her composure. "How did you find me?"

"Every Fire Elf knows this is your favorite place when you want solitude."

And here she thought it to be her secret place.

Many of her people had suffered and died. Those who had survived were now homeless. Displaced. Lost. Even she was displaced and lost. The Fomorians had come and gone with such a fury it was over almost as quickly as it had begun.

"What news?"

"The death toll continues to rise, your highness. Most of our noble leaders are dead."

Her stomach twisted tighter. It sickened her. She knew it was news he had to deliver but she was not prepared for it. The royal palace had been decimated. Only burned out walls remained standing. Still smoking. She had not heard if her parents or her betrothed had survived the attack nor had she seen them among the survivors.

"My parents?" The lump in her throat thickened again making it nearly impossible to swallow past it this time.

"They did not survive." Hiram looked away, blinking furiously. His voice wobbled.

Shock and pain slammed into her. Dead. They were dead. Her parents were gone. The king and queen. That left her as ruler of a ruined realm. Ruler of a kingdom that had nearly been wiped out.

Laerwen sat hard, her head on her knees. Hiram squatted next to her and patted her shoulder. She blinked away the tears that threatened and made a valiant effort to keep it together. To stay strong. She had to for her people. For herself.

"I'm so sorry. There was nothing the healer could do." He said it softly near her ear. Hiram was not always the most heartfelt person but she could hear the sincerity in his voice.

She had to know if her betrothed had survived. He and his family had come to their kingdom to begin the wedding festivities when the Fomorians struck. She was to be married today. "Lord Randir and his people?"

"He has not been found. Most of his people were slaughtered. I pray to the gods he escaped with his life."

She squeezed her eyes shut. She knew she shouldn't feel guilty but she couldn't help it. It was nothing but a senseless act of violence and she knew that. Pain sliced through her. Regret. Guilt. It all pressed on her, threatening to suffocate her.

"Please let me know the minute you find him." Her voice was muffled against her knees. She didn't want to look up yet. She didn't want to see the pain and anguish on Hiram's face. She didn't want his sympathy—it was not something she could handle. It'd make her crumble into a thousand pieces and right now, she needed all her strength.

"Of course."

She sensed movement next to her and knew Hiram stood once again. But he didn't leave her side. Laerwen took two deep breaths before she at last lifted her head. She looked across the expanse of charred earth and a little piece of her died inside all over again.

"What happened, Hiram?" She was still reeling from the horror of it all, trying to piece together what had actually happened and still she could not.

"The Fomorians, highness. They came in the night. Destroyed the outlying villages. Burned the homes, killed the women and children and any man who tried to fight back."

It was hard to believe only hours ago they were at banquet, feasting on roasted meats to celebrate the upcoming wedding. A wedding that would never happen now.

"Your father sent for you. Asked that you and your mother be secreted to safety," Hiram continued, his voice shaky with emotion.

Aye, she recalled that. She had retired for the night to her chamber after the wedding feast. She had yet to prepare for bed and will still dressed in her finery.

"But I never saw my mother," she whispered. She pressed cold fingertips to her lips, forced away the bile that wanted to rise into her mouth.

"Nay," Hiram agreed. "The Fomorians had already stormed the palace by then. It was…too late for them. They…killed the queen while your father watched."

She wanted to retch. Laerwen put her head in her hands. How awful. How awful for her father to watch as they…did things to her mother.

"They killed him next." Hiram paused as he tried to collect his emotions. She heard him take a long breath, expel it.

"How do you know all this, Hiram?"

"You mother's lady-in-waiting was there. Hiding in the wardrobe. She managed to escape. She…saw the whole thing happen. Heard them saying they wanted to do the princess next."

Gods. A wave of nausea hit her. She would have been next. She should have been next. But she had been spared. She hadn't time to gather anything before the man-at-arms—what was his name? Lord Brand? Aye, that was it—and Hiram were at her door, ushering her away from her chamber, taking her through the hidden corridors to safety. Or what she thought was safety.

"You saved my life." She lifted her head and looked at Hiram but he refused to meet her gaze. His cheeks were damp with tears.

"Lord Brand saved your life."

Lord Brand. The brave knight who stepped in front of the oncoming arrow that would have pierced her heart. He died in her arms. She would never forget him.

All the memories pounded into her now and her chest constricted. Her throat tightened. Tears burned the back of her eyes. Gods, no. She would not cry. Not here. Not now. Later. Only when she had time to process her grief and sorrow would she cry.

Laerwen had no idea how the Fomorians had been released from their bonds. But they had landed at the edge of her realm, thirsty for bloodshed. They had been attacked without cause and now the princess was left to pick up the pieces.

"These Fomorians are far more powerful than we," Hiram said. "How is this possible? How is it they escaped the Sorrow Lands?"

"I know not, Hiram. Our meager weapons were no match for them."

The Fire Elves were a people of peace. They had not amassed weapons or an army for they never had the need. Their realm was far remote from the other Elven races. Mayhap in their solitude, they had become lax. They certainly paid the price for that as their weapons were not enough. When the bloody path of the Fomorians led them to the palace doors, the guards had tried desperately to fight against them. To no avail.

But sitting here feeling sorry for herself would not change anything. She lifted her head and pushed to her feet next to Hiram. The breeze ruffled her honey-brown hair, making it blow into her face. Fear and anguish pressed into her. It was as though a fist had punched her in the gut. How could this have happened? What was she going to do with her people now? Many had gathered at the bottom of the mountain, huddled together as they looked to her for guidance.

She had no guidance to give them.

"The Fomorians. Have you identified where they are headed?"

"No, your highness." He halted and looked at her, a thoughtful expression on his face. "Though I should call you 'your majesty' as you are queen now."

"No." Her voice was sharp. "Do not call me that."

"But—"

"No, Hiram." It was too soon.

In the distance, she could see riders approaching. She tensed. Hiram saw them too and took her by the arm. "We must get you out of here."

"Who are they?"

"I cannot say but you must be taken to safety."

She jerked her arm free. "I am the only living royal, Hiram. I must greet them." She may not wish to be queen but she still had a royal duty to perform.

Without waiting for his reply, she started down the slope of the volcano. There were four riders. They didn't seem like Fomorians. Instead they were dressed as Elves which gave her relief…and pause.

She made it to the bottom of the slope as they reared to a halt not far from her. Most of her people had stopped to stare. To see who was coming to them. Hiram joined her, his breath see-sawing in his chest as he puffed to catch it from hurrying down the steep incline.

"Who are they?" she asked, not even winded.

"I don't know highness."

The leader dismounted and walked to her with a confident stride. Though she could see the sorrow on his face as he looked around. He was definitely Elven with the high pointed ears and the angular face. His aristocratic features bespoke of someone highborn, though who he was she didn't know. He dressed in finery but his boots and long riding tunic were covered in dust. The horses were foamy with sweat as though they'd ridden at breakneck speed to get there.

"I am Lord Navin of the Wood Elves. Brother of Crown Prince Andahar and son to King Urdithane." He bowed to her with a flourish. "I'm here to speak with Queen Lucinda and King Aleron of the Fire Elves."

Laerwen stiffened and Hiram did the same next to her. "I'm afraid you're too late, Lord Navin. The king and queen were killed in the attack on our kingdom. How can I assist you? I am their daughter, Laerwen."

His jaw clenched. "You have my condolences, Princess. I'm truly sorry for your loss. I regret my arrival is far too late but we rode as quickly as we could when we discovered the direction the Fomorians had taken."

"You knew of their attack?"

Lord Navin shifted from one foot to the other. "I'm afraid so, your highness. But we were unable to stop them. They are led by a powerful mage named Lorcann. He placed our palace under a dark spell that was only recently lifted. He's also responsible for leveling your kingdom. Once we realized where they headed, Prince Andahar sent me to warn you."

"And you can see for yourself what they did to my kingdom and my people." She swept her hands out to indicate the destruction, unable to keep the bitterness out of her voice. "How were they released from the Sorrow Lands?"

He lowered his head in reverence. "One of our own turned into a Dark Elf. He invoked the dark magic and awakened the mage. The Woodlands suffered too though I confess not as greatly as the Hin'dar Rhule."

She drew in a long breath. If a Wood Elf was responsible for this then she would have the king's explanation. She would know what they intended to do about these Fomorians. Their deeds could not go unpunished. Her family was dead. She wanted vengeance. And she would have it.

"Bloody Wood Elves," she muttered so he wouldn't hear. "And where is this mage now?"

"No one knows, your highness. He has all but disappeared."

"Then I suggest your people find him since you are the ones responsible for these deaths. The blood of the Hin'dar Rhule is on King Urdithane's hands."

Hiram gripped her arm again as though he prepared to pull her away. "Princess—"

"I will not be silenced, Hiram." She spat out the words as she glanced around the wreckage. Then she met Navin's level gaze. She knew what she wanted to do. They couldn't stay here and wait to be slaughtered again. She saw only one other option. "The destruction of the Hin'dar Rhule is the Woodlands fault. I wish to speak with your king at once."

"My king?" Navin repeated. "But your highness, the king—"

"I do not wish to hear excuses. You will take me and all remaining Fire Elves that wish to go to your kingdom for refuge. And I will say my piece to King Urdithane and demand an answer."

Navin pressed his lips together and then gave her a slow nod. "As you wish, your highness. I should be glad to escort you and your people back to the Woodlands."

"I need a moment to speak with my people. We'll gather what we can and leave as soon as possible."

With a nod, he returned to his mount and the other three riders to wait.

Laerwen stared a heated hole in the back of his head. The bloody Wood Elf. "Hiram, are there horses left?"

"Aye, Princess, I believe there are a few remaining."

"Good. We'll take all we can. Gather the people. I wish to speak to them."

"And tell them what?" Her eyes must have flashed fire for he ducked his head. "Forgive my insolent tone. I merely ask what you intend to tell them."

"I intend to tell them we're going to pay a visit to the Wood Elves."

"Are you certain about all of us?" His voice held a note of shock and he blinked wide brown eyes. She didn't miss the surreptitious glance he gave to what was left of their realm.

"Aye, all who wish to go with us to the Woodlands. They're

responsible for this." She waved her hand to encompass the charred land before her. "And they will answer to it."

"Do you think that wise, highness?"

"We have nowhere else to go, Hiram," she snapped.

"It could look as though you're abandoning your kingdom," he warned. "With the king and queen dead—"

"I know. I'm the sole ruler now. But I make the decisions."

She heaved a heavy sigh. She didn't want to think of her parents' deaths. Not now. In time, she would have to face it, but she had to think of her people and what their next steps should be. And at this moment, she knew the only place for them was the Woodlands. Certainly King Urdithane would grant her request for assistance.

"Aye, your highness. I will gather the people as you requested." He bowed his head low, then turned and left.

She watched him go and the hollowness in her chest persisted. She had so many unanswered questions. If the Fomorians had marched across the land, killing, then what of the outlying areas? What of the other people in the realm? How many survivors remained?

She glanced skyward. Would the Skye Elves come down from their demesne to aid in their battle? Because Laerwen knew they would be going to war. It was only a matter of time before they would have to face the Fomorians on the battlefield. And she wanted the Wood Elves to help them fight. They owed it to her and her people.

"Laerwen."

She knew that voice and slowly turned to see Lord Randir behind her. Relief sputtered through her. Her breath hitched in her throat at the sight of his familiar face. She was happy he was alive. Happy to know not all the nobles in the castle had perished.

His face was dirty. His clothes torn and covered in blood—his or someone else's, she couldn't tell. His gaze met hers and time stood still between them as they looked at each other, as though they couldn't believe the other still lived. He started toward her and it was then she noticed his right arm hung limply by his side.

He must have fought them. She could tell he struggled with every step and hurried toward him. As she reached him, he seemed to lose his strength and fall toward her. She threw out her arms and caught him, holding him against her. Her hand landed on his shoulder, touching the sticky blood there. He winced.

"Randir…"

"I will live. Though it's quite painful." He gave her a playful smile, hiding behind his bravado.

"What happened? I must find the healer."

"Arrow grazed my shoulder. Funny thing too. It wasn't one of the Fomorians."

Gods. He was hit by her people trying to defend the castle. She lowered him to the ground. "Stay here. I'll be back."

"Laerwen." Randir caught her hand before she took off. His fingers closed around hers and squeezed. "Be careful."

"Don't move."

She slipped her hand from his and hurried away to find the healer. Her emotions sizzled through her as she looked for him. He had finished tending a woman and her baby when she finally spotted him and waved him over.

"Come quickly. It's Lord Randir."

"He lives?" His voice held a note of relief and hope.

"Aye, he does. And he's injured."

"His people?" he asked as they headed back to Randir.

"I don't know. I haven't seen any of them. I think they may all be dead."

"Quite likely. Not many survived the attack on the palace."

He gave her a sidelong glance as if to say she was one of the lucky ones. And she was. She knew that. They returned to Randir and the doctor fell to his knees, immediately going to work. He shoved aside the material of Randir's tunic to reveal the bloody shoulder. There was so much blood it was hard to see the wound itself.

"You were lucky," the healer said. "The wound isn't bad. With some cleansing and a clean bandage, you should heal quickly." He reached for his bag and pulled out a bottle of clear liquid and doused a rag. "I'm sorry I don't have anything clean but this is the best I can do."

"Wait." Laerwen ripped a piece from the end of her sari and handed it to him. Though it too was soiled, it was still better than what the healer had. "You can't use that on him. Try this."

"Thank you, princess. But I'm afraid there is a great need for more clean cloths."

"I'll see what I can find."

She didn't want to stick around to watch him clean Randir's shoulder anyway. She darted off back through the crowd to bellow orders to give up whatever clean clothes they had—skirts, tunics, saris, trousers, anything they could spare. The healer had appointed several nurses to help with the wounded. People were quick to respond and help gather materials.

As she went from person to person, they questioned her on what would happen next. Who would rule? What would happen to their kingdom now? She told them to meet at the foot of the volcano so she could address them and answer all their questions. Most of them agreed but remained skeptical.

When she returned to Randir, the healer had placed the bandage on him.

"Keep it clean," the healer ordered. "Or it will get infected."

Randir nodded agreement and the healer left to tend his other patients.

"I'm glad you're alive," she confessed. She'd given up all hope.

"It all happened so fast," he said. "I heard the commotion in the palace and went to investigate. I saw those people attacking. Who were they, Laerwen?"

"Fomorians. A vile, bloodthirsty race."

His gaze took on a faraway look as he remembered his ordeal. "I'd left my chamber and went down to the great hall. That's when I saw all the fighting. I tried to help. I took up arms with your people. I made it outside somehow. Into the outer bailey. But there were so many…dead. So many…dying. The palace was going up in flames. I wanted to go back inside. To find you, but I couldn't. It was…too hot. I knew at that point I had to save myself." His dark gaze flickered back to her. "I thought you were dead."

Though their race could withstand the heat of fire, they were not totally immune to it. He would have turned back when it became unbearable.

"We're safe now. At least for the moment." It was all she could think to say.

"The king and queen?"

Her stomach knotted. She would have to say it again. "Dead."

He closed his eyes and shook his head. "Gods. I'm sorry, Laerwen."

"As am I. And for your loss as well."

His eyes blinked open and met her gaze. "Aye."

Mayhap it was all he could think to say. She had never faced death on such a large scale before. She didn't know what to say or do. But Randir had noticed the gathering crowd and focused on that, mercifully changing the subject.

"What's happening?"

Laerwen helped him to his feet. "I asked them to meet here so I could address their concerns."

"What do you intend to do?"

"I intend to pay a visit to King Urdithane."

"You believe he is responsible for this?"

"I know he is. Lord Navin of the Woodlands paid me a visit." She nodded in his direction. He stood apart from her people, unwilling to join the crowd, and she couldn't blame him. "He will have some answers."

"I'm coming with you," he said.

"No, Randir. That's not necessary. I can handle it myself. You should return home."

"I'm sure you can handle it yourself. Of that I have no doubt. But my people were killed too and I deserve answers as much as you do."

She couldn't deny him that. He was right. Still, she tugged her bottom lip through her teeth as she looked out at the growing crowd.

"I know we have not been on the best of terms. We hardly know each other, after all." He put his hand on her shoulder. "But I cannot let you go alone, Laerwen."

Her eyes fluttered closed as she forced away the sudden hot tears that burned her eyes. Not yet. She could not cry yet. Knowing he was there with her, though, gave her strength. Gave her hope. He was right—they hardly knew each other. They'd been betrothed as children in the hopes it would strengthen the kingdom. But she had not seen him in nearly twenty years and it had only been days ago she'd met him as an adult.

Despite his declaration that he couldn't allow her to go alone, her isolation was palpable.

"Thank you. I appreciate your help."

"I'll stand with you."

Again, that gave her peace and comfort. She wanted to lean into him but instead, stood her ground and turned to her people. As Hiram returned to her side, she took a deep breath. Sweat beaded his brow as he paused next to her.

She scanned the faces smudged with dirt. Their clothes were splattered with blood. Some of the women had tried to save their men and their hands were stained red. Again, that hollow pang went through Laerwen as she looked upon their faces. What could she offer them but solace?

"My people," she greeted. "You have all fought bravely in a losing battle. For that I commend you. I also send my heartfelt condolences for your family members who have been slain in our realm." Her hands closed into fists, her nails sharp against the skin of her palms. "Our homes have been destroyed and there is no guarantee these Fomorians will not return."

"What if they do?" someone called. "What do we do now? We have no place to live. No food. No water. Nothing!"

"I know," she nodded. She met the gaze of the man standing in the middle of the group. He held a young girl with blonde curls surrounding her face. "I know our resources have been depleted. Our livestock has also been slaughtered, leaving us to face a winter with nothing. That is why I propose we go into the east. To the Woodlands. Lord Navin has graciously offered to lead us there."

She motioned toward him. Murmurs erupted within the group of survivors. They looked to each other, questions in their eyes. She knew their thoughts because she had the same questions.

One spoke up. "We do not wish to leave our home, Princess."

"You will address her as your majesty," Hiram said, his tone harsh and unforgiving.

"Hiram, it's all right. I'm still their princess. I'm also the leader of this realm now with the death of the monarchs."

"What do you intend to do about our realm?" the commoner demanded. "They took everything."

"That's why I want to go to the Woodlands. I will ask for aid from King Urdithane. We cannot defend ourselves against another attack. Therefore, I invite you to come along."

Silence descended as they stared at her through round, wide eyes as though she'd lost her mind. And mayhap she had.

"You ask us to abandon our realm?" one asked. "To turn and run? To flee?"

"Not flee," she corrected. "Seek assistance. We must push aside our pride and ask for help. The Wood Elves are the closest to us. I have never known King Urdithane to be unreasonable. He will assist us in rebuilding our realm if he can. The Hin'dar Rhule will not stay this way forever." She met Lord Navin's gaze. He merely nodded to her as if in agreement.

"I'm not leaving."

"You have that right," she said and nodded. "I merely offer the chance to go with me and my royal court to show the Wood Elves what sort of devastation our realm incurred. Those who wish to remain here in the Hin'dar Rhule are certainly welcome to," she continued. "But I intend to pay the king of the Wood Elves a visit. The sooner the better."

"I intend to join her." Randir spoke up for the first time. "Let us stand together to show the king we are united in our tragedy."

She granted him a smile. She may not know this man, but he clearly had her best interests in mind. Hers and the Fire Elves.

"I will go." A woman with two small children stepped forward. "I will go and support your effort to ask the king for help."

"Thank you, Marda."

Marda. The baker's wife. The baker who was now dead in a pool of his own blood. Marda who had hidden with the children in the basement of her house at the behest of her husband while he fought the dirty Fomorians. Marda who was now a widow and a single mother of two.

Another pang of sorrow hit Laerwen.

More volunteers stepped forward to follow Laerwen on her journey to the Wood Elves. Most were women and children. There were a few men. A few angry men who wanted to seek justice for their dead families. And who could blame them? They were angry and had every right to be. For if it was the fault of the Wood Elves, then they should answer for it.

"Gather what belongings you can carry," Laerwen said. "We leave as soon as you're ready."

Her people scattered while Hiram looked at her with worry etched on his face.

"What, Hiram?" He flinched. Her tone was sharper than she intended. Her shoulders dropped as she exhaled. "Apologies, my old friend. What troubles you?"

"Do you believe going to the Wood Elves will help us? Honestly?"

She stared into the distance, watching black smoke curl upward from one of the burned out cottages. "I don't know. But I hope. I hope King Urdithane will be sympathetic to our plight."

"And taking survivors with you? What do you hope to accomplish?"

She reeled on him. "To show him what my people have gone through!"

He took a step back, his eyes wide. Guilt swarmed her and emotion clotted her throat again. She bit her lip to keep the tears at bay. "Hiram...I..."

"If you believe that will help our cause, then I will follow your lead. I will be ready to leave when you are. But we must care for the dead."

"I agree. See to it, Hiram."

He gave her a stiff bow before turning on his booted toe.

"As will I," Randir said. "I'll collect what's left of my things."

They walked away and the emptiness nearly consumed her. Squaring her shoulders, Laerwen vowed not to let this defeat her as she strode back toward the palace. All around her, the people gathered the dead for burning in the fires of the Hin'dar Rhule, as was their way. Her feet crunched over the charred remains of the earth. A billowing white material caught her eye. Reaching down, she pulled the length of veil from the debris. As she held the delicate material with edges trimmed in fine lace, her hands shook.

This was all that remained of her mother.

Despite its soiled appearance, she wrapped it around her head.

Chapter 2

Prince Andahar stood on his balcony and stared across the expanse of treetops, watching as Wood Elves rebuilt the kingdom. It had suffered some damage with the attack of the Fomorians but the reconstruction hadn't taken long. Only a few weeks. He was pleased with the progress.

Still they had not heard any news of Lorcann, the Fomorian mage who had caused so many problems. At least Lord-Regent Marath was dead but the damage he left in his wake was done. The people were different now. More skittish. Unable to trust. He had doubled the guard presence at each and every gate to keep those unwanted visitors out.

He had sent word to every kingdom to warn them to protect themselves from the attack of the Fomorians. But he had no idea which way they had gone. Nor had any of his men returned. His brother, Navin, had volunteered to go west to the volcanoes but even he had yet to return. Andahar had tried to talk him out of going and instead staying at the gate. But it was necessary to do more after the debacle with Marath. He wanted to be more than a mere gatekeeper. Andahar couldn't blame him.

He heaved a sigh. Loneliness pressed through him, leaving a hollowness he didn't know if he could fill. His father, King Urdithane, had yet to recover from the poison the lord-regent gave him. He still lingered in a coma. Allanna was happily married to her human knight and Lord Eldrin had found bliss in the arms of the Lady of the Skye.

The prince could not deny the isolation that pressed him. Certainly he had his duties to attend to, but speaking about the state of the realm with his advisors did not constitute socialization. He longed for…well he wasn't quite sure for what he longed. Only that he needed something. Or mayhap someone.

A stiff knock on his chamber door brought him out of his deep thoughts. His noble advisor entered and paused inside the doorway.

"A moment, your majesty?"

"Aye, Leopold, what is it?" He waved him to the balcony.

"One of our scouts from Lord Navin's party has returned. He rode nonstop to get here." He paused, his jaw clenching tight. "I'm afraid the news is not good."

Andahar stiffened, his hands closing into tight fists. "Tell me." Though he didn't want to hear, he knew he had to. He had to know.

"The Fomorians marched across the Heartlands, your majesty. The death toll is quite great."

An icy ball of fear formed in his gut. "And?"

"And I'm afraid they destroyed numerous villages. I understand the Fire Elves were hit the hardest. Their kingdom fell."

Hearing the words was like a fist in his gut. "The kingdom fell? Explain."

"The Fomorians attacked the Fire Elves, though the reason is not known. One can only speculate it is because they are, quite simply, Fomorians and nothing more than savages. They destroyed numerous villagers' homes as well as killed many of those who fought back. They dared to attack the palace." He paused, cleared his throat. "It pains me to report Queen Lucinda and King Aleron are dead."

A fist closed on his innards and yanked. "What of the princess?"

"He says she was the only one of the royals left alive. She insists on speaking with King Urdithane."

"About what?"

"She blames us for the Fomorians' attack. She's bringing her people here to demand assistance from us. And answers."

"She's coming here?"

Leopold nodded.

"When do we expect them?"

"Anytime, your highness."

The blood drained from his head as he rubbed his forehead. "Did he say how many she's bringing?"

"About two hundred."

His brows drew together. Two hundred? He didn't have room for two hundred more people. And how would the Fire Elves interact with the Wood Elves? They weren't used to their humid climate. They needed the dry, arid environment of the Hin'dar Rhule. But why come here? What could he possibly offer?

What was left of the Hin'dar Rhule aside from the volcanoes? If the palace had been hit then Andahar could imagine the worst. They needed help. The Fomorians would not be satisfied with wiping out one race. And what of Lorcann? The mage had yet to surface. What would he do when the he returned to lead the Fomorians? They still had unsettled business. They still had to find a way to defeat them and put them back into their prison in the Sorrow Lands.

"What do you intend to do about the Fomorians?"

"We cannot fight them alone. They clearly are more powerful than we knew. Especially if they wiped out an entire race." He turned back to his balcony and gripped the railing, his knuckles turning white. "We must send out a call for help from the other clans as well as the Fae."

"You believe it to be war then?"

"I believe the Fomorians' deeds should not go unpunished. They have attacked our land and now we must do something to stop them before there is more bloodshed. The Skye Elves will help us, as will Queen Elyne."

With his brother married to the Lady of the Skye, Andahar knew he could call upon them for assistance once again. As for the Fae, Queen Elyne and King Derron had become allies. He knew they would not hesitate to answer the call for help.

"Shall I send a messenger to Queen Elyne?"

"Aye. I will write the letter with a plea for help. And I will send one to Lord Eldrin myself as well."

"And what do you propose to do about the Fire Elves, Majesty?"

indeed? He gripped the railing tighter, his muscles cramping. "Prepare for their arrival. There isn't room in the palace for them all so see what space you can find at the inns. The princess will stay here and any other nobles she brings with her."

"I'm told most of them were killed."

Gods, how awful. A royal family wiped out. An entire kingdom annihilated. And all because of one Wood Elf who had dared to invoke dark magic. Even dead, that bloody Lord Marath continued to wreak havoc on the Otherworld.

"I will take care of all the arrangements, your majesty. Shall I prepare some sort of feast as well?"

"Aye. No doubt they'll be famished after their journey." With a nod, Leopold left to carry out his orders.

Andahar pinched the bridge of his nose, the tension weighing heavily on him. He stalked to his desk, sat and picked up a quill. He scratched a hasty letter imploring the Fae queen for help with the Fomorians, explaining the dire situation. He rolled the parchment, sealed it with wax and pulled another sheet out to write a similar letter to his brother in the sky. Once he was finished, he sealed it with wax and left to find Leopold.

He found him in the great hall and delivered the letters with instructions to send them with a messenger as quickly as possible. Once he was assured they would be sent, he headed back to see about his father.

It had been several days since he'd checked on him. He wanted to see what progress, if anything, had been made. Marath had poisoned Urdithane but until recently they hadn't an antidote. The king didn't seem to be improving at all. When he arrived, his sister, Allanna, sat by his side.

She rose when he entered but he waved her back down.

"How is he?"

"The same." She clutched the king's pale hand. "He hasn't improved. But he hasn't declined either. I suppose that's something."

Andahar stood at the bedside and looked down at his father. Worry clawed through him.

"How are you?" Allanna looked at him, her blue eyes bright with emotion.

He knew his sister worried about him too. Marath had dealt him a near fatal blow. It still ached. He pressed his arm against his side.

"I'm healing." Though that was true, he was still in some pain.

Allanna looked back at their father. "Marath took a lot from us that day. I'm glad he's dead."

Her face turned dark for a brief moment as she remembered the fear she'd gone through. Andahar couldn't blame her for the anger she must be feeling. Marath had tried to kill her beloved Sir Drake and marry her by force. When that failed and he knew he'd been defeated, he'd tried to take her life. He'd nearly plunged to his death with Allanna. Drake and Lord Eldrin had rescued her from certain death.

"It's all over now though, and we won't worry about that any longer." He squeezed her shoulder, trying to reassure her.

She held onto his hand so tightly, her knuckles leeched of color, matching that of the king's. "Are you certain? Lorcann still has not been found."

"We cannot worry about that, Allanna."

"But he can flash. He could come here—"

"I know. If that happens we will deal with it then." He pulled her away from their father with a gentle tug. "Come away. You look tired. You should rest."

Reluctantly she stood and turned to him. Her eyes searched his face. "As do you, brother. Mayhap you should take your own advice."

"There is much to be done."

"I know." She gave him a faint smile. "Will you let me know if there's any change?"

He nodded. "Of course."

She seemed satisfied with that and left him alone with the king. There had been someone by his bedside every hour keeping vigil. Andahar didn't know how long Allanna had been there but she had dark circles under her eyes. No doubt, even her husband could not drag her away.

He perched on the edge of the bed. He glanced up at the guard standing by the door.

"Leave us."

With a nod, the guard left the room, closing the door behind him. Andahar often came to his father's chamber, sat by his side and talked to him. He didn't know if it did any good or not, but he didn't want the guards overhearing him. He didn't want them to think he'd lost his mind talking to an unconscious man.

"Ah, Father, I do hope you recover soon. Your presence is greatly missed in court."

He made no move. Not that Andahar expected him to.

"We have searched everywhere for the Fomorian mage, Lorcann. To no avail. I know not where he's gone. All I do know is that they have attacked those in the Heartlands. I understand the Hin'dar Rhule was nearly destroyed." He paused, glancing at his father's still face. "The king and queen are dead but the princess survived. Thank the gods."

Andahar scrubbed his hands down his face. "It's my fault. I should have done something about Marath when I had the chance, yet I let him continue to stay here. I feared him. Feared what he could do to us. I was so wrong. I regret that now. He could have killed Allanna."

He looked again at his father and immediately jumped away from the bed. Urdithane's eyes were open, staring sightlessly at the ceiling. He hadn't blinked. Andahar's heart pounded wildly as he ran for the door.

"The healer! Get the healer at once!"

The guards on the other side of the door scrambled to do his bidding. When Andahar turned back to the king, he had closed his eyes again. He rushed to his bed, grasped him by the hand and searched for a pulse. It was weak. Fluttering just below the skin. The same as it had always been.

Brom entered the chamber with Allanna on his heels.

"Did something happen? Is he awake?" she asked.

The healer nudged Andahar out of the way to check the king's pulse. "What happened?"

"He opened his eyes."

"Is he awake?" she asked again.

"He is not conscious," Brom said.

"Why would he open his eyes like that?"

"I know not. I will talk with Turin and see if he knows. He is the only one who is familiar with the poison he ingested." Brom straightened and looked at the two of them. "I'm afraid there is no change."

"Even though he opened his eyes?" Andahar asked.

"Aye."

With regret etched on his face, Brom left them to seek council with Turin, the Skye Elves healer. He had remained to assist with the king's recovery.

"Did he say anything?" Allanna asked.

"No. He only had them open for a moment. Come, Allanna. Let's go. There is nothing more we can do here."

"I don't want to leave him. What if he opens his eyes again? I want to be here."

He heaved a sigh. There was no way he would get her away from their father. "I will send your husband to check on you."

Mayhap Sir Drake could talk some sense into her.

She didn't move as he left. He walked through the halls of the palace, looking for the human knight. He inquired about his whereabouts and was told he was practicing below with the rangers. He wasn't entirely used to the idea his sister, the Elven princess, had married a human knight. But she had been determined to never leave his side. And he could tell the two greatly cared for each other.

Andahar descended the staircase in the ancient tree and wound his way down to the ground. He found Drake quickly. The knight spotted him and set aside his sword.

"You must have news for you to leave the palace walls," Drake said.

Indeed, Andahar had not left the treetops since the tragedy with Lord Marath. He had been too busy reassuring his people and trying to rebuild. The strain of it all would eventually catch up to him, he knew, but for now there was still much to do and much he had to oversee.

He took Drake by the arm and led him from anyone who might eavesdrop. "The king opened his eyes but only for a moment."

"Is he awake now?"

He shook his head. "No. He didn't speak. But Allanna is rather distraught and refuses to leave his side in case he wakes again. I fear it gives her false hope."

"You believe the king will not recover?" he asked.

"I believe it is a strong possibility, Sir Drake." The grim truth hung over him like a dark storm cloud ready to burst any moment. Though he served as regent for now, he had no wish to take the throne as king. Not yet.

"Allanna…I worry for her. She looks fatigued these days."

Drake looked into the distance, unable to meet his eyes. "She still has nightmares."

The events with Marath must have affected her more than he knew. Again, guilt assailed his senses. "I thought mayhap you could talk to her. Try to coax her away from Father's side long enough to rest and break her fast."

Drake grinned. "I daresay she rarely listens to me but I will try to get her to rest. Thank you for your concern."

"If she needs a sleep aide, I'm sure Brom could assist her."

"She refuses to take such things. She says they cause the nightmares to be more intense. I'll do what I can. Any word on

Lorcann's whereabouts?"

"None. One of my scouts has returned with news of the Heartlands, though."

"Not good news?"

He shook his head. "Villages were wiped out. I don't know how many are dead."

Drake clapped him on the shoulder in comfort. "Let me know what I can do."

"I will."

Drake headed off to the palace stairs while Andahar stood there, watching the men and women of the Woodlands. They had managed to recover quickly from the havoc Marath had wreaked on them. The rangers resumed their practice before heading off to Ranger Hall. Two of the stable boys were busy exercising the horses by trotting them through the grasslands. He could see them just beyond the loch. It gave him hope they could get through anything.

As he returned to the palace, Leopold intercepted him before he made it to his private chamber.

"Your highness, I have news." Leopold cleared his throat, a look of unease on his face. "Princess Laerwen has arrived at the gates of the Woodlands."

"Let her in. The last surviving member of the royal Fire Elf family is welcome here."

Leopold shifted from one foot to the other. "As we discussed earlier, she's brought many of the survivors with her. I have found suitable accommodations for most, if not all, of the survivors."

"Good. Please make sure the nobles have rooms in the palace. Show her to the private chamber in the throne room. I will speak to her there at once."

"By your command, your highness."

Andahar entered his father's private receiving chamber and poured two tankards of honeywine and waited. He sipped the sweet liquid to stay calm. He needed to stay calm. He had no idea what he would say to her, this princess he'd never met. Nor did he know what help he could offer her. Asylum? Or did she want something more? Leopold said she blamed the Wood Elves for the attack on her kingdom. Mayhap she'd come to demand answers. To demand who was responsible for the release of the Fomorians. He was not looking forward to that.

Leopold opened the door and admitted the princess. She followed him in, pausing inside the doorway. Andahar had not seen such a dark beauty as her. Whiskey colored eyes fringed in dark lashes met his straight on, peering at him out of a beautiful, perfect face. Eyes that made him thirst for the drink he had never touched. Her skin was the color of brown sugar, making his mouth go bone dry and long for a taste—just one taste—of it.

Her clothes had seen better days—her emerald and garnet gown was dusty, dirty and blood-stained. He thought he could see a hint of her tawny skin between the waist of her skirt and the top that was hidden by the length of material tossed over her shoulder, hiding all those womanly curves he so desperately wanted to see.

He wished he could see her hair but an opaque veil covered it, hiding the length. His fingers twitched with the want of pulling it away, to unwrap her like a present as though she were a gift delivered just for him. But he didn't. He closed his hands into fists and gave her his best welcoming smile.

Despite her beauty, he could see the fatigue shadowing her eyes. The lines of worry and fear etched on her features. She looked as though she hadn't slept in weeks and mayhap not if they traveled all the way here from the Hin'dar Rhule.

"Her highness, Princess Laerwen emer'Aranhil Bloodfire of the Hin'dar Rhule."

She curtsied low and deep before rising and meeting his gaze again with those pale, mesmerizing eyes. "Your highness." Her melodious voice was so sweet he wanted to weep.

"That will be all, Leopold."

His servant quietly closed the door, leaving them alone. Andahar motioned toward one of the chairs. "Please sit. You must be exhausted from your travel."

"I thank you." She moved to the chair with grace, as though she floated instead of walked, and sank into it with such a flowing motion, it was almost as though she melted. When she leaned back into the cushion, she expelled a soft breath and closed her eyes. No doubt relishing the comfort.

"May I offer you honeywine?"

Her eyes blinked open and she met his level gaze. She reached for the outstretched goblet and held it between her hands, staring down into the liquid a moment before taking a long quaff. She drained the cup and set it aside.

"I'm afraid we haven't had much in the way of rations on our way here." Her voice was quiet, raspy. She cleared it and forced a faint smile.

"Those that travel with you are the survivors of the attack?"

"You've heard then." When he nodded, she continued. "I thought coming here was our only option."

Andahar perched on the edge of the chair across from her. "Why here?"

Her gaze never wavered as she leaned forward, a sharp glint of anger flashing there. She didn't move as she folded her arms across her chest. That billowy material didn't budge and instead become more voluminous around her. Still hiding her. "I'm told one of your people released the Fomorians from the Sorrow Lands."

Her voice was so cold he nearly shivered.

He understood she blamed him and his kingdom for the attack. He set aside the goblet and clasped his hands together, leaning back into the chair and crossing his legs. Lord-Regent Marath's ghost continued to haunt the halls of his palace. Would he ever be able to exorcise him from this place?

"I have great regret Lord Marath released the Fomorians from the Sorrow Lands. But I assure you he's been dealt with accordingly."

"I certainly hope so. Where is he? For I wish to express my outrage to him directly." Fire flashed in those whiskey eyes, sparking gold flashes of light that made him want to dive in and never leave.

"He's dead," Andahar said flatly.

She dropped her arms and then nodded. "I see."

"We've had our own problems with the Fomorians and their mage."

"Have you? Did they burn your villages to the ground? Rape and murder your women? Kill innocent children?"

Hearing that was like a knife to the heart as he stared at her in stunned silence. He'd been so involved with what was happening in the Woodlands, he hadn't known about what the Fomorians were doing to others in the Elven realm. He knew of the attack, aye, but not of the other horrid acts.

"I thought not," she snapped. "By the looks of it, your kingdom fared well in the attack. Or did you assist these men in their quest to destroy the Heartlands and the Hin'dar Rhule?"

"My heartfelt and sincerest condolences, your highness. I understand your outrage but I can assure you we had nothing to do with the Fomorians' senseless violence. Those who travel with you…is that all that remains?"

Her eyes took on a faraway look "No. A few opted to remain in our realm. But most of my people have been massacred."

"Gods…"

"They are all I could convince to travel here with me. The Fomorians murdered my parents and destroyed our castle." She met his level gaze. He could see all the weariness, the worry, the fear.

"Then you're the sole ruler?"

"I am."

His throat constricted and he took a deep breath. He too was facing the loss of his father. He too would be the ruler of the Woodlands. But for the moment, he served as regent. He could imagine her emotional state and understood her weariness. She must have traveled here with the weight of grief on her shoulders.

"Then I should address you as your majesty."

"You should address me as Laerwen as I have no kingdom."

A pang of sorrow hit him so hard he wanted to double over. "What can I do to help?"

"We hoped to come to you for refuge…and revenge. You can help us by fighting with us against the Fomorians. They are nothing but barbarians. And you owe it to us to help since it was your man who released them from their prison."

"I understand your feelings, Princess, but it is war you speak of. We are not prepared for that. At least not yet." Despite her wish to address her by her given name, he refused. She was still a princess, even if she didn't believe it.

"Then you must prepare yourself. The Fomorians will not disappear long. They will come back for more bloodshed."

"I know," he said. "I've asked the Skye Elves and the Queen of the Fae to help."

"The Queen of the Fae?" she scoffed. "I fail to see how they can help us."

"Do not discount them, Princess," he said. "We have a mutual enemy and one the queen will be happy to help us dispose of."

"Well then. When you receive your reinforcements from them, mayhap we can schedule a meeting of the war council."

"I have no war council."

"Then form one," she snapped. "And quickly. The Fomorians will not wait for you to be ready before they attack. I assure you. They will come quickly and kill anyone in their path."

Annoyance flickered through him as he pressed his lips into a thin tight line. He knew that, of course, but he couldn't explain that to the princess. The Wood Elves had lost many men in the Battle for the Otherworld as well as the fight against the Goddess of War. His father saw no need for the war council once that was over.

Andahar swiped a hand over his chin. "You need rest. Allow me to show you to your chamber."

"No," she snapped. "I wish to speak with King Urdithane. Where is he?"

"I'm afraid the king is indisposed."

Her sharp assessing eyes landed on him again. "Indisposed?"

"Aye. Lord Marath did more damage to our kingdom than you think, your highness. With the help of the Fomorians, he gave a valiant try at wiping out the entire royal family to take over the kingdom himself. He attacked me and my brothers and tried to marry my sister, Allanna. He also poisoned my father. He has yet to recover."

Her face drained of color. "My apologies, Prince Andahar. I had no idea the king was ill. Has your healer not been able to find an antidote?"

"The Skye Elves healer was gracious enough to offer one but it hasn't seemed to help much. I fear the poison did too much damage before the antidote could be administered."

She clasped her hands together. "I hope your father recovers, your highness."

"As do I." He stood and held a hand down to her. "Come, Princess. Let's get you to a chamber where you can bathe, get a change of clothes and rest."

"Aye, thank you. I would like that."

Laerwen didn't even hesitate when she slid her hand in his. He closed his hand around her cold fingers and gave a gentle squeeze. Her gaze lifted, their eyes met and something skittered through him. He loved staring into those whiskey-colored eyes.

"I…appreciate your help." Her voice was but a whisper.

"It is my pleasure, Princess."

A knock on the door sounded, breaking the spell.

Chapter 3

They jumped apart as though they were locked in a lover's embrace. But Laerwen couldn't deny the warmth that cascaded through her as his hand closed on hers. She looked into those mesmerizing pale green eyes and wanted to know him. Wanted to see what he was all about. Wanted to learn all his deep, dark secrets.

She didn't know why. She had never had that reaction with a man before.

Andahar's servant, Leopold, entered with Lord Randir on his heels.

"There you are," Randir said, his voice full of relief. "When I couldn't find you, I feared the worst."

"Prince Andahar, this is Lord Randir of the clan emul'Valahuir. He is my betrothed and was visiting the Hin'dar Rhule when we were attacked. His people were also killed in the attack." Laerwen introduced him as her betrothed because she knew that's what he wanted. That's what he insisted upon. Though why they were still betrothed, she didn't know. It didn't matter anymore. Their marriage would do nothing for her vanished kingdom.

For a brief moment, she thought she saw a shadow of jealousy pass across Andahar's face. Which would have normally made her laugh if she hadn't been in such a state of exhaustion. Her nerves were raw with emotion. Talking to the prince about the king had nearly been the catalyst that made her crumble into a thousand pieces. All she could think of was at least he still had his father. While she was now nothing but an orphan.

The two men sized each other up. Randir straightened and puffed out his chest. Andahar had suddenly turned stiff and formal.

"Pleasure to meet you, Lord Randir. You have my condolences on your loss."

She resisted the urge to explain to Andahar their betrothal meant nothing to her. She didn't know the man. Not really. She was marrying him out of duty and responsibility. Not because she was in love with him. Why she wanted to tell the prince all that, she had no idea.

"I'm afraid the entire incident has made me worry for the princess. She's quite fragile you know."

Laerwen stared at him as though he'd grown a third eye. Was he mad? What would make him say such a thing? She was far from fragile and hadn't allowed herself to fall to pieces when she learned the death of her parents, though that's all she wanted to do. Her pain and anguish during the fortnight they'd traveled to the Woodlands had been closely guarded so no one—not even Hiram or Randir—would see it.

She kept her outward appearance as one of calm while inside she tamped down the hysterics that so wanted to control her. Grief was a constant companion and it was only when she was alone she allowed her feelings to surface so she could deal with the loss of her kingdom, her parents, her people. All the while fending off Randir's subtle advances.

Randir moved to stand next to her and clasped her hand. Did he think they would continue to marry even after she'd lost everything? He was only marrying her for her title and her kingdom. Why would he still want her?

"I'm quite protective of her in light of recent events."

Ah, so that was it. He was showing Andahar he was the alpha male and she belonged to him. Almost as though he were marking his territory. She belonged to no man, betrothal or no.

"As you should be. I'm sure the entire ordeal has been difficult. I know I'd want to keep the princess safe if I were you."

She could see the visible tension in Andahar's neck, shoulders and arms. Irritation emanated off him in waves. Randir stiffened beside her, his hand closing into a tight fist. So tight his knuckles turned white.

She jumped in before they came to blows over…her? That was silly. "It has been difficult and I'm quite tired. Prince Andahar, I'd like to take you up on that offer of a hot bath and a bed."

Randir's chest puffed out even more. He nudged forward, putting himself between her and the Wood Elf. She wanted to roll her eyes. But Andahar wasn't even flustered by his behavior. He gave her a sincere smile.

"Of course. Leopold, please make sure her highness and Lord

Randir have appropriate accommodations." Then to her he said, "We've prepared a feast for you. After you've had time to rest and clean up, mayhap you could join us?"

"We'd like that." It was Randir who answered for her.

She suppressed a scowl.

He pinpointed Randir with his pale green gaze. And then, as he kept his eyes on her betrothed, he reached for her free hand. Her heart stilled and her breath caught in her throat as he bent and placed a delicate kiss on the inside of her wrist. It sent delicious warm spirals through her, leaving her skin tingling where his lips had touched. When he straightened, a lock of silvery hair fell across his forehead and her fingers twitched. All she wanted to do was brush it away but she didn't. She kept still and rigid.

"I will see to it your people are well cared for, your highness."

Warm shivers went through her again and her skin still had not stopped tingling. The breath she held shuddered out between her lips. Randir turned his head to glare down at her but she didn't care if he noticed or not.

"I greatly appreciate that."

She granted him a smile as she followed Leopold from the king's private chamber, through the throne room and into the corridor.

"He's quite generous, isn't he?" Randir asked as they walked through the hallways.

"He has my utmost respect for granting us refuge in his kingdom."

"Is that all he granted you?" Randir cast a sideways glance of suspicion.

Her lips pressed together as her jaw tightened. She knew what he implied and she didn't appreciate it. "Aye. That is all." She enunciated each word, her tone hard and unforgiving.

"Here we are," Leopold announced. Mayhap glad to be rid of her. "Your chamber, your highness."

"Thank you, Leopold." She backed into the door, bumping it open with her rear and standing in the doorway. "I'm sure you can follow Leopold to your own chamber, Lord Randir, can't you?"

Without waiting for a reply, she shut the door with a snap.

It was a slap in the face. She saw the expectant look on Randir's features. As though he meant to share her chamber. Her bed. Her skin tightened with revulsion at the thought. She knew she'd insulted him by not allowing him inside. Betrothed or not, she was still her own person and she wasn't ready to share anything with that man. They hadn't even shared as much as a kiss. Why would she allow him to room with her?

She pressed cold fingers against her lips. Gods, the prince was gorgeous. She had never seen another quite like Andahar. With all that silvery hair long enough to touch the collar of his tunic. It looked thick and soft and she desperately wanted to run her fingers through it. And those eyes! They rivaled that of the most precious jade jewels in the Hin'dar Rhule. She had never seen eyes quite that shade of green before.

When he kissed her wrist, it was like a brand. She rubbed her fingers over the spot. His lips had been like velvet and she couldn't help but wonder how they'd feel against hers.

A sharp knock on the door startled her out of her reverie, making her jump. She opened the door and several servants brought in a copper tub. They filled it with steaming water. Two girls set about building a fire in the huge fireplace across from the bed. Another group of girls came in with a giant trunk and placed it near the foot of the bed. She dismissed them, though, wishing for solitude. They each curtsied to her before leaving her alone with the steaming tub.

Laerwen removed her hair covering and dropped the gauzy material on the bed then stripped. She was grateful to be out of the sweat and blood-stained clothes. Grateful for the hot bath. She stepped in and let the water sluice over her skin as she sank into the tub.

She languished there until it was cold. Until she was forced to step out and dry off with the thick towels the girls left her. For the first time in days, she was clean. She wrapped the cloth around her and combed out her long wet hair. As she did so, she toed open the trunk, kicking off the lid.

Inside were miles and miles of material in fabulous colors— garnet, sapphire, chocolate, onyx.

How drab.

She was used to wearing bright colors—orange, yellow, teal, fiery red. Plus these were gowns. Not her native sari. She frowned. She dug through the trunk until she came upon a gown the color of sunset. This could work but it still wasn't what she wanted. She would need help. She tossed the garment on the bed as she headed for the door and cracked it open. Peering out, she saw her door was guarded by two Elven soldiers.

"You there. Get me the royal seamstress at once."

When he nodded, she closed the door. All that was left to do was wait.

A short time later, the royal seamstress arrived with a crisp knock on the door. Laerwen didn't want to put on the soiled clothes she'd traveled in, so she'd pulled on the sunset-colored gown. It was form-fitting and clung to her curves, something she wasn't quite used to. The sleeves were long and wide and the skirt had a short train that trailed after her when she walked. With a scooped neckline, it plunged a little lower than she was accustomed.

"Princess Laerwen." The seamstress dipped a curtsey. "I'm Nell, the royal dressmaker. How may I serve you?"

Laerwen ushered her inside and closed the door. "I'd like some clothes made, if you please. Something that is more traditional than these gowns."

"More traditional, your highness? You look ravishing in that color. It does well with your beautiful complexion."

"My apologies. I meant more traditional for my clan." She motioned toward the discarded clothing on the bed. "Something like that. Except without all the jewels of course."

"May I?" At her nod, Nell reached for the blouse and held it up, giving it a critical once over. "I believe I could have something like this made."

"And this? This is a sari." Laerwen held it up. "It goes over one shoulder."

"Aye, I could make that."

"Wonderful. And the colors should be bright and cheerful. Yellows, reds, oranges and the like."

Nodding, Nell said, "We have material such as that. I'll have the ladies get started on making you some suitable outfits right away."

"Thank you. There are a few more things I require, if you can accommodate me."

She gave an elaborate description of the trousers with the wide legs and a long tunic that hit mid-thigh. Nell listened intently, nodding with understanding. Laerwen could see Nell's mind working as she described what she wanted. Then the lady scooped up her skirt and top and, before Laerwen could stop her, picked up her mother's tattered veil that had seen better days.

"I'll get rid of these for you, Princess, since they're so soiled."

"No, wait." Laerwen's heart pattered wildly as she jerked the veil from Nell's hands causing her to drop the rest of the clothes. She didn't hide her look of surprise as Laerwen blushed and clutched the veil to her chest. "My apologies but this veil is very dear to me. I wish to keep it."

Nell blinked understanding and then softened, giving her a brief smile. "Then allow me to have it cleaned for you, Princess. I will personally see to it and make it good as new."

"You can do that?"

She nodded. "I can."

Laerwen relinquished the veil back to her after a moment's hesitation. But Nell assured her she would make sure it was well cared for.

"I will, of course, pay you for your services."

"Don't you worry about that," Nell said. "You're under the prince's care now. He's instructed me to make sure you have all that you need."

"He has?" It was Laerwen's turn to be surprised.

With a nod and a smile, Nell left her to begin sewing her new clothes. Prince Andahar was turning out to be quite a surprise indeed.

Her stomach rumbled with her hunger. She couldn't remember the last time she ate.

Laerwen stepped out into the hall and paused there, chewing on her lower lip as she tried to recall which way to go. Then she spotted Andahar heading her direction, which saved her from having to speak to the guards who merely gave her sideways glances. They weren't exactly conversationalists and anyway, they were not her men—they were Andahar'.

The prince's step faltered a brief moment when he saw her before he started toward her again. A slow smile spread across his handsome features and her silly heart skipped a wild beat.

He was dressed in finery—a royal blue tunic trimmed in gold, black pants and knee-high black boots polished to a high shine. His sword swung at his side. And that silvery hair fell across his forehead as though in invitation. Those jade eyes reflected the torchlight in a way that made her want to never look away. Gods, he was beautiful for a man.

He halted in front of her and he didn't bother to try to hide his appreciation of her new clothes. He gave her a small bow. "Princess Laerwen," he greeted. "May I say you look ravishing in that gown?"

Much to her chagrin, she couldn't stop the flush that crept over her cheeks and throat. "You may."

"I understand you made use of the royal dressmaker."

"Aye. I do hope that's all right."

"But of course. Nell and her group of seamstresses are some of the best in the kingdom." He smiled, his eyes twinkling with mirth. Her fingers twitched, dying to brush away that lock of hair that curled over his forehead. "I'm glad they could be of service. My kingdom is yours. While here, you and your people will want for nothing."

"You are most kind, your highness."

"I would be honored if you'd call me Andahar."

His given name? A spark of desire ran through her. "As you wish."

"I've come to escort you to dinner. You must be famished." He held out his arm to her.

She glanced down the hall, looking for signs of Randir.

"He's already made his way to the dining hall," he said, as though reading her thoughts. "I saw him earlier."

With a faint smile, she slipped her hand in the crook of his elbow and he pulled her close. His body heat radiated over her, warming her. Charming her.

"I am, actually. Thank you for all that you've done. I do hope it's not an imposition."

"Not at all." Andahar gave her a sideways glance full of heat and need.

She had to keep steady. Not allow herself to be pulled in by his good looks and his charms. She had to keep him at a distance. It was for the best. After all, by the laws of her land, she was still technically betrothed to Randir.

"How's your father?"

"No better. Though he's no worse, either. I suppose that's something."

"I wish there was something I could do to help. I've always admired King Urdithane. He's always very no-nonsense."

"His illness has been difficult for everyone. Especially my

sister."

"It's often hard on the only daughter."

"My sister has a special ability. She has visions of the future. She told me what would happen to him and I wouldn't listen. I blame myself."

"I'm sure it's not your fault."

"But I could have prevented it from happening if I'd only listened to her."

"Sometimes fate cannot be changed, Andahar."

He halted and looked at her. Smiled. "I do like hearing my name on your lips." His gaze dropped down to her mouth before meeting her eyes again.

Her blood warmed at the small gesture. Making her cheeks heat and she worried he would see her blush. But he seemed not to notice. She knew there was an attraction to him and, she hoped, him to her. Now she knew that was not simply a figment of her imagination. It was real.

"Come. Let us dine together. The others are waiting."

He led her into the dining hall. It was crowded with people and right away, she spotted Randir and Hiram. And they spotted her. They both had a chance to bathe and dress in clean clothing of the realm. A dark glower covered Randir's face when he saw her on the prince's arm. Andahar must have seen his dark look too for he released her and gestured toward the room.

"Here we are." He granted her another knee-melting smile.

But she wasn't so ready to be gone from his side. "I'd be delighted if you'd introduce me to your sister."

"Of course."

He led her deeper into the room to a young, fair-haired girl with sparkling blue eyes. She stood next to an ox of a man who was clearly human. It was odd to see a human in this realm. They were often not wanted or welcome.

"My sister, Princess Allanna and her husband, Sir Drake. I present to you Princess Laerwen of the Hin'dar Rhule."

Allanna curtsied as Sir Drake bowed low. The princess took Laerwen's hand in hers and stepped toward her. Her eyes bright and clear. "We've heard much about you, Princess. Welcome to the Woodlands."

She glanced to Sir Drake. "You are human."

"I daresay I am." He flashed a broad smile. "I hope that doesn't bother you, your highness."

"Sir Drake came from the human realm and helped the Fae and the Elves fight numerous battles," Andahar said. "We're grateful for him. I'm afraid fighting those battles is how he won my sister's heart. She couldn't bear to be parted with him and so he remains."

"Aye, my brother speaks true." Allanna flushed, moving closer to her husband and giving him an adoring look. "Sir Drake is one of the very few humans allowed in our realm."

"There are more?" Laerwen asked. It was most unexpected.

"Sir Finn and his wife, Maggie, have returned to his time," Andahar explained. "She is with child."

"Sir Finn?" She met Andahar's gaze, those crystalline eyes seemed to penetrate right through her.

"Another knight who honored us by fighting with us. And another tale for another day. There is a great deal you do not yet know about the Woodlands or the Fae. When the time is right, I do hope you'll allow me to brief you on that."

She wasn't sure what had transpired in those few moments but suddenly her body tingled with anticipation. Gooseflesh rose on her arms and she was glad for the long sleeves so he wouldn't see. And was it hot in here or was that simply her imagination? Laerwen sensed Randir's presence before she saw him. He moved to stand next to her, his arm sliding around her shoulders. Andahar eased away from her.

"Princess, I have to say that gown is quite becoming." Randir looked down at her, his eyes fixing on the low-cut neckline.

She resisted the urge to fidget, forcing her fingers to remain still at her side. It seemed everyone had the same opinion about the damn gown and she'd be glad to be rid of it as soon as possible.

"Thank you. Prince Andahar, I'm sure you remember my betrothed, Lord Randir." She introduced Allanna and Sir Drake to him. He shook the knight's hand and kissed the princess's.

"I'm honored to make your acquaintances," he said.

"I don't know about everyone else, but I'm famished," Andahar announced. "Shall we make our way to the tables? I'd love for you to sit at the high table with me, Princess. You and Lord Randir would be my honored guests."

"We'd be delighted," she said before Randir could object. And she knew he would. He had opened his mouth to do that.

Andahar waved them toward the table and then made his way

there. Randir took Laerwen's hand and folded it into the crook of his elbow as they followed.

"He seems quite taken with you," Randir said.

"Aye, he does."

She liked it. More than she should. She was quite taken with him as well. With those gorgeous green eyes and all that silvery hair. She could see the family resemblance between him and Princess Allanna. They shared the same pointed chin and high cheekbones.

"I don't like it."

He wouldn't. He still claimed her as his own. "He's merely being friendly." But she knew it was more than that. The spark between them flared bright. She knew there was something there. Something that begged to be explored.

"He should back off," Randir said.

"Or you'll pummel him?" She glared at him. "Leave him be, Randir."

Understanding stained his features. "You like him."

She huffed and jerked her arm free. "That is none of your concern."

"Don't play me for the fool, Laerwen." His tone was sharp and commanding. It sent a chill up her spine. She had never heard him speak to her that way before. "Tread carefully, Princess."

"Or what?" she demanded. "What do you plan to do? My guess is nothing. Any hostile move against the prince is a hostile move against the kingdom and I won't have you putting what's left of my clan in jeopardy. Not like that."

Randir's hand gripped her upper arm, his fingers digging into her flesh. "But you are still betrothed to me. Never forget that." His eyes were hard. Cold. Icy. "Never."

"How could I when you won't let me?" She shoved away from him. "Do not threaten me, Randir. Our betrothal was null and void the moment the Fomorians destroyed the kingdom. You have no claim left on me."

"That is not what the laws of the land say and you know that."

"Aye, but the laws of the land did not account for total annihilation now did they?" she snapped. "You cannot say that you love me, Randir, for I know different. Our marriage was one of arrangement for the good of the kingdom. And since the Hin'dar Rhule has been destroyed...well, I doubt there is any reason to continue with the betrothal."

"You act as though all hope is lost and I know that's not like you." He stepped closer, his voice a low timbre so only she could hear. "I also know that means you want something else. Or should I say someone else?"

"You are a fool, Randir. There is much rebuilding that must be done before the kingdom can become whole again. And before we can do that, the Fomorians must be destroyed. Now, if you'll excuse me, I intend to join our host for dinner."

She turned on her slippered toe and headed for Andahar. But Randir had shaken her resolve. It was clear to her he would not let her go so easily. She would speak with Hiram soon to see what could be done. As she took her place next to Prince Andahar, a servant filled a silver goblet with wine.

Grateful for the drink, she snatched it up and drained the cup. Licking her lips, she replaced the goblet to allow it to be filled again.

"Everything all right?" Andahar asked, one brow raised in concern.

"Aye, I'm fine. Thank you. It's kind of you to ask."

Randir joined them a moment later, sitting on the other side of her. He leaned across her and glared at Andahar. Andahar, in turn, glared right back. Unflustered. Like two hellhounds about to get into a pissing match.

Laerwen knew this would be a very long night.

Chapter 4

When Lorcann left the Woodlands, he made his way south away from Lord-Regent Marath. Away from the kingdom of Elves. Away from the realm of the Fae. He had sent a silent command to his Fomorians to do as they willed. He had been delighted when he discovered they had destroyed most of the Heartlands and the Hin'dar Rhule.

It would send the right message to that stupid King Urdithane. He would understand at last that they were not to be trifled with. Nearly killing an entire race of Elves should be warning enough, but his blundering idiots hadn't killed them all. Some survived. They would have to be dealt with in time.

At least that fool, Marath, was dead. Disappearing and leaving his fate in the hands of his enemies was the best decision Lorcann had made. He had tried to control him. What a mistake that was. He had watched from the shadows as Lord Eldrin shot an arrow through the man's skull, killing him. Pleasure swarmed through him at the memory of watching Marath plunge from the rope bridge to the ground below. It had been a sweet victory.

Things were not over with the Wood Elves. And now the Fire Elves. He sent a silent message to his Fomorians to stand down until he was ready to attack. Until he had help from the underworld.

Cormac was the most powerful Fomorian mage. It had been a great loss when the Goddess of War killed him in the underworld. But what no one seemed to know was that his spirit still roamed free. Lorcann intended to resurrect the man and bring him back to the land of the living. It would not be easy, either. He would have to travel to the underworld and then find him.

He had never performed such a feat before but he knew he could do it. He had confidence he could bring back Cormac.

Lorcann found the caves he was looking for in the southernmost part of the realm. The violent surf crashed against the rocky outcropping that hid the caves but he knew this was the place he needed to be. This was the place where he would be able to travel to the underworld and return with Cormac, alive and in the flesh.

He stood on the edge of the cliff and looked out across the frothing waves. Overhead, the sky darkened from pink to indigo back to pink again. The sun was setting on the western horizon and the waves reflected silvery against the shimmery light.

Taking a deep breath, Lorcann wound his way down the path toward the rocky shoreline. By the time he'd made it to the caves, the setting sun bounced off the water and turned everything a golden color. But he turned a blind eye to the beauty of it all and entered the dark, dank cave.

It smelled of the sea, rotting fish and fecal matter from nearby creatures. It was a disgusting place but then, the entrance to the underworld would hardly smell of roses or perfume.

He held his hand out, palm up and a fireball formed, tossing out light to guide his way. Not many knew of the existence of these caves or if they did, they didn't realize they led to the underworld. Only a few knew—Lorcann being one of them. It was not far from the Sorrow Lands where he and his people had been imprisoned for thousands of years.

Lorcann made his way deeper into the cave, winding along the sharp downward path. His ankles and calves burned with the pain of trying to maintain his footing without slipping. The farther he went, the damper it got. The colder it got. The smell seemed to die as well. Mayhap most of the creatures that inhabited the cavern stayed close to the opening and didn't venture deep into the bowels. They were wise not to. It was a dangerous place.

The path leveled out and he knew he was closer to the bottom. Not quite where he needed to be but getting there. He walked for what seemed like hours, holding the fiery ball of flame in the palm of his hand the entire way. The light flickered on the walls. It had become so dark inside the cavern he could hardly see even with the flame.

At last, he came to a crossroads. One path led off to the right while the other steered to the left. Turning left, he headed downward again, following it farther into the dark. The air thinned down here and his flame snuffed out on a strange breeze. A breeze that should not be here in the darkest depths.

He halted and strained his ears to listen. Silence deafened him. And then there was a warm puff of air on his cheek.

"Why have you come, Fomorian?"

The words were a whisper on the lips of a female. The demon who guarded these walls.

"You know." He didn't need to tell her what he intended to do. Likely she already knew why he was there. She knew he would have come for Cormac.

"Your mage is dead, you know."

She fluttered around him, her heated breath on his face. Her body brushing against his. He knew she was a hideous thing. That she likely had horns protruding from her head. Her tongue was forked. Her skin scaly.

"Keep your distance, demon," he warned.

She laughed a deep guttural laugh that echoed through the empty darkness. "I promise not to hurt you…much."

Her sharp, long nails scraped across his chest. He clamped down on her wrist and pushed her away. "I'm not here to play with you."

"Pity." She moved behind him. He could feel her heat warming over his back. Her breath trickled over his ear. "Why should I let you in?"

"I've come for Cormac. His body may be gone but his spirit is not," Lorcann said. "You know this as well as I."

"Indeed." Again that guttural chuckle rumbling her throat. She slipped her hands over his shoulders. "It has been far too long since I've had anyone to play with. Why won't you let me play with you?"

"I could kill you here. Now."

"But you won't," she taunted. "You need me to open the gate. You need me to let you inside. You need me to lead you into the underworld. Quite simply, my Fomorian friend, you need me."

Her hands were on him. Roaming. Touching. Petting. She cupped his crotch and squeezed. She was right. He did need her to open the gate but he could find his own way into the underworld without her. He didn't need her help to find Cormac.

The demon's scaly hand slipped beneath his pants. Her long fingers wrapped around his cock—his already hardened cock. She had managed to make it come to attention with her touches. Damn her. She would have her way with him whether he wanted her to or not. She would take what she wanted. But when she was done, he would take from her.

"Mmm. Nice and thick. Nice and hard. All for me?"

"I will give you want you want," he said, "if you will open the gate for me in return."

She purred. "It would be my pleasure."

Then she slithered around him, dropped to her knees and pushed down his pants. Her mouth closed on his cock, sucking him into her hot mouth to the back of her throat. At that point, it had become too difficult to control his reactions. Her mouth did all the work and his body responded.

When he finished, she rose to her full height. She stood nose to nose to him, her eyes red as she licked her lips.

"You are tasty."

"Open the gate."

"And demanding. I like that about you."

"Open the damn gate!"

"Patience." She licked his cheek with her forked tongue, leaving a sizzling path in her wake.

As soon as they were through the gate, he would kill her.

She turned, moving away from him. He could hear her movements. Her shuffling. And then the gate opened. Light exploded into the confines of the cavern. He could see her for the first time.

The demon was revolting, as he had pictured. He was right about one thing—her skin was covered in scales. Green ones. A long tail snaked out behind her. Her hands were long, slender ending in blood-red claws. Her tongue was indeed forked. Once she might have had delicate features but now her teeth were nothing more than sharp points and her face covered in the same green scales. She had two horns protruding from her forehead. They looked like nothing more than stumps.

"By your command, Fomorian."

She motioned for him to follow her. Through the gate they went and then it shut immediately behind him, closing off the damp darkness. He stood in the garish light of the cavern, surveying his surroundings. He could feel Cormac's spirit and knew which way he had to go.

The demon wound her arms around his neck from behind, then licked his ear. A sensual purr reverberated through her.

"I let you through the gate. Now I need payment."

"Payment?"

"Mmm." Again she purred against him.

"I'll give you payment."

He spun out of her arms and clamped a hand around her throat. With his free hand, he retrieved that dagger and stabbed her once, twice, three times in the gut. Her eyes bulged. He released her, watched as she stumbled backward, her hands covering the holes in her stomach. Blood seeped through her fingers.

"You will pay." Her breath came out in a deep hiss.

"We'll see about that."

He lunged, plunged the knife into her throat and watched as the life ebbed from her. She gurgled her last breath. A satisfied grin crossed his lips as he turned toward hope.

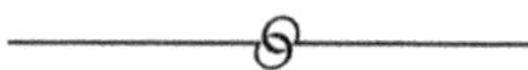

It had taken several hours to walk through the underground. To find Cormac's wandering spirit. The man sat on an outcropping of rock, his elbows propped on his knees. His head hung low with his chin touching his chest.

He was not a corporal being. Not yet. He was merely a presence. But Lorcann could see him.

"Cormac."

He lifted his head, his gaze meeting Lorcann's. There was no life left in his eyes.

"Lorcann." Hearing his name on his lips gave the mage hope. "What are you doing here? How did you get here?"

"I walked." Lorcann approached slowly. "I came for you. To resurrect you."

Cormac laughed, a bitter laugh. "You can't. The Goddess of War killed me."

"Aye I know. But your spirit still lives. You can be free. Free to walk the land again."

Cormac stared at Lorcann long and hard before he put his feet on the ground and rose to his full height. "You cannot reverse something the goddess has done. You are not that powerful."

"No," Lorcann agreed. "But you are."

Cormac blinked surprise. "But I am not…of the living."

"You will be."

"How?"

"Come with me. We will find you a body and you will live once again."

"You know how to leave the underworld? Only a few can do that."

"Give me your hand," Lorcann said. "Come with me, my old friend."

He could see the hesitation in Cormac's face. He knew he didn't believe him. Knew it was a leap of faith for him to accept the truth.

"For what purpose?" Cormac asked. "I will not be an agent of evil again."

"We need someone to lead us. Our people are free, Cormac." When the mage refused to take his hand, Lorcann dropped his arm. "A Dark Elf released the rest of us from our bonds."

"What does that mean to me?" Cormac folded his arms across his chest.

"It means you can exact revenge on all those who forced you to do their bidding. You can rule our people once again. You can lead us into war. We can gain control of the Otherworld once and for all. And there is magic in the Hin'dar Rhule. Magic we can harness as our own."

"No." He shook his head. "I wish only to be left alone. I have no desire for more fighting. The ones who forced me to work for them are both dead. The Goddess of War and Lord Kieran." He sat once again on the rock. "I will not go back to that. What do I care about magic?"

Lorcann's eyes narrowed. He peered out of slits at the mage. "It pains me to do this. If you will not come willingly, I will have to take you by force."

Before he could react, Lorcann charged. As his hand landed on Cormac, he invoked the spell to take his spirit into his own body. It would be temporary until he could find someone suitable to take on his spirit. Cormac saw him coming and tried to move out of the way but he wasn't quick enough. Lorcann sucked the spirit into him.

He fell to his knees. Cormac was not a willing participant and banged against his skull, calling him vile names. As soon as Lorcann found a body for him, he would bind Cormac to him, making him docile. Forcing him to do this bidding. The man said he would not be a party to evil again. But Lorcann needed him.

And soon Cormac would know that too.

Lorcann trudged back through the underworld to the cavern gate.

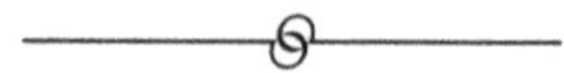

It was dawn when Lorcann stepped out of the cavern and onto the rocky shore. Cormac still banged against his skull, shouting curses. It made Lorcann weary. His mind was fatigued. His body just as tired. But he knew he had to keep going. He wended his way back up to the cliff. Exhausted, he fell to the ground, staring up at the morning sky turning from a deep indigo to pink.

He could not keep Cormac inside him for much longer. The mage was stronger than he had accounted for. His powers were strengthening. Lorcann could tell he was feeding off him and he had to get him out as soon as possible.

He called upon one of his men, Balor, to come to him. He would transfer Cormac's spirit into his man's body. Balor was a weaker mage. He would be able to handle Cormac's power. He would be easier to control.

Balor answered the call immediately, flashing to his location. He knelt by his side.

"Lorcann, what's happened?"

"I've…retrieved Cormac."

Balor glanced around. "Where is he?"

He grabbed his friend by the tunic and dragged him close, his lips against his ear. "His spirit. Inside…me."

Horror flashed over Balor's face before he managed to regain his composure. "You took his spirit inside you? How?"

Cormac exploded against his skull again, the pain bursting through Lorcann's mind. He pressed his palms against his temples and gritted his teeth. The bastard would never stop. He had to get him out of his head. He had to convince Balor to take Cormac's spirit into his body. For the good of their people.

Lorcann shook his head. "No time."

"What can I do?"

There. Balor made it all too easy. "Take him."

He blinked confusion before dawning overcame his features. "Take him? From you into me?"

Lorcann nodded. Cormac was draining his strength with every

passing moment. He didn't know how much longer he would be able to hold out.

"Get…the others. Daroch and Phelan. They'll help."

And he knew they could flash there. Balor rose to his full height, his arms by his side and his hands fisted. Through his haze, Lorcann could hear Balor calling to the others. A flash. Two. And the men stood in the semi-circle around them.

Through the noise in his head, he could hear the three men arguing about something. He couldn't quite make out the words. All he knew was their voices were angry.

"Enough!" Balor said, his voice sharp enough to cut through Lorcann's haze. "I'm doing this. Will you help me? Will you help us?"

There was a pause before Daroch replied. "I will."

"Daroch, you fool. We don't know what removing the spirit will do to Lorcann." Phelan. His voice angry.

"We have to try." Daroch's quiet voice filtered through Lorcann's mind over the din of Cormac.

Lorcann reached for Phelan, his hand landing on his dusty boot. "Aye…try."

Phelan's gaze dropped to his. Lorcann could see the indecision and then the acceptance. He gave a quick nod.

"Aye then. Let's do it."

Balor dropped to his knees again and placed the pads of his forefingers on Lorcann's temples, applying a slight pressure. Phelan and Daroch stood on either side of Lorcann with their arms spread wide, palms open and upward to the sky. They each chanted the ancient words that had not been spoken in eons. Words they still knew from their time when they walked the realm before they had been exiled to the Sorrow Lands. It seemed not so long ago. Time had stood still for them.

Cormac quieted in Lorcann's mind. He couldn't hear him anymore. He had stopped banging against his skull and shouting. It was almost as though the chanting soothed him.

Mayhap it did.

As the men chanted louder and louder, Lorcann could feel the presence ebb from him. It moved quickly from his body into Balor's. And then Cormac was no longer part of him.

Balor screamed and reared back. He landed on the ground with a thud, his hands on his skull. Lorcann sat up quickly. Pinpricks of light danced in his eyes as blood surged to this head. He doubled over, groaned, and pinched the skin at his temples to stave off the dizziness and weakness. When he regained his composure, he scrambled to Balor's side. The man's eyes were pinched shut, his mouth curled back in a snarl. He rolled from side to side, as though in terrible pain.

Phelan growled his contempt. Daroch tried to get control of Balor but he kicked him, rolled away and pushed to all fours.

"I knew this was a mistake," Phelan said.

"He's all right. He's taking in the spirit. He will be fine," Lorcann assured. But he couldn't ignore how drained his body was. It had to be from losing the spirit of Cormac and transferring it to another host.

Balor stilled. He took in several deep breaths before he sat back on his heels, his chest heaving. Sweat dotted his brow and upper lip. His eyes were clouded over and he blinked, as if trying to see clearer. After several moments, they returned to the shade of blue they once were and then colored with an inkiness that set in, changing them to black orbs. So black, the pupils were lost in the pools.

Daroch scooted closer to him. "Balor?"

Balor reacted with violence. He reached out, clamped a hand around Daroch's throat. Daroch gasped, trying to suck in air.

"Release him," Lorcann demanded.

"No. He will die." Balor's voice was different. Deeper. Darker. More authoritative than ever before. It did not sound like the man they once knew. Rather, he sounded like someone else.

Lorcann knew the transfer had worked and was complete.

"Daroch is of your kind. We are of your kind. We are Fomorians. We're here to help you."

Balor snarled. "No one can help me."

"I did. I brought you back from the underworld. I have given you renewed life."

His fingers slowly relaxed their grip on Daroch's throat. When he dropped his hand, the man fell forward, gasping in air and coughing.

"Why?"

"Because you can lead us." Lorcann and the others bowed their head out of respect.

"The transfer is complete," Lorcann said. "Welcome to the land of the living once again, Balor."

"How do you know? How can you tell?" Phelan glanced between the two of them.

Balor turned his head to meet his gaze. "From now on you will call me Cormac."

"Cormac," Lorcann corrected. "You were once a powerful mage. You will be again."

"I was imprisoned in the Sorrow Lands before being released by Lord Kieran."

"Aye," Lorcann nodded. "And then Morrigan, Goddess of War, released more of us. And still more were freed by Lord Marath. Now we are going to conquer the lands and become the most powerful in all the Otherworld. We have already begun with our march through the Heartlands and the Hin'dar Rhule. We have much left to do."

Cormac's gaze focused first on Daroch, then Phelan and finally rested on Lorcann. There was a darkness there that wasn't there before. And Lorcann knew the eyes staring back at him were Cormac's. He pushed to his feet.

"Good. Now tell me. Where are our people?"

Chapter 5

The banquet ended on a sour note for Laerwen. Whenever she had a moment alone with Andahar to exchange pleasantries, Randir would intrude. He did his best to keep her away from the prince as well as continue with his unwanted advances.

She couldn't help but reflect on the way Randir acted. They had been betrothed when she was a girl. Her parents had chosen him because he was the son of one of their Lord-Regents. He would make a fine husband, her father said. A fine king, her mother said.

He had never pursued her romantically before. And now suddenly when there was no kingdom left to her, he doubled his efforts to want her.

She relished the moment when she could excuse herself and retreat to her chamber. To silence. As she leaned against the door, taking in deep breaths, she saw two stacks of neatly folded clothes on the edge of her bed. Beside them, the veil. Nell must have left the clothes. Laerwen was impressed they had managed to make the clothes so quickly.

She rushed to the veil and grabbed it up, letting the length of it fall to the floor. It was in perfect, pristine condition. Cleaned, just as Nell had promised. She was grateful she had rescued it from the rubble and held the softness against her cheek, remembering all that was lost.

Thinking of her parents, her lost kingdom, overwhelmed her control. Her calm. She sank to the edge of the bed and then curled into a ball. She pressed her forehead into her knees, letting her emotions overcome her. She hadn't allowed that the entire trek through the Heartlands to the Woodlands. She had been strong. She had been commanding. She had been in charge. Randir had stood by her side.

And yet…it hadn't changed anything. Her parents were still dead. Her kingdom was still destroyed. Hot tears flooded her eyes and spilled down her cheeks. The dam had broken. At long last.

She didn't know how long she sat there, weeping for what was. Feeling sorry for herself. Nor did it truly matter. When she finally regained her composure, she buried her face in the coverlet.

What was she to do? She didn't want to marry Randir. She didn't want to marry anyone. She hadn't a kingdom.

But she had her life.

What she saw in her travels through the Heartlands with the remaining Fire Elves had shredded her heart. So many dead. So many gone. Entire villages wiped out. Homes burned to the ground. Women and children murdered. It had been awful to go through the rubble to find survivors. There were none. They never found any.

Laerwen rolled to her back and stared up at the knotted ceiling. She examined it, marveled at it. It was made entirely of tree wood. Her tears had dried but she couldn't kick the despair that pressed against her. Somehow, she had to find a way to go on. Mayhap even rebuild the Hin'dar Rhule.

Shoving from the bed, she stumbled over to the windows to peer out. Dawn was breaking, turning the indigo sky into that of the pale pink she had long loved. As she leaned against the window frame, a knock sounded on her door.

Who could be calling so early? Unless it was the servant girls.

One quick glance in the looking glass showed her face smudged with tears. She splashed cold water on her face. The knock sounded again.

"One moment," she called.

She hadn't even changed from the gown she wore last evening. It was crumpled around her body. Creased and wrinkled. As if she'd slept in it. And she would have if she'd been able to sleep. When she finally opened the door, she was startled to see Prince Andahar standing on the other side.

He took in her appearance in one swift glance. "My apologies, Princess. Is it…too early?"

"I…" She glanced down at her clothes, smoothed her hands down her skirt. "I had a long night."

"I should let you rest." He turned to go.

"No!" At her sharp response, he turned back. Curiosity etched his face. "I mean…please come in." She swung the door wider and stepped aside.

Andahar entered and she closed the door behind him. He

walked to the window and shoved open the draperies to let in the early morning light. "Your room faces east. I do hope you like the sunrise."

When he smiled at her, her stomach did a flip.

"I do. Thank you." She inclined her head and watched him prowl the room. Looking for someone, mayhap? "Is there something you needed, your highness?"

"Aye." He halted, his highly polished boots—riding boots, she noticed—scraping on the wood floor. "I must insist you call me Andahar."

Heat warmed her cheeks as the blush crawled across her skin. She couldn't help but smile.

"I've never been one to stand on rules of decorum." He winked.

She grinned. "Very well then. You must call me Laerwen."

Andahar closed the space between them in three steps. He scooped her hand into his. Her breath caught in her throat as he bent and his lips brushed across her skin. When he straightened, his eyes held a twinkle of mirth.

"I would be honored."

She was reluctant to remove her hand and allowed him to continue to hold it. "Good. I'm glad that's settled." Her heart did a wild thump.

"As am I. Mayhap you'll tell me what troubles you."

Laerwen pulled her hand free and turned away. He had seen her face. He must have known she had been crying. Damn it all to the gods. "Nothing."

"Come now, Prin—Laerwen. You and I both know that's not the truth of it."

He moved to stand behind her. She could feel the warmth of his body press over her, through her, comforting her. Her eyes fluttered closed but he didn't touch her. Not again. He stood there as though he were nothing more than her rock. Her steadfast supporter.

Wouldn't it be nice to let him take some of the burden? Nay, she couldn't. It wouldn't be right to tell him. To ask him.

"Please tell me." His voice was soft and low next to her ear. The deep timbre sent goose bumps skittering through her.

"I...I'm so...alone."

"You are not alone," he said firmly. "As long as you're in my kingdom you are never alone."

"I know. I appreciate that. But you cannot know what it's like to be without a home."

"I don't know. You're right. I want to help you. And I swear on my honor we will find these Fomorians and exact justice."

She smiled. He sounded so sure of himself. "I hope so."

And then his hands landed on her shoulders. Warm, strong, sure hands. "When all this is over, I should like to help you rebuild the Hin'dar Rhule."

Her heart squeezed at his words. How kind of him to want to do that. Tears threatened once again and she blinked them away. "That's a gracious offer."

"One you'll accept, I hope."

Gods, she would be a fool not to. "I do."

"Good. I'm glad to hear it."

He released her and moved back toward the window. She angled her body to see him. To watch him. He moved with the stealth and grace of a cat. Or a creature of the night.

"How about a bit of fun?" he asked as he looked out the window.

"Fun?"

"My brother will be visiting soon with his new bride, Lady Talaiel of the Skye Elves. I intended to ride out to meet them." He turned to look at her then. "Would you like to accompany me?"

A slow smile lifted the corners of her mouth. "I would love it. I just need a moment to change." She swept her hands down her crumpled gown.

"Of course. I'll wait for you in the dining hall. When you're ready, meet me there."

She watched him walk to the door, all fluid grace. As though he walked through water. He was so unlike Randir who was nothing more than a big, bumbling oaf of a man with more muscles than sense. Mayhap that's why she never really liked him. He wasn't her intellectual equal and he never would be. He was merely someone with whom to produce an heir.

And now even that didn't matter so much. Her kingdom was gone.

She quickly changed into something more suitable. Instead of changing into another gown, she opted for long billowy pants that floated around her legs and gave the illusion of a skirt. She pulled on a long tunic that fell just below her waist. Then she covered her hair with the opaque veil she'd arrived in, the last vestige of her beloved mother, letting it cover her hair and fall down her back.

One glance in the looking glass, though, told her she looked far from rested. She had dark circles under her eyes. Laerwen couldn't deny how tired she was from her night of fitful sleep, however she didn't want to refuse the company of the prince. She would be alone with him for a ride through the Woodlands. Her heart did a strange skip as she smoothed her veil.

She was as ready as she would ever be. When she opened the door to her chamber, she nearly ran into Randir who stood on the other side, his arm raised as if to knock. Her excitement skittered into dread and annoyance.

"Lord Randir, what are you doing here?"

"I came to escort you to breakfast."

"I'm not hungry." She pushed past him and into the hallway. Even as she said it, her stomach rumbled in response. She was suddenly ravenous at the thought of food.

Randir fell in step beside her. Damn him. "Where are you going then?"

"Not that it's any of your concern, but I'm going for a ride."

"Do you think that's wise with the Fomorians still on the loose?"

Halting, she turned to him and drew in a sharp breath before releasing it in a huff. "Let's get one thing straight, Randir. I do not report to you. I appreciate your concern, but I'll be fine."

She started back toward the dining hall trying to think of a way to shake him. He still followed her and she didn't want him to know she was meeting Andahar. Otherwise, he would bully his way into their private time together and she wasn't willing to give that up.

"Are you taking a guard with you? How do you know it will be safe? Mayhap I should go with you."

Frustrated, she whirled on him. She put her hands on his chest and shoved him back. "Stop. Just stop it. I don't need you hovering over me."

"Laerwen—"

"I mean it! Go away, Randir."

His face fell and she didn't miss the look of complete devastation he gave her. She couldn't care about that right now. All she could think about was getting to Andahar. She hurried her pace and found him right where he said he'd be. He smiled when he saw her.

She took his arm and steered him toward the door.

"Are we in a hurry?"

"We are now," she said, trying to keep her voice light.

"Someone following you?" He didn't look over his shoulder to check. Instead, his gaze focused on her.

"Oh, you know. The usual."

"Randir?" he asked, his voice low-pitched so only she could hear.

She bit her lip and nodded.

"Then let's see if we can lose him, shall we?"

Oh, she liked the way he thought. She squeezed his arm as they exited the palace walls and headed down the rope bridge, the wooden slats clanking together with their hurried steps. They made it to the ancient tree with the winding staircase a moment later and started their descent. Andahar had a quicker pace than she did, but she managed to keep up. As they headed down, the giggle started to bubble up in her throat. By the time they made it to the bottom, she was out of breath with laughter and exertion. She leaned against the tree, her heart racing at a furious beat as she gulped in air to catch her breath.

"That…was…exhilarating." She looked at him standing near her, smiling and barely breathing hard. It wasn't fair. "Why aren't you…out of breath?"

"My dear princess, I'm quite used to the stairs." He held out his hand. "Come. I have just the horse for you."

Laerwen loved that idea. She loved that he wanted to touch her. To hold her hand. To keep her close. She slipped her fingers in his and they hurried off. It seemed silly to be walking so fast to get away from Randir when she wasn't even sure he followed. She was sure she'd hurt his feelings, though, and for that she would have to apologize. She tried to ignore her pangs of guilt. The man didn't mean any harm. He merely thought they were still betrothed and he would continue to think that until she had it broken.

She must speak with Hiram soon.

"Have you ever seen a Skye Elf?" Andahar asked, breaking into her thoughts.

"No, I haven't."

His jade eyes twinkled with anticipation and mischief. "Then you're in for a treat."

"I thought the Skye Elves never left their realm."

"They don't. Not usually. But my brother, Lord Eldrin, has been slowly changing their mind."

They arrived at the stables and four horses were already ready and waiting. One of the stable boys waited for them and bowed low when they arrived.

"Your mounts are ready, your highness."

"Thank you, Phillip."

"Four horses?" she asked. "Are you expecting company?"

"Horses for my brother and his wife," he said. "And this is Moonshadow, my sister's horse. A fine mount for you to ride."

"Oh, I couldn't."

"She won't mind. Besides, she's distracted by her husband at the moment." He winked.

Ah, yes. Her husband the human knight, Sir Drake. "Well, if you're certain."

At his nod, she stuck her sandaled foot in the stirrup and swung her leg over the saddle. A moment later, he was mounted and ready to go. They wasted no time in heading for the gates and exiting. Lord Navin, Andahar's younger brother, gave them a silent nod of farewell as they left.

So Andahar had two brothers, Lord Eldrin and Lord Navin, and a sister, Allanna, who was the youngest. Laerwen was aware of the guards following at a discreet distance. They also led the spare mounts.

"I'm afraid I can go nowhere unattended. Especially with the Fomorians still in hiding," Andahar said. "I've asked the guards to stay back."

"The Fomorians are in hiding?"

"From what information we've gathered, once they destroyed the Hin'dar Rhule, they disappeared. We're not sure where they are. Mayhap to regroup and prepare to attack again. I don't know."

That was unsettling. Her gut twisted at the thought they would destroy another realm. Another kingdom.

"It's strange, really," Andahar continued. "It's almost as though they disappeared out of the Otherworld."

"But surely they haven't."

"I doubt that," he agreed. "But I do believe they still pose a threat to us. That's why I've asked Lady Talaiel and my brother to come down. I have also sent word to Queen Elyne and King Derron. I expect they'll be joining us soon as well."

"You've been able to convince the Fae rulers to come here?" Certainly she knew Queen Maeve had relinquished the throne to her daughter but she had no idea the Wood Elves were able to call upon them and they would answer that call.

"Aye," he said. "Has news reached your realm about the Treaty of Separation?"

"No. I'd heard Queen Maeve stepped down but nothing more."

"The Treaty was put in place between the Fae and the Wood Elves. The Fae are our closest neighbors and we had a long-standing feud that has now been abolished as well as the Treaty. Queen Elyne is quite amicable."

She hadn't even thought to ask the Fae for help. New hope surged within her. "So you believe the Fomorians aren't finished? That they'll be back?"

"I believe that, aye," he said with a nod. "It's only a matter of time. Lorcann is a powerful mage. He's the one Lord-Regent Marath awoke from the Sorrow Lands."

"And the one who is their leader."

"We think so."

"Those Fomorians who attacked us didn't seem to be led by anyone. It was merely a senseless act of violence. One the Fomorians seemed to relish. Where is he now?"

"No one knows. He disappeared shortly before Marath was killed. And that's what scares me the most."

"And me."

He reached out to her, clasped her hand. "I'll make sure you're safe. You and your people. You have my word."

She believed him. She could hear the conviction in his voice. Knew he spoke true. And when she looked into those eyes of his, those beautiful green eyes, she could see the truth of it there too. It put her at ease. And stirred deep feelings within her she had never experienced for anyone before.

"I thank you."

They rode on through the grasslands down the Banríon Road—the King's Road. The road that led through the Heartlands and back toward her home. She wondered if she would ever see it again. If she would ever be able to rebuild like she hoped. But while her parents were still dead, his father's life lingered. He still had the hope that Urdithane would recover.

"Any news on the king's illness?" she asked.

"No change." His mouth formed a thin line. She could tell he didn't like talking about it.

"I'm so sorry, Andahar."

"He hasn't come to again. Allanna thought for certain she would see him wake if she stayed by his side. Drake had to force her away." Andahar kept his gaze on the road ahead. Never looking at her. She could hear the emotion in his voice, knew it troubled him. "I don't know what's to become of him. If he doesn't wake up…"

It was her turn to reach for him. She wrapped her fingers around his wrist, her thumb caressing the soft skin there. "He will."

Their slow trot came to a halt. He edged his horse closer to hers. When he lifted his eyes to meet her gaze, her stomach fell to her knees. Which was quite a feat while sitting atop a horse. She started to remove her hand but he clamped his other one on top of it. Holding her there. Keeping her pinned.

No, not pinned. Warmth from his skin rippled through her. Her breath hitched when she realized he leaned toward her, his lips parted slightly and his eyes half-lidded.

Oh, gods, he was going to kiss her.

And she was going to let him.

She angled her head to one side as his lips brushed hers, leaving behind a tingling sensation she had never anticipated. It shuddered through her entire body right down to the ends of her toes.

When he started to move away, she knew she couldn't let him. Her hands came up to his face, pressing against each cheek. She pulled him to her, kissed him with a sort of voraciousness even she didn't expect or know she possessed. Their mouths collided, lips pressed against lips. Her tongue seeking his. Tasting. Teasing.

His mouth was like a velvet recess made solely for her. He tasted of wild berries and something sweet. Like honeywine. He let her take her time exploring and when he decided he wanted to be in charge, his hands lifted to her face, cupped her cheeks and tilted her head back. To deepen the kiss. To take more pleasure.

Her fingers curled into the silky strands of his hair, twining the locks between her fingers. She couldn't stop the mewl vibrating through her throat. When his lips wandered from hers, he kissed a trail across her jaw and down her throat. Her head fell back to give him more access.

"I shouldn't…" His breath was hot on her tingling skin.

"You should." All thoughts of Randir, her parents, the Fomorians fled her mind. Nothing mattered but the here and now as he kissed her.

"You taste like spun sugar." His heated words whispered across her skin.

"You taste like wild berries."

Another kiss landed on her neck under her earlobe. "I wondered what you would taste like."

"Did you?" Her heart picked up the pace in a wild beat that threatened to drown out any other sounds.

He hummed against her skin, which sent her senses into overdrive. He was simply driving her mad. He had to know that. When he pulled back, she could see the desire reflected in those gorgeous eyes of his. Desire, need, lust. Want. All the same things pounding through her veins.

"I did." One corner of his mouth lifted in a half-smile. "Now I know."

"I hope you're not terribly disappointed."

"Never, Princess." He lifted her hand to his mouth, kissed her knuckles. "I think you would never disappoint me."

Warm pleasure spread slowly through her. But much to her dismay, he released her hand and picked up his reins. Their romantic interlude was clearly over. He clucked at the horse and they resumed their slow pace. She'd rather be kissing him. And doing other things.

"I should apologize for my lack of decorum, though." He kept his eyes forward as he spoke.

"No apology necessary." His sudden regret pushed the joy right out of her. She didn't regret it. Why should he?

"Aye, it is. You belong to another. It isn't right of me to take such liberties."

Still he kept his gaze forward and it maddened her. "There is no reason to express such remorse, Prince Andahar. For the situation with Lord Randir is no one's concern but my own. And, as I recall, I took it upon myself to take those liberties, as you call it."

Anger spilled through her. She gripped the reins in her hands and kicked her horse into a gallop. It seemed as though the breath was being sucked right out of her as she rode away. Though where she was going she had no idea. All she knew was she needed to get away from him.

With some trepidation, she realized he followed her. He galloped after her as though she were on a runaway mare. When he caught up to her, he reached for her reins and pulled her to a stop. Moonshadow didn't particularly appreciate that and reared her head, whinnying with her disapproval.

"Laerwen, look at me."

"No."

She turned her head away from him. She wouldn't look at him. Why did it bother her so much that he could hurt her? He meant nothing to her. He was nothing to her. But she had begun to have feelings for him. She had begun to allow him to inch his way into her heart. And she knew it was wrong. He was not of her clan. Not of her kind. It could never work between them. A Wood Elf and a Fire Elf? She must be mad to even think for a moment it would be a possibility. But then, his brother married a Skye Elf. Was that so different?

And why were her eyes suddenly pooling with tears?

"Look at me," he repeated, though this time his voice was more demanding. When she still refused, he cupped her chin and turned her head to face him. She blinked away the tears as quickly as possible, hoping he wouldn't see. "I didn't mean to hurt you."

"You didn't," she lied. But he had. Why, she didn't know. She couldn't explain. *Aye, you can, you dolt. You do like him. You like him more than you should. More than you ever can.*

"Laerwen, I—"

"Please do not try to explain. I don't need an explanation of anything. I understand how you feel. Truly I do. And you're right. There can be nothing more than friendship between us as long as I'm betrothed." She should forget her fancy for the prince and marry Randir. He was of her kind and mayhap over time, she would come to love him. Hiram would never allow her to break the betrothal anyway. He would try to talk her out of it and he would be right to.

"I should like to remain your friend," he said. "And my offer to help rebuild your kingdom still stands."

She nodded understanding.

Overhead, the clouds parted and two moon dragons emerged

from the sky, saving her from any more uncomfortable conversation with the prince. Andahar looked toward them and smiled.

"Ah, my brother and his wife have arrived."

Laerwen was relieved to have the distraction.

The moon dragons landed not far from them, their wings silent on the wind. They were iridescent, catching the light just so and making colors she had never seen before in a dragon's wing. It was breathtaking and beautiful. The two dragons lowered their heads. First Lord Eldrin landed then Lady Talaiel.

Laerwen had never seen anyone more beautiful than the Lady of the Skye. Coppery hair fell in long waves over her shoulders and down her back. Her eyes were the same color as the moon dragons—a lovely silver. Laerwen wondered if they would catch the light like the dragons' wings. Her alabaster skin was a contrast to Laerwen's own light brown coloring. They could not be more opposite than light and dark.

But she and the Lady of the Skye did have one thing in common—Wood Elf royalty.

Andahar dismounted and Laerwen followed his lead. The two of them walked in front of the horses where they waited for the lord and his lady.

Lord Eldrin held his hand out to Talaiel and she placed delicate fingers on the back of his hand. They walked toward them, the lady with a smile on her pale pink lips. Eldrin looked like a proud peacock strutting his feathers with his chest puffed out, clearly delighted with the woman at his side.

"Hello, my brother," Eldrin greeted them and gave a small bow of the head. His gaze landed on Laerwen then.

"Lord Eldrin, Lady Talaiel, I should like to present to you Princess Laerwen Bloodfire of the Fire Elves," Andahar said.

Lord Eldrin took her hand and kissed it. "Greetings, Princess. Welcome to the Woodlands. I hope my brother has been treating you well."

"He's been most gracious, my lord," Laerwen said.

Lady Talaiel stepped forward and stretched out her hand. Laerwen shook it as the Lady of the Skye smiled at her. "Such a beautiful name. It's lovely to meet you, Princess."

"I feel quite privileged to make your acquaintance," Laerwen said. "It isn't often one meets a Skye Elf."

"My people are quite reclusive. Lord Eldrin and Prince Andahar has been helping them overcome that though," Talaiel said with a warm smile. "You'll find the Wood Elves are most kind and generous."

"Thank you for coming on such short notice," Andahar said, changing the subject. "I am sorry I had to disturb you so soon after your wedding."

"My wife and I understand our first duty is to the realm." He gripped her hand in his. When he looked at her, Laerwen could clearly see the love passing between them.

"Aye," she said. "How can we assist?"

"Let's return to the palace first," Andahar said. "I've brought horses." He waved to the guards. "We can discuss the details while we dine tonight."

The ride back to the palace was in relative silence. Relative for Laerwen. She listened with a keen ear while Andahar and Eldrin discussed the state of the realm. Eldrin had heard of the attack on the Hin'dar Rhule only too late. The Fomorians had come and gone before they could send anyone to help.

Such was the case with the Wood Elves.

"My sincerest condolences, Princess," Eldrin said. "I heard of the death of the king and queen."

"Aye, it's been difficult." And that pang of sorrow hit her in the middle of the chest again. She didn't think she would ever get used to the idea her parents were dead.

"Where does that leave the Hin'dar Rhule?" he asked.

"It's currently destroyed. There is nothing left of the palace except a burned out shell."

"I've pledged the help of the Woodlands to see the Hin'dar Rhule is rebuilt to its former glory," Andahar said.

"Then I pledge the same of the Skye Elves," Talaiel said. "You have my word, Princess. I will send every available hand to your realm."

"I thank you for that. It means more to me than I can express."

And it did. Their generosity was more than she had ever expected. When she came to the Woodlands, it was to seek revenge for those who had sent the Dark Elf to destroy her land. Now she was starting to feel the beginnings of friendship and respect and mayhap something more with Andahar.

No, she would not allow herself to become attached to the

prince. It was folly to believe there could ever be more than one kiss between them. It was also folly to expect Hiram to willingly break her betrothal with Randir. He would fiercely object. She knew the duty she faced. She must forget Andahar and that kiss.

They arrived back at the stables and relinquished their horses.

"The midday meal will be served in an hour," Andahar said. "That should give you both time to refresh I should think."

"More than enough time," Talaiel answered. "Thank you."

The two brothers took the lead ascending the winding tree staircase. The Lady of the Skye fell in step with Laerwen.

"If there is anything I can do for you, Princess, I hope you'll let me know," the lady said.

"I appreciate your offer, but I don't know what you could do to help me."

"Losing your kingdom and your family in one blow is more than difficult, your highness. I was quite saddened to hear of your loss and even more distressed we could not help you in time."

"I did not know you had come to help."

"When my people arrived, the realm was deserted. There was no one left. Only the dead."

Laerwen's heart stopped. She came to an abrupt halt. "There was no one left alive?"

"No, your highness."

Her knees gave out and she dropped to the step, no longer able to stand. She fell back against the wall, her stomach clenching with the disbelief and horror of the truth. She had left many Fire Elves back in the realm when she came to the Woodlands. If the Skye Elves found no one alive… Her chest tightened as she made a valiant effort to force away the threatening tears.

Ahead of them, Eldrin and Andahar paused mid-stair. They each looked back, question on Eldrin's face. Concern creased Andahar'. He stepped down to her, dropping to a knee and sliding an arm around her shoulders.

"Laerwen?"

"Oh, gods," Talaeil breathed. Her fingers pressed against her lips. "You didn't know, did you?"

She shook her head. Had the Fomorians returned and finished them off? They must have arrived shortly after her departure. In hindsight, leaving the Hin'dar Rhule was probably not the wisest decision but it was the only one she could make at the time.

"They're all dead," she whispered. "All of them. And it's my fault. I should have insisted they come with us."

"It's not your fault. There must be a few survivors. Mayhap they were able to get away," Andahar insisted. "I'll send a search party."

But she was already shaking her head. "No. It's no use. There were only a few dozen left behind. They would not have been able to defend themselves. The attack would have come on as suddenly as before."

"You don't know that," Eldrin said. "Andahar is right. Let us send men out to search. They could be trying to make their way here to you."

She looked into Andahar's eyes, saw the determination there and knew she couldn't say no. She nodded. "All right."

"I will send a scout on a moon dragon," Talaiel said. "That way we'll know sooner rather than later."

Laerwen nodded as the prince helped her to her feet, still holding onto her. But Laerwen shrugged away from his grasp. He tried to hide the hurt look but she saw it as he turned and headed back up the stairs. The Lady of the Skye did something Laerwen never expected—she hooked her arm in hers as they took the final steps and walked toward the palace.

"All is not lost, Princess."

"I fear my people will never be able to recover from this," she said.

"You must have hope." She hugged her arm. "I should like to be a friend to you."

"I should like that. Thank you."

In a time like this, Laerwen needed all the friends she could gather. And Lady Talaiel would be not only a good friend, but a powerful ally.

"There you are, you impetuous woman."

Lord Randir's voice rang out across the span of rope bridges. He charged toward them, a stormy look upon his face. Laerwen flinched. A confrontation with him was the last thing she wanted yet she knew it was inevitable.

Chapter 6

Andahar saw the fierce look staining Randir's features as he stalked across the bridge, the ropes swinging with his weight and every angry step. Eldrin turned to face him, brushing Andahar's shoulder almost as though he knew he intended to block the man from getting to the princess. Behind him, he could hear Laerwen suck in a sharp breath and knew standing as a blockade was the right decision. She'd had enough stress for the day.

"Move aside, highness," Randir said, his eyes boring into Andahar.

But Andahar wasn't swayed. "What business have you with the princess?"

"That is none of your concern. I wish to speak with her so move aside."

"I fear I cannot," Andahar said. "For the princess is attending official royal business with me, my brother and the Lady of the Skye."

Randir leaned around Andahar to see Lady Talaiel who merely smiled sweetly and kept her cool. Laerwen's face was still pale as she tried to recover from the news the rest of her people were dead. She wouldn't meet Randir's gaze and instead kept her eyes lowered. Now was not the time to confront Randir. But he wasn't to be pushed off so easily. He looked at Lord Eldrin.

"And this is?"

"My brother, Lord Eldrin." Andahar's voice was ice cold. "Surely you've heard of him? One of the best rangers. He helped lead the Battle for the Otherworld."

Randir took a step back and then stopped. He charged forward. "Move aside. I wish to speak with my betrothed."

As he charged, Eldrin removed his sword and pointed it at the man. "You threaten the crown prince of the Woodlands, sir. Stand down."

Randir held up his hands in surrender, consternation look of consternation crossing his features. "I meant no harm. I merely wish to speak with Princess Laerwen."

"Now is not the time," Andahar said.

The last thing she needed was an altercation with Randir. Learning those who had left behind were killed had left her in shock. Her face had paled—he had never seen her so pale—and she had crumbled to the stairs. All he wanted to do in that instance was comfort her and hold her. He had tried but she had rebuffed him.

"Be gone before I have the guards arrest you."

His eyes narrowed to slits. "You wouldn't dare."

"Try me."

They stared at each other for a long moment in a silent standoff. Until at last Randir took several steps back. He positioned himself so he could make eye contact with Laerwen.

"I will see you soon, Princess."

He stalked away, leaving the rope bridge swaying once again in his wake. Eldrin put away his sword. Andahar relaxed his fists, realizing only then he had clenched them. Behind them, the princess blew out a low breath of relief.

"Who was that?" Eldrin asked.

"Just who he said. My betrothed," Laerwen said, her voice cool and controlled. She sounded as though she'd regained some of her composure. Andahar admired that she could pull herself together so quickly. "Thank you for begging him off for me. I don't believe I have the energy to speak to him yet. I'm not ready to tell anyone else about the fate of those left behind in the Hin'dar Rhule."

"He seems rather forceful," Talaeil observed.

"He doesn't mean any harm. Not really. He wouldn't hurt me, though I believe he thinks he still holds a claim to me no matter that my kingdom has been utterly destroyed."

"Has the marriage contract been dissolved?" Eldrin turned toward her when he asked the question.

"No." As she answered, she met Andahar's gaze.

Hope prickled through him. As much as he wanted to look away, he couldn't. He held her gaze. He could see fear and pain and anguish in those whiskey colored eyes and it squeezed his heart. He wanted to help her. He wanted to see that marriage contract dissolved as much as she did. Or, rather, he hoped she did. Because he couldn't stop the need for her from racing through his blood.

He couldn't stop the want for her from skittering through his veins. No more than he could stop the desire from clouding his brain.

He meant what he said earlier—he shouldn't take liberties with her. But that kiss was oh-so-sweet. He could still taste her on his tongue.

He was quickly losing himself to her.

Eldrin cleared his throat, bringing Andahar's attention back to the marriage contract. "Well, mayhap you can help her with that, brother." He clapped him on the shoulder then held his hand out to Lady Talaiel. "Come, my love. Let's rest before we meet for dinner."

Without a word, she placed her hand in his and they walked away, leaving Andahar alone with the princess. She clasped her hands and looked away, unable or unwilling to hold his gaze any longer. He could see a faint flush creep into her cheeks.

"You'll have to excuse my brother," he said at last. "He often speaks his mind before he should."

"It's…it's all right." She turned away, her hands gripping the rope handhold and staring off into the distance.

He had never seen such a faraway look before and it made him ache. He moved to stand beside her, keeping a fair amount of space between them. Not wanting to get too close. Not wanting to acknowledge the feelings pressing into him.

But he had to acknowledge it, didn't he? He had to talk to her about the kiss they'd shared. He had to know where he stood with her. The look she gave him when discussing breaking the marriage contract told him she wanted that. She didn't want to marry Randir.

"Princess, about that kiss—"

"Please don't." She whispered it so softly the wind nearly blew away her words.

"Why not?" he demanded a little more forcefully than he intended.

She closed her eyes for a long moment before opening them again. "I cannot."

"You cannot what?" Andahar couldn't stop from reaching for her. He took her by the shoulders and turned her to face him. "You can't break the betrothal? Laerwen, if that's what you wish then I can help you. I can see to it—"

"Stop it." She shrugged his hands off her and stepped back. Away from him. He could see the pain in her eyes and he didn't understand it. Did she love Randir and she was keeping it from him? "You don't understand."

"Then make me." He took a tentative step toward her, closing the space between them. He had to be close to her.

"Lord Randir is…he is a Fire Elf." She clasped her hands together, holding them in front of her as though she tried to keep them still. To keep from fidgeting. "The betrothal cannot be broken."

"Aye, he is and I am not. All betrothals can be broken in some way. I can—"

"No." She looked at him then, her gaze piercing through him. Her eyes glinted with a hard edge. "It cannot. And you are not a Fire Elf. That is why this thing between us can never be."

"Princess, I fail to see why that matters. My brother married a Skye Elf."

"My kingdom was destroyed!"

She spun from him, shoving the veil from her hair. It fell back against her shoulders, showing her beautiful hair. He resisted the urge to reach out and stroke her hair.

"My kingdom is gone and Lord Randir is one of the few remaining nobles. I know what my parents would want me to do. What I should do."

"But not what you want to do." Again that hope pressed against his chest. This time it coiled there, hiding.

"No," she whispered.

"Laerwen—"

"The kiss meant nothing." She turned to face him, the color high in her cheeks and her eyes shiny with tears. "Nothing. Do you understand? I'm going to do the right thing. I'm going to marry Randir and once this…this war is over, we will return to the Hin'dar Rhule and rebuild. Together. There's nothing you can do to stop me."

Nothing? Challenge accepted. "I understand." He closed the gap between them, stepping so close to her he could see the freckles dotting her nose. Freckles he had never noticed before. How truly delightful. "But because I understand doesn't mean I have to like it. I will fight for you, Princess. He doesn't love you."

She stared at him a long moment before putting her hand on

his chest right over his heart. Right over that coiled up hope. "Neither do you."

The words were like a stab in the heart. No, mayhap he didn't love her thus far. But he knew he was attracted to her. He knew he liked her fierce strength and her courage. He gripped her hand in his, brought her delicate fingers to his lips and kissed the tips.

"Not yet, Princess." He smiled.

She slipped her fingers out of his hand and stepped away. This time he let her. But she never took her eyes off his as she continued to back from him until at last she turned and darted inside the palace.

Laerwen hurried through the palace halls until she made it back to her chamber. She slammed the door and leaned against the Elven wood, her heart hammering a wild beat.

What had just happened? Everything had spun out of control so quickly she hadn't a chance to process it all. First Randir appeared, demanding to speak to her. She could guess what he wanted. No doubt to chastise her for disappearing from him earlier that day. The anger was clearly written on his face.

It was at that point Laerwen knew what she had to do. He was her betrothed. Her parents had made the arrangement long ago to strengthen the line. They were both Fire Elves, of the same blood. She owed it to them and her people to do the right thing and marry Randir, returning to rebuild.

But Andahar…when he looked at her. She could see the fire in those jade green eyes. She could feel it too when she placed her hand over his rapidly beating heart. Desire and need was clearly etched in his face. Burning in his eyes. Like he might die if he didn't hold her in his arms.

She might die if he didn't hold her in his arms. An admission she would never speak aloud.

And she could not forget that kiss. She had urged him on like some wanton wench. That searing kiss full of need and want and yearning. She could still taste the sweetness of his lips. The wild berries and honeywine on his tongue.

You taste like spun sugar.

His words echoed in her head. Her heart did a wild beat as she pressed her fingers against her lips.

She squeezed her eyes shut to block out the vision. To make her forget his words. When she saw Randir's face, his rage, she knew she had been selfish. She knew she would have to make it right with Randir.

Laerwen pulled herself together, changed into a royal blue sari she had from the dressmaker. She covered her hair in the veil, throwing one end over her opposite shoulder. She would be the perfect princess. She would most certainly not make eye contact with Prince Andahar and she would never use his given name. Not again.

Taking a deep breath, she opened her chamber door and headed to the dining hall. When she arrived, she was greeted with the sight of several nobles she had yet to meet. She hadn't expected that. In fact, she was under the impression the dinner was for the four of them when the prince mentioned it.

Prince Andahar and his brother, Lord Eldrin, were already there. Lady Talaiel was at Eldrin's side looking radiant and beautiful and elegant in a gown of sapphire trimmed in silver. Laerwen would look like a wilting flower next to her. She took a step backward to disappear out of the dining hall before anyone saw her.

But Prince Andahar caught a glimpse of her and smiled, waving her over.

Too late. No escape now.

Taking a deep breath, she headed toward them. Lady Talaiel greeted her with a smile and a hug.

When she pulled back, she held her at arm's length. "How lovely you look in that color. It's quite flattering."

Andahar nodded agreement, his gaze slipping over her before meeting her eyes. "You do look quite ravishing, if I may say."

Laerwen couldn't stop the blush rising. "You may. Thank you."

Andahar waved toward the long table in the center of the room. "Now that we're all preset, shall we dine?"

He started for the table. Laerwen fell in step with the Lady of the Skye who hooked her arm through hers.

"He's quite taken with you." She spoke low so only she could hear.

"I'm sure that's not true, my lady." Laerwen didn't want to think about that. She didn't want there to be anything to change her already made-up mind about marrying Randir.

"Oh, but it is. Have you not seen the way he looks at you?"

"I choose not to see." She kept her gaze forward and off Andahar. The last thing she needed was meeting his gaze yet again.

"Why is that?"

"My lady, I don't believe anything can come out of a liaison with the prince."

"Because you are from two different clans?" When Laerwen nodded, she squeezed her arm. "That can be overcome."

"You only say that because you have managed to overcome it with Lord Eldrin."

But what she wanted to say was Lord Eldrin was not crown prince. He was not next in line for the throne. Lady Talaiel was leader of the Skye Elves and though her position was not much different as princess to the Hin'dar Rhule, there were vast differences. The Skye Elves were known recluses. Whereas the Fire Elves were not. Her land in the west was one of the first kingdoms travelers came to from the shore.

"Give it some time, your highness." After another gentle squeeze, she released her to join her husband.

Before she could find a place as far from Andahar as possible, his hand clasped her by the elbow and steered her toward a seat next to his.

"As my honored guest, I have a place for you near the head of the table," he said and then lowered his voice. "Near me."

A cool shudder shifted through her. There was no getting away from the prince this night.

Several candelabras adorned the table, their candles blazing brightly. There were platters of freshly baked bread, wheels of cheese, piles of fruit. They took their seats and the first course was served. A roasted boar and several roasted fowls. A servant poured honeywine in each goblet.

"Thank you all for coming," Andahar said. "I'm sure you all know why you've been asked here this evening." Nods and murmurs of agreement before he pressed on. "Princess Laerwen's realm, the Hin'dar Rhule, has been destroyed by the Fomorians. We believe that threat is not over."

"What's being done about it?" It was one of the nobles sitting farther down the table. She didn't know his name but she knew he was high-ranking with the Wood Elves.

"I have asked the Skye Elves for their assistance as well as the Fae," Andahar said.

"And we have agreed to help any way we can," Lady Talaiel said.

Laerwen couldn't help but admire her. She was cool and confident. A leader she would like to emulate.

"And I've received word from Queen Elyne in response to the missive I sent her a few days ago. She has agreed to send troops as soon as we need them," Andahar said.

"All that is well and good, Prince Andahar, but what is our position?" the same nobleman asked. "Why have you called us here this night?"

"I've called to ask you to for your approval to form a war council. With my father's failing health, it is left to me to find a solution to this matter with the Fomorians."

"So it's to be war, is it?"

"What Lord Malack means to express is that war is costly. Not only to the royal coffers but to lives," another nobleman said.

"Aye, I agree, Lord Calnon. But I believe it's a necessary war. An unavoidable war. One that we must face." Andahar gripped his goblet, his nail beds turning white. "If we do not prepare now, we will be ill-equipped for battle. I will not risk lives of innocents. I will not stand by and do nothing."

"Nor I." Lord Eldrin leaned forward and pinpointed his gaze first on Lord Malack and then on Lord Calnon. "It is our duty to respond to this new threat."

"What makes you so sure the Fomorians are coming back?" Malack fiddled with his knife, spinning it round and round as though bored with the entire discussion. "It could be they were sated with the destruction of the Hin'dar Rhule. Though I can't see why they wanted to destroy such a desolate area."

"A desolate area, my lord?" Laerwen spoke for the first time, her voice cold as the first snowfall. "Should I remind you the Hin'dar Rhule has provided you and other realms precious jewels? Some were even forged from the first fires of the volcanoes."

"And not much else. We can get jewels just about anywhere." Lord Malack didn't bother to hide his snooty tone. He even punctuated his insult with a sniff of derision.

"So are you then saying the Hin'dar Rhule doesn't matter?"

Malack looked right at her, his eyes dark and shadowed. "Aye.

That's what I'm saying." He pressed his lips together to punctuate his sentence.

Anger surged through Laerwen's veins so immediate she fisted her hand and bashed it against the table. Plates clattered in the aftermath. "My people were murdered. Does that mean nothing to you?"

"Lord Malack, do not downplay the tragedy at the Hin'dar Rhule. For it is a tragedy." Andahar reached for her, placing his hand over her fist. She relaxed then, his touch calming her. "The women were raped. The children were killed. The men who tried to defend them were slaughtered. The Fomorians did not take mercy on anyone. Even the king and queen were not spared. This is not something to be taken lightly. They will never be sated with that. They are nothing but barbaric brutes. A real threat to the Otherworld."

She glared at Lord Malack from her place at the table. His eyes touched on their twined fingers before meeting her gaze. He swallowed hard. Mayhap swallowing his pride as he said, "You have my condolences, your highness. I deeply regret my words here this evening. However," he paused and looked at Andahar then, "I cannot give you my vote for a war."

"I can," Lord Calnon said. "You have my support, Prince Andahar."

"And mine," Lord Eldrin said.

"Then shall we take an official vote? All those in favor of the war, say aye."

It would have been unanimous had Lord Malack voted but he abstained. The bastard. Laerwen would remember that, for now he had become her enemy.

"Now that the business has concluded, mayhap we can continue to dine with more pleasant conversation." Andahar had yet to release her hand and she was reluctant to remove it. He picked up his goblet and held it aloft. "To Princess Laerwen and the Fire Elves. Your fight is not yet over."

"Huzzah!" they cheered and toasted her.

All but Lord Malack who shoved his chair back, the legs scraping along the wood floor. He flung his napkin into his seat as he stalked from the dining hall. Everyone watched his retreat. Andahar squeezed her hand.

"Do not let him ruffle you, Princess," he said. He lifted her fingers to his lips and kissed the tips.

"Aye, ignore the bastard," Lord Eldrin added. "He's a crotchety old man who needs nothing more than a good lay with a woman to fix his bad attitude."

"Eldrin!" Talaiel scolded on a gasp. "That's not appropriate dinner conversation."

But Laerwen laughed. And it felt good to laugh, releasing all the pent-up tension and anger allowing her to enjoy her food.

The heavy meal included leek soup followed by roasted pheasant, roasted mutton, mushrooms in a cream sauce, as well as other vegetables and oat cakes. Dessert was some sort of frozen delight covered in chocolate sauce. She had never experienced anything like it but devoured it. When she scraped the bowl clean, a smiling Andahar pushed his bowl to her. She gave him a questioning look.

"You seemed to enjoy it."

She attacked it with relish. Far more than she had in years. She loved the way the cold dessert froze her tongue.

"We have nothing like this in my realm," she said. "What is it?"

"My human friends call it ice cream. One of them—a lady named Maggie—taught us how to make it."

"You mean you have more human friends than Sir Drake?"

He chuckled. "Aye. It's quite a story if you'd like to hear it someday."

"I would."

The light moment was interrupted with Leopold, Andahar's servant. He seemed to appear out of nowhere and leaned down to whisper something in Andahar's ear. Laerwen watched as the color drained from his face and his brow was immediately creased with worry. He nodded and rose, his gaze seeking Eldrin's.

"Lord Eldrin, would you come with me at once, please?"

Eldrin rose. "Is something wrong?"

"I'll tell you on the way."

Laerwen watched as they left abruptly. Fear crept over her. She had a terrible feeling it had something to do with the king.

Andahar hurried from the dining hall with Eldrin at his side.

"What is it?" Eldrin asked. "Is it Father?"

"Aye." Andahar couldn't stave off the fear gripping him.

"What did the message say, Andahar?" Eldrin's tone was demanding. He grabbed him by the arm and pulled him to a stop. "Tell me before we arrive."

"He woke again. He's stayed awake but he doesn't look well. We must hurry."

By the time they got to their father's chamber, Allanna was at his bedside. She perched on the edge, holding his hand. Navin stood on the other side, staunch yet stiff. Brom, their healer, stood at the foot of the bed waiting for them to arrive. But seeing his other siblings already there, Andahar knew nothing good would come of this.

"You're here at last," Brom said on the breath of relief.

"Thank the gods you came." Allanna jumped from the bed.

"Is he coherent?" Andahar asked.

"Aye...I am." The king himself answered. He lifted his hand and waved Andahar toward him. "Come closer...my son."

Andahar stepped toward the bed, took his hand and sat. Allanna and Eldrin crowded around him. He had to admit his father didn't look well at all. His skin was pale and thin. So thin, he could see the veins running a wiry path. His lips were stark white. While he held his hand, Andahar could swear he could feel every bone, he was so frail. It saddened him because he knew what was to come next. He knew his father would not live to see another sunrise.

"Father, you had us all worried," Andahar said and forced a smile.

He coughed a deep raspy cough before he got it under control. He squeezed Andahar's hand. "I'll not live much longer." His voice was a whisper.

"Don't talk like that. You'll be fine."

But Urdithane was already shaking his head. "You know it...to be true." He gasped for a breath, as though trying to suck as much air into his lungs as he could.

"Father..."

"Andahar....you will be king now. You...must protect the realm from...that monster. And...break the betrothal."

"That monster?" Andahar glanced back at Eldrin.

"He must think Marath still lives," Eldrin said.

Aye, of course. He wouldn't know the lord-regent had been killed or that Allanna had been saved from marrying him. "Father,

Marath is dead. Allanna is safe. We are all safe." It was a kind lie. One that would send his father to the gods with peace in his heart.

Urdithane patted his hand. "Good. That's good." He closed his eyes and leaned back into the pillow. "I know…the kingdom is safe…with you on the throne. And your brother…leading the rangers."

"Aye, Father."

Behind him, Allanna sniffed and hiccupped with a sob. She knew, as they all did, this was the final time their father would speak. He stole a glance over his shoulder, saw tears streaking down her face as Eldrin stood beside her, his arm around her shoulders for comfort.

"You will be a good king, my son," Urdithane said. His eyes fluttered open once more. He took a moment to look at each one of them. His gaze lingered on Navin first, then Eldrin, the Allanna. "You have all made me proud. My children."

With that he closed his eyes. His hand relaxed in Andahar'. He knew without a doubt his father had gone to the gods.

"Is he…" Eldrin started but stopped.

"Aye. He's gone."

Allanna turned into Eldrin and wept openly.

"May he find peace," Brom said.

They all bowed their heads in their own silent prayer.

Chapter 7

It seemed hours later when Andahar and his siblings left their father's chamber. Navin stalked off back to his post at the gate. Drake waited outside in the hallway to comfort Allanna. Lady Talaiel was also waiting for her husband to comfort Eldrin. But who would comfort him? When he walked from the king's chamber and out of the palace, the ach of loneliness pressed against his chest.

Night had fallen. The moon was bright and white in the sky, beaming down in shafts of light along the rope bridge. The very one where Marath had fallen to his death and Allanna had been saved by Eldrin and Sir Drake. He stood there now, gripping the rope handhold and staring out across the vast darkness.

His father was dead. He was king. In the morn, he would announce the passing of King Urdithane to the people. He would take the crown and sit on the throne. He would comfort his people as they began planning to lay the king to rest.

He wanted none of that. He did not wish to be king. Not yet.

He had fully expected his life as crown prince would continue. That his father would recover.

As he grappled with his grief and reluctance to rule, he thought of Laerwen. It did not compare to what she must have suffered when she learned her parents were gone, but he could understand her better now. Why she was unwilling to take the title of queen.

The bridge shifted underfoot and he knew someone had stepped out to join him. He smelled her before he saw her. Sensed her before she announced her presence. She had freely come to him. To console him. He turned to face her before she could speak.

She stood bathed in the silvery moonlight. Her hair seemed to sparkle beneath the opaque veil she still wore on her head. She clutched her elbows close to her body as she looked at him with those eyes that so mesmerized him. When she turned her head just right, he could see the stars dancing in her eyes.

"I heard from Lady Talaiel. Is it true?"

He could only nod.

A breath rushed out of her. "Oh, Andahar. I'm so very sorry about your father."

"Thank you, Laerwen."

They stared at each other a long moment and he watched as she shifted from one foot to the other, as though suddenly unsure what to say or do next. He should be grieving. He should be planning to take on the kingdom, to be crowned as king. But all he could think about was her hair. Gods, how much he wanted to see her hair and run his fingers through those long silky locks. Why was he thinking of that instead of his father? He should be ashamed that he wanted her. That he wanted to forget so soon.

But deep down, he knew Urdithane's death had been inevitable. He had never fully recovered from the poison. He had never awoken. Andahar had known he would die and, mayhap, he had mentally prepared for that eventuality.

Laerwen looked away, her hands fiddled with the edge of her veil. "I don't wish to disturb you. I just wanted to…offer my condolences. Good night." She dipped a quick curtsey.

"Wait. Please."

He stepped toward her before she could move away. She waited and watched as he approached.

"I don't wish you to leave. Stay with me. Stand with me." He offered his hand.

She hesitated. He couldn't see her expression, didn't know if her face held indecision but he could feel her emotions colliding around her. She tentatively reached for him, took her hand back.

"Please."

Again, she hesitated but at last reached for him, slipping her fingers into his. He gripped her hand, pulled her to him. Together, they turned and looked out onto the treetops while holding hands. It soothed him. Comforted him. Made him feel whole again.

"Thank you for coming," he said.

"I don't know why I did. Only that I needed to."

He glanced at her. "I'm glad you did."

"I know how…difficult this must be for you."

"Aye, I know you understand. Having experienced it yourself not so long ago."

Her hand tightened in his grip. "Aye." Her voice was quiet and wavered on the one word response.

His heart broke for her. She had lost so much and come here to him for help. As he stood there, the two of them staring out at the night, failure pressed against him like the night.

"I understand how you must feel now, Princess. Why you're reluctant to take on the title of queen."

She stiffened next to him, though she remained silent. Her hand didn't move from his but she knew it was a subject she avoided like a terminal disease.

"I am king now. As you are queen." He looked at her and marveled at the way her veil sparkled in the moonlight. Like tiny stars dancing over her head.

Her bottom lip trembled and she refused to look at him. "No. I am not queen."

"But you are." He reached for her, turning her to face him. "Laerwen, I understand. I do not wish to be king but it is my birthright. It is who I am. It is who you must now be too. You are the only ruler left of the Hin'dar Rhule, of the Fire Elves. You are the one who can lead your people back to greatness."

Tears had filled her eyes. He hadn't meant to make her cry. "Why are you saying this to me?"

"I want you to know I understand your loss."

She jerked her hands away. "You could never understand my loss."

"I do. My father was poisoned. Murdered as your parents were."

She stared at him, her eyes black orbs in the shadows. "Aye. They were." Her voice was so quiet he had to strain to hear her.

Andahar reached for her again, took her hands in his. "Have you grieved yet? In the time you have been here, I have not seen you grieve."

"I've dealt with my pain in my own way."

"Have you?"

"What do you wish of me, Andahar? You wish me to break down and cry here? In your arms?" She shook her head. "No. I'm stronger than that. I cannot crumble. I cannot break down. I cannot lose faith that someday I will be able to reclaim the Hin'dar Rhule."

"I know you are strong. One of the strongest women I have

ever known. Mayhap that's why I admire you so. Why I find you irresistible in every way." A slow smile spread on his lips.

She shivered. "You find me irresistible?"

"Completely."

He moved closer to her so he could smell her soft scent. She tipped her head up to him and in the darkness, he could still make out the shimmer of tears in her eyes. One slipped down her cheek. He brushed it away with his thumb.

"You are beautiful."

"Stop." Her voice was breathy. "I've already told you—"

"I know what you told me."

"And does that not mean anything to you?"

"A man sees what he wants and takes it." He pulled her to him, cupped her face and brushed her lips with his.

"You cannot take what does not belong to you."

"But I can try to steal what does not belong to me."

She sucked in a sharp breath between her slightly parted lips. She didn't pull away or try to stop him when his lips met hers. The kiss was soft and sweet. He didn't want to take too many liberties with her for she had already told him she would marry Randir.

"Andahar, please, you mustn't." She turned her head away from his wandering lips.

"Why? Why did you come to me tonight if not to comfort me?"

"I did come to comfort you. To offer my sympathies. Not to kiss you."

But her hands had landed on his chest. And she continued to stand there and let him hold her close.

"But you let me kiss you anyway."

"*Puthair.*" She flung the Elven curse at him as she pushed out his arms and stepped away. "You are incorrigible, sir."

"Aye, I am. One of my better qualifies." He grinned.

"You cannot mean to seduce me."

"I can. I will. I will fight Randir for you if I must."

"You will not fight him." She folded her arms over her chest. "I forbid it."

"Is that a challenge you've issued? I accept." He bowed with a flourish.

Footsteps on the bridge interrupted their banter. Andahar saw Leopold heading for him and straightened. He knew what that meant. He was needed.

"Your majesty." Leopold bowed. "Your presence is requested in the throne room."

"I'll be right there." The man nodded and left, giving them a few more minutes together. "I've been summoned. I take my leave of you." He took her hand, lifting it to his lips and brushing a kiss over it. "Until next time, my queen."

He left her on the bridge and headed for the throne room.

Cormac had never felt more alive. Though he had resisted Lorcann, he willfully accepted Balor. And, though the foolish mage didn't know it, he'd taken more of Lorcann's magic with him. It had been a painful transition. But once he realized he could take away the magic of the mage, he had calmed and accepted his new body.

Now Lorcann led him from the caves southward toward the Sorrow Lands. They had returned there to make their camp, to regroup and plan the end of the Otherworld. It had been on the mage's orders but now that he was back, it would be up to Cormac.

Cormac gladly took the responsibility. Being alive again—albeit in different skin—meant he could take control of his destiny. He had been a pawn of evil for first Kieran and then Morrigan. He had escaped eternal damnation from the underworld. His family may be dead but he would start anew.

The Sorrow Lands were called that for a reason—it was a desolate area in which no one wanted to live. It had once been part of the Hin'dar Rhule but the last volcanic eruption had destroyed it, laying it to waste. Leaving nothing behind but scarred land. Nothing could grow there. No creature, great or small, could survive there. No one wanted to live there. Here the sky was pink and the sun was bright.

On the westernmost edge, their watery prison was a reminder of where they'd come from. They had been there for thousands of years, only surviving due to the curse that held them in place. Morrigan had broken the spell, releasing a few of them so they could walk the land again. A few together were not a threat, but many made a formidable army that could not be defeated.

And so came Marath and his fascination with dark magic. He had released most of their kind. Lorcann had taken it upon himself to liberate the remaining prisoners. Or so the mage had told Cormac on the journey to their temporary home.

When they arrived, Cormac paused to survey the land. A few tents dotted the landscape. The harsh wind blew across the cracked earth, billowing dust along with it. Here, there was not much protection from the elements. But they hadn't planned to be there long.

"This is all that is left of our people?" Cormac asked.

"No. There are others waiting for your command," Lorcann said.

"Assets?"

"Weapons, gold, jewels."

"Gold and jewels do not interest me. Liabilities?"

"We lost some men at the battle at the Hin'dar Rhule."

"What battle?" Cormac turned to him, met his watery gaze. "You attacked?"

"When Lord Marath died in the Woodlands, it released the dark spell he had on the kingdom. Most of our people managed to escape. Some did not. We traveled west to the Hin'dar Rhule. Through the Heartlands. You must understand, my friend, the men were restless and in need of encounters."

"You destroyed innocents."

"We destroyed most of those people who lived in the Heartlands, aye. And the Hin'dar Rhule suffered." He smiled, well pleased with himself.

But Cormac didn't like the thought of innocent men, women and children dying. He had seen it all too often in his battles while working for Kieran and Morrigan. He wanted no more part of it.

"How did you leave it?"

"Destroyed. The king and queen were killed."

Cormac scowled. They had senselessly destroyed a kingdom. And for what? They had taken nothing but gold, weapons, jewels.

"Prisoners?"

"None."

"Survivors?" Cormac asked.

"A few. I'm told they scurried to the Woodlands, which is where we intend to attack next."

Cormac never let his gaze leave the land in front of him. His pulse throbbed an angry beat. He could feel the vein pulsating on the side of his head. He wanted to turn to the man, grab him by the collar and beat in his face. Instead, he stood there looking at the group of people gathered and nodded, maintaining his calm façade.

"Good."

He hated the thought. He hated the thought of attacking the Woodlands and killing more. And for what?

"What is your end game, Lorcann?"

"End game?"

He turned to the mage, pinning him with his stare. "What do you intend to do with the Woodlands should your attack succeed?"

"Take what we want." He pressed his lips together in a fierce line.

"Such as?" Cormac pressed.

"Such as all the women we want. Any resources we need. Anything."

He intended to rape the women and steal from their realm. Why did this anger Cormac so much? Before he had gone along with the plan to kill the Fae with Kieran. That Dark Elf wanted total domination over the Otherworld, both the Seelie and Unseelie realm. Cormac had gone along with it because Kieran had captured his wife and children. He had threatened to kill them unless Cormac helped him. As a mage with his own power, Kieran used him to do his bidding.

But Kieran had died and Cormac had been captured by the Fae princess before he could find out the location of his family. Before he could rescue them. He had been such a fool to think he could find them himself. When Morrigan offered him her help, he had taken it. And, again a fool, he had lost them. He had lost his life in the underworld.

And now…he was nothing but another pawn of evil. He had no interest in destroying the Elves or the Fae. The only difference this time was, he was in command of his own people. Things could be different. Mayhap he could find a way to get free of this madness. To live his life in peace.

"And the Fire Elven princess is with them. We need her," Lorcann said.

"Why?" Cormac folded his arms over his chest.

"Because once we have her, we can sacrifice her. Her blood will release the magic from the fires of the Hin'dar Rhule. Magic we can take for ourselves."

"So you wish to attack the Woodlands, kill those who would

protect her and capture her?"

Lorcann nodded.

Senseless killing. All for magic.

"We will discuss the plan more later. First let us rejoice you are back among the living."

"I wish to meet my people," Cormac said. "Take me."

"Our people you mean."

Cormac did not appreciate the correction and ignored it as he stepped toward the small cluster of tents. Already Lorcann was trying his patience.

As the mage led him into the maze, people emerged to see him. Lorcann made the introductions and they responded with a kind of reverence Cormac had never seen before. As though they thought of him as a god. Mayhap he was to them since he'd risen from the dead—a feat not many could accomplish.

At the last tent in the line, a woman stepped out and paused. Her eyes the color of spilled ink landed on Cormac as her long black hair blew in the breeze. She reminded him of Morrigan with all that hair. She had a perfect heart-shaped mouth and high cheekbones. Something about her was different than any Fomorian woman he had ever encountered. His gaze narrowed as he looked at her. She never looked away as she watched the two of them approach.

"Gweneth," Lorcann said and moved to stand beside her. He slid his arm around her waist and pulled her to him. "My woman."

A sensuous light passed between Cormac and Gweneth, though. Something he could not explain. Had she felt it too? Her gaze never left his face as she peered at him with her interested gaze.

"More of our people are in the Heartlands and other realms," Lorcann said. "We will regroup with them later."

"Good. I wish to discuss a plan of attack on the Woodlands." He wanted to know exactly how they intended to kill off the Wood Elves and steal the Fire princess. A quick glance at the sky told him dusk approached. "We will convene in the morn."

"Aye, you'd want to rest after your long journey. There's a tent for you there." He nodded across the way.

How convenient.

Lorcann turned toward his tent, pulling Gweneth along with him. She turned her head to keep her gaze on Cormac as they entered, disappearing through the flap of canvas.

Cormac remained there a long while staring at the place she'd stood looking back at him. There was something distinct about the way she regarded him. As though she intended to find him later and seduce him. He had been seduced by evil women before—Morrigan for one. Did he want to tempt fate with Lorcann's woman?

He didn't think so.

Even so, he couldn't get her face out of his mind as he headed back through the encampment. Someone had begun to roast meat over a fire. The succulent smell wafted to him on the slight breeze, making his stomach rumble in response. He joined several of the others who stared at him with wide curious eyes, as though he were something out of the tales of old.

He couldn't blame them. He had been resurrected from the underworld after all. With his belly full, he located his empty tent save for the mattress, a few blankets and a lantern. He lit the lantern and fell to the bed, his arms propped behind his head as he stared up at the canvas.

Now that he was truly alone, he could admit that he missed his wife. He hadn't seen her face in a very long time. So long he couldn't even remember what she looked like. It pained him. And his children. Though their faces were emblazoned on his mind, they would forever remain young. Morrigan, that bitch, had killed them.

A rustle outside his tent made him lift up. He saw the shadow move across the material then return to the entrance and pause. It was a shapely outline and undoubtedly female.

Gweneth shoved aside the flap and entered. Cormac propped himself up on his elbows and looked her over with a curious eye. She stood there, staring down at him with those dark round eyes.

She stepped toward him and fell to her knees beside the mattress. Her hands pushed her hair back and a moment later, she pulled the dress from her shoulders.

Cormac sat up and grasped her wrists. "Don't."

Her hands stilled but her gaze never left his. "Is this not what you wanted?"

"You belong to another." He nodded toward the tent across from his. Lorcann. Though he didn't fear the man, he respected him enough not to take his woman. Though she clearly wanted to be taken.

"He sleeps."

"He'll wake."

"Not for a while." A slow smile spread on her pretty lips. "I put him under a sleeping spell."

Surprise flickered through him. Most of the women in their race did not have magic. But she did. "You have power."

"And a lot of it." She leaned toward him, her lips parted ready to kiss him.

"You are not a Fomorian." He pushed her back. "Who are you?"

"No, I am not." She made to kiss him again but again he pushed her away.

"Tell me who you are."

"I am a woman who wants you. That is all that matters."

"A woman of power."

"A woman of lust," she whispered. "Take me, Cormac. Let me slide under you."

"No."

"Because I belong to him." He nodded. "Lorcann is a weak fool. He doesn't possess the power you do. He thinks he does but he's wrong."

"And how do you know that?"

"Because he gave it all to you when he brought you from the underworld. He doesn't know it yet."

How did she know he had taken it?

"And you do?" He cocked his head to the side and looked her over. She wasn't a Fomorian, he knew that. She was far too beautiful for that. So who—or what—was she?

"He needed a sorceress. He asked for my help. I gave it." She leaned into him, brushed her lips against his. She tasted sweet and sinful. Like dark chocolate melting on a hot summer day. "But his request came with a price."

Damn her. He couldn't resist taking a sip of her. He brushed a kiss against her lips and his shaft thickened into a painful erection. He couldn't deny he wanted her. "One you failed to mention."

She grinned. "He did not ask. I did not divulge."

"You robbed him of his power."

"It was necessary." She slipped her wrists from his grasp and shoved her dress down her shoulders, exposing her breasts topped with dark red nipples, peaked and ready for him. "He had to give up something to give you life."

"His power."

So mayhap it wasn't Lorcann's power but Balor's. He must have absorbed it when he took over his body.

"You are a smart mage, aren't you?"

"And you are a sorceress."

Unable to resist her anymore, he pulled her to him and they tumbled backward. Their mouths collided. His tongue dipped into her mouth, tasting all that she was. Her mouth was willing and ready. Pliant. Giving. Wanting. Needing. Taking all that he had and more. She landed on top of him, her legs open and straddling him. Her heated inner core rubbed against his hardened length, making the pain of wanting her even more excruciating.

"I helped bring you back to life. You owe me."

She licked her way along his jaw, making him groan. Then nipped her way back to his lips. She took her time kissing him, tasting him. Her breasts crushed into his chest, the perfect mounds soft and supple, while her hips rocked against his.

"What do you want?"

"I thought that obvious. I want you." She sat up, pushing her core against him and rocking again. Her fingers trailed down his chest.

"And Lorcann?"

She shrugged a shoulder. "He matters not."

Her hands slipped under his tunic, shoving the material up and out of the way. He shrugged out of it.

"If he doesn't matter, then remove the dress and get on top of me."

Another grin. She stood, shimmied out of the dress and kicked the material out of the way. While she did that, he pushed his trousers down and freed his erection. She straddled him again and lowered herself down into his thickened shaft, sliding her warm wet center over him. Her breath hissed out of her. His fingers dug into her hips.

She rode him hard. He let her take control. Her body was soft and wet. Demanding and yielding. It had been so long since he'd caressed the flesh of a woman and he'd forgotten how damn good it felt. He'd forgotten so much about the intimate experience.

But she was willing to give herself to him. Her back arched as she tossed her head back, the ends of her long hair tickling his thighs. He watched as her breasts bounced while she moved against him, her body milking and sucking him until he could no longer hold back. They climaxed together and when it was all over, she collapsed on his chest.

"You can command them, you know," she said, her voice thickened with contentment.

"Them?"

"The clan. Lorcann does not hold their loyalty."

"And what will I do with their loyalty?"

"They will follow you into battle."

"Is that what they want? To kill? To destroy?"

Her fingers traced a lazy circle along his chest. "That is what any Fomorian wants."

He didn't want that. He wanted away from the fighting, the killing, the evil. He wanted to live in peace.

"But not what you want," she said as though she'd heard his thoughts.

He grabbed her by the upper arms and jerked her up so she had to look him in the eye. "How do you know what I want?"

"By your reaction when he said we would attack the Woodlands. If you do not go through with it, he will think you a traitor and have you killed."

"Let him try," Cormac said through clenched teeth.

She was unfazed by his threat. Her hands flattened on his chest. "You can have anything you want. Even the Otherworld. Why don't you take it?"

"I do not want to rule the Otherworld. Let the Elves and Fae have it."

"Then what will you do?"

His hands tangled in her long, soft longs. "Forget it for now. I want to feel you again."

He gathered her to him and rolled, pushing her down into the mattress. Her legs opened again and he nestled between them, plunging his shaft deep into her core. Tonight he would do with her as he pleased. On the morrow, he would consider what he'd do later.

Gweneth was gone when he awoke in the morning. Too bad. He would have had his way with her once again if she had been there. It was probably for the best she wasn't since she still belonged to Lorcann. She must have slipped out in the night and returned to his tent.

He couldn't stop from feeling disappointed and jealous.

He rose, dressed and left his tent. The morning was bright and shiny. His first morning in the Sorrow Lands. His first morning alive and well once again. He inhaled the fresh scent of the dry air, letting it fill his lungs and rejuvenate him. He was whole once again.

Lorcann stepped out of his tent with Gweneth. He grasped her hand in his but she eyed Cormac the entire time.

"Good. You're awake. We have much to discuss."

Before he could reply, the mage headed off. Cormac followed, keeping his gaze fixated on the girl's swinging hips. He couldn't forget the way she moved under him last night or the way her velvet mouth tasted. He longed to taste her again.

Lorcann joined several others in another tent with a low table and a line of cushions. These were the same men who had journeyed with them to the Sorrow Lands from the underworld. They had assisted with Cormac's resurrection for which he was grateful. They feasted on porridge in bread bowls and drank ale or mead. All conversation halted when the three of them entered the tent.

"Now that we're all gathered," Lorcann said, "we can discuss how we will take the Hin'dar Rhule."

"I thought you said it had been destroyed," Cormac said.

"I did. And it was mostly destroyed. A few remained behind. They are now dead. The survivors fled to the Woodlands. That is where we will find the princess."

"Why do you want her?"

"Because she is the key to our survival." Lorcann waved him to a seat across from him.

Once he was seated, a servant brought him food and drink. He quaffed the ale in one long swig. It seemed a lifetime since he'd had a strong drink of ale.

"The lovely Gweneth has been gracious to share some information with me about the volcanoes of the Hin'dar Rhule."

She sat beside Lorcann, her sultry gaze never leaving Cormac's face. "Ancient legends tells us the volcanoes of the Hin'dar Rhule erupt every eight thousand years when the moon and sun align. A fortnight from now, they will align at precisely the same moment when the eight thousand years are up."

"When the volcanoes explode once more, the lava can be used to harness power," Lorcann said. "Once we do that, we will be invincible."

"That's why you drove out the Fire Elves?" Cormac asked.

"It is." He smiled, showing his toothy grin. One that was riddled with yellow and black teeth. "The magic in the Hin'dar Rhule is unprecedented. Those Fomorians who have yet to come into their powers will have it once they feel the power of the lava."

Cormac's brows drew together. "I fail to see how anyone can 'feel the power' of the lava. It's deadly to all but the Fire Elves."

"It's even deadly to the Fire Elves, though they have a higher tolerance to it than us," Gweneth said.

"That is why I intend to capture the princess. She is of pure noble blood. We will take her to the volcano and use her. But she's fled to the Woodlands with the remaining Fire Elves."

"That's why you want to attack the Woodlands. To capture the princess of the Fire Elves?" Cormac asked.

"It is the only reason. Once we have her, we will travel back to the Hin'dar Rhule."

"And how exactly do you intend to use her to harness this power?" Cormac asked.

"She will have to die," Gweneth replied. "When the lava begins to flow, her blood must be spilled to mix with the molten rock to release the power within."

"She and the rest of the Fire Elves will be destroyed," Lorcann added.

"You intend to commit genocide?" Cormac looked at him then and saw him for the evil he was. "Why? The Fire Elves have harmed no one."

"They have the valuable land we want and need."

Cormac didn't like this plan. He didn't like killing for the sake of killing. Or killing for the sake of magic. And to wipe out an entire race? It was too diabolical, even for Fomorians.

"We leave today for the Woodlands. Once we have the princess, we will immediately start our journey to the Hin'dar Rhule."

"And what makes you think you'll be able to capture her?" Cormac asked. "The Woodlands are guarded by a warded gate and gatekeepers."

"And wards by the Skye Elves. Aye, this I know already. But these are merely obstacles, nothing that can stop us from our ultimate goal." Lorcann waved away the idea as though it were a gnat. "Aside from that, King Urdithane is dead. He was never able to recover from the poison Marath gave him. That leaves the realm virtually unprotected."

"There will be a new king named by now."

"Andahar," Lorcann said. "The eldest and first in line. He is nothing but a weakling. He will be dealt with." He leveled his gaze at Cormac. "I expect you to handle him."

"Which means?"

"I want you to kill him."

"Killing Andahar will serve no purpose other than killing him. There will be someone else to step in as king once he's dead."

"Andahar poses the most threat. He has connections to the Fae Queen and the Skye Elves."

"Those connections won't be severed just because he's dead," Cormac said.

Lorcann narrowed his eyes. "Are you saying you won't kill him?"

"I'm saying it's not necessary to kill him."

"I want him dead. And you'll do that." Lorcann narrowed his gaze at Cormac. "Or do you want me to send you back to the underworld?"

Under the table, Cormac clasped his hands tightly, his knuckles leeching of color. His muscles tensed as irritation clawed through him. He didn't appreciate being threatened. He had been bullied by enough power-hungry war-mongers and he was done with all that. He glanced at Gweneth whose eyes sparked with what looked like anger.

"Don't threaten me, Lorcann."

"Then do my biding and I won't have to."

There would be time enough for him to get back at Lorcann. He would. He just needed to figure out how.

"Let's get back to business," the mage said.

With the discussion back on track, Cormac let them work it out. He had other plans.

Chapter 8

He had said he would fight Randir for her if he must. He had kissed her as though he meant it.

Laerwen still could not get Andahar's words out of her head as she stood at the window and stared out at the morning. It was a bright day with a clear pink sky only dotted by a few clouds here and there.

She thought of Andahar all night. She couldn't get the devil out of her head. Nor could she stop feeling his kiss. She pressed her fingertips against her lips, remembering the way his mouth pressed against hers. First on horseback to meet Eldrin and then later on the rope bridge outside the palace.

How could he have affected her so deeply and so quickly? It was as though that intimacy spoke to her soul.

Laerwen had told him she intended to marry Randir. She owed it to her people to make sure the royal bloodline stayed true. Why, then, did she allow him to kiss her last night? Why did she find it terribly romantic to have him want to fight for her?

The answer was indisputable—her feelings didn't lie. Andahar had awakened her deepest desires. When he'd kissed her, there was a curious swooping in her lower abdomen. Longing rushed through her with a fierceness she could not deny—though she must. She was committed to Randir whether she liked it or not.

She knew Andahar grieved for his father, though he held his emotions in check. Laerwen had done the same when she'd learned of her parents' deaths that fateful night in the Hin'dar Rhule. And though their situations were not the same, they were similar. She understood his reluctance to rule. Her feelings were much the same.

Andahar had been crowned king in a small, private service with only his family and the High Druid to preside over the ceremony. No outsiders were allowed, not even the commoners. Today he would stand before his people as a newly-crowned king while they paid their final respects to Urdithane as he laid in state. Andahar had moved from crown prince to king in a matter of minutes while she still resisted the title of queen. She still resisted the idea of ruling her realm.

She just…couldn't.

A knock interrupted her thoughts. "Come."

Lord Eldrin stepped inside. "Princess, would you like to go with Lady Talaiel and me to the throne room?"

"Aye, I would. How kind of you to escort me."

She forced her feet to walk from the window to Eldrin's side. He granted her a smile as he swung the door wide for her exit. The Lady of the Skye stood in the hallway, wrapped in a grown of snowy white, her coppery hair spilling over her shoulders. She was the type of woman who outshone everyone in the room. She made Laerwen feel like a waif and troll.

"How is Andahar?"

"He fares well," Eldrin said. "My sister, however, is not."

"What do you mean?"

"He means the princess is taking the death of the king hard," Talaiel said. "She's quite distraught."

"Their last words to each other were not so cordial," Eldrin supplied. "I'm sure she bears some guilt for that."

Laerwen considered her last words to her own parents. They were nothing to be remembered, to be sure. They had bid each other good night before retiring. Before the attack came and they were killed. But she would often recall them with a fondness, happy for the time they had together.

"Surely she knows her father loved her to the very end."

"She does. And he did. But she still has regret." Eldrin didn't hide the sadness in voice. "I feel for her. I wish there was something I could do to help her."

"Time will heal her," the lady said.

They arrived at the throne room where all the nobles and commoners alike had gathered, waiting their turn to pass by the old king and say their final farewells. Eldrin and Lady Talaiel, though, walked to the front of the room where the rest of the royal family stood.

Lord Randir and Hiram were off to the side from the family, but still in a place of honor. Andahar had brought them together since they were visiting dignitaries. She was touched by the gesture.

She had never expected him to include them in such a personal memorial.

The king lay on a raised platform, his hands clasped over the hilt of his sword. He was dressed in his finery. The translucent burial shroud had been draped over him in preparation for his entombment.

She hadn't even been able to do that with her parents. According to Hiram, no one wanted to see what was left of them. He wouldn't let even her see them before they departed the Hin'dar Rhule. They had left behind a small band of men to take care of the dead. She hoped they were able to burn them in the fires. But what of those left? They were dead with no one to put them to rest.

Princess Allanna stood to the left of Andahar, her husband on the other side of her. She leaned into him, a kerchief crushed in her hand as she dabbed at her falling tears. Lord Navin was on the right of the crown prince. He stood stiffly, his back ramrod straight as he stared straight ahead looking at nothing. And everything.

Andahar met her gaze, his eyes watery. But when he saw her, he straightened. He smiled, as though glad to see her.

Navin stepped aside to allow Eldrin and Lady Talaiel their place beside the new king. Laerwen intended to join her people when she heard Andahar speak her name in a soft voice. She looked at him over her shoulder. He held his hand out to her.

"I would be honored."

Gods, he didn't mean to have her next to him, did he? But he hadn't dropped his hand and he stood there with that wounded look. How could she resist him? She took his hand and he pulled her to his side. He laced their fingers.

And there they were for the remainder of the service, hand in hand. As though she stood with him as his queen. Her cheeks warmed at the thought. Had that been his intention or did he not think what the outward appearance would be? What it would speak to his people? As the citizens of the Woodlands came one after the other to say goodbye to their king, they glanced in her direction. Some with curiosity in their gaze, others with an aloofness that bespoke of their displeasure.

She did not miss the look of disdain that passed on Randir's face as he watched them together. A pang of guilt flashed through her as she quickly looked away. She would have to make it up to him, to explain to him she had no choice but to accept his offer. She could not have refused him in front of his family or his clan.

It seemed they stood there forever. She shifted from one foot to the other and after a while, her feet and back ached. Even through it all, Andahar never released her hand. When the last of the men, women and children had passed by, Andahar moved to the king's side, gazing down at him. Allanna joined him, as did Eldrin and Navin. Laerwen remained where she was since she didn't want to interfere in the small family gathering. The princess placed a long-stemmed pink rose on top of the king's body before turning away, her face buried in her kerchief as her husband took her in his arms.

All Laerwen could think about was her own parents. How they had died at the hands of those bloody Fomorians. Heated tears burned the backs of her eyes. She blinked furiously, trying to keep them away but knowing she couldn't. They spilled down her cheeks as Andahar turned toward her.

When he looked at her, she crumbled completely. He moved to her, reaching for her and brushing away the tears with the pads of his thumbs. He cupped her face and for a moment, she thought he might kiss her. Here, in front of his family and what was left of hers. But instead he smiled.

"Thank you for being here." He said it so only she would hear.

Laerwen wrapped her arms around his neck and hugged him. She knew she shouldn't but she couldn't stop herself. He held her close, his arms around her waist, their bodies pressing against each other. And all the while Randir and Hiram looked on. She could practically feel the daggers of jealousy Randir stared at her.

Before Andahar released her, he placed a soft kiss on her temple.

And then he stepped away from her and watched as several pallbearers lifted the king's body from the dais and walked with a slow gait toward the palace exit. One by one, the royal family fell in step behind them. She stole a glance at Hiram and Randir.

Randir did not look pleased with her at all. Nor did Hiram. But she would not relinquish her place at Andahar's side, even though she knew she would bear the wrath later with both of them. So be it.

The king would be laid to rest today.

Once outside on the rope bridge, she watched as they placed his body in an elaborate basket and slowly lowered him to the ground with the pulley system they had in place. It was something she had never really noticed before. Several stood at the top while there were others at the bottom to take his body. The royal family continued to the winding tree staircase.

When they were on the ground, another set of pallbearers took the king and headed through the Woodlands, past all the homes to the other side of the loch to a large mausoleum. She didn't feel right following Andahar and his siblings, so she waited with Randir and Hiram as they disappeared inside.

Randir stood next to her, his body rigid and stiff. Hiram was on her other side, his arms folded over his chest. She whisked away the remaining tears, thinking of her parents and how Andahar must be feeling with the loss of his father.

"What happens to us now, Princess?" Hiram asked.

"I do not know," she said. "Andahar is king now. He understands our plight. He will help us. I'm sure of it."

"Are you sure, Laerwen?" Randir's voice held an angry edge to it.

She knew he was jealous. "Aye, I'm sure. He promised to help rebuild the Hin'dar Rhule. I believe he will keep that promise."

"Because he's in love with you."

She stared at him, dumbfounded. "Lord Randir, his offer of help does not mean he's in love with me. It simply means he intends to help us rebuild."

"I've seen the way he looks at you. And you at him." He crowded her, standing so close she could see the anger in his eyes. "You are still betrothed to me."

"And I intend to marry you." She lifted her head, her grief and tears forgotten. "That has not changed. That will not change."

"And when will we marry, Princess? You have yet to commit to a date."

A surge of anger flowed through her. The Fomorians attacked on their wedding day. Had it not been for that, they would have been wedded by now. "Now does not seem the time. Need I remind you of the extenuating circumstances?"

"You do not. The Fomorians destroyed our land but it doesn't mean we have to allow them to destroy our marriage." Determination etched on his face. "Marry me now, Laerwen. Here in the Woodlands."

She balked. She was not ready for that. Not yet. In the back of her mind, she had intended to see the battle with the Fomorians won before marrying Randir. She wanted to be wed in her own realm. "I am committed to you and our people, Randir. I intend to marry you. To return to the Hin'dar Rhule once the threat of the Fomorians has been neutralized. And together we will rule the realm."

"You wish to wait then?"

"Aye, until we can return to the Hin'dar Rhule."

"I don't think that's a wise decision," Hiram said. "Randir is right. You should marry at once."

"No." She would not be bullied into it by either of them. "We will wait."

Randir huffed out a breath and relaxed, his shoulders drooping. "Pushing you will only make you all the more stubborn. Forgive me. I shouldn't have."

"I made a promise to you. I intend to keep it."

"I'm glad to hear you say that." He granted her a smile.

"As am I," Hiram added. "It is clear the new king of the Wood Elves has taken a fancy to you."

She couldn't stop thinking about Andahar telling her he would fight Randir for her. Laerwen knew he meant it, but she hoped it wouldn't come to that. She knew Andahar's feelings for her. He'd made it clear with his words and his kisses.

"I assure you there is nothing between us," she said. "We should return to the palace and await the royal family. I don't think they'd want us standing around waiting for them to come out."

The three of them headed away from the loch putting distance between them and the mausoleum. Randir moved to walk beside her. He grasped her hand, holding it much like Andahar had.

"I know you do not love me, Laerwen," he said, his voice low so Hiram would not hear. "But I hope in time that will change."

She met his gaze and looked at him. Really looked at him. He had a regal face with chiseled features. He had perfectly shaped lips and long dark lashes framing his dark blue eyes. His nose was perfect. His dark hair was thick and wavy with a lock brushing his forehead. He was not unattractive and yet there was something about him that didn't mesmerize her as Andahar did. The Wood Elf had roused something inside her she hadn't known existed until she met him.

Her gaze landed on Randir's lips and she wondered how he would kiss her. Like Andahar? Would she feel that same swooping sensation in the pit of her gut? He paused and turned her to face him, taking her face in his hands. Her heart sped up to a quick beat as she waited, breathlessly, for what she knew was to come.

His mouth slowly descended to hers in a tentative yet sweet kiss. A kiss of hesitation. As though he wasn't sure he should be kissing her. She let him capture her mouth and taste her. When their mouths fused together, there was…nothing. Absolutely nothing. But it was clear to her Randir enjoyed the kiss for he groaned deep in his throat. His arms slipped around her waist and pulled her to him. All the while, all she could think about was how Andahar had tasted like wild berries. How Andahar had kissed her with reckless abandon. How his mouth had moved over hers with exquisite tenderness and caressed her lips more than kissing them.

Randir did not kiss her that way. His mouth was warm and light, his lips slow and thoughtful. But there was no passion, no fire, no yearning. It was nothing more than his mouth pressed against hers. He didn't even try to taste her with his tongue.

How disappointing.

Suddenly his body was jerked from hers and he stumbled backward. The next thing she saw was Andahar throwing a punch and landing his fist on Randir's jaw with a loud crack. Fury burned in his eyes, as though he couldn't believe the man had the audacity to kiss her.

Randir staggered backward, as surprised by the blow as she was. But Andahar wasn't finished with his assault. He threw another punch at her betrothed but this time he was ready for him. He blocked it and swung back, his fist connecting with the king's gut. Andahar expelled a muffled "oof" before regaining his footing and attacking him once again.

"Stop it! Stop this at once!" she shouted.

But it was to no avail. The two men had collided again in an all-out war with fists flying. Andahar landed a punch on the side of Randir's head. He grunted and grasped the king's tunic in one hand while swinging at his head with the other. His fist connected with his nose. They pounded each other while Laerwen stood there, mouth agape, as the two of them acted like boys fighting over her.

Lord Eldrin and Sir Drake ran toward them. Eldrin grabbed his brother by the collar and yanked him away, pulling him off Randir.

Drake wrapped his arms around Randir from behind, clamping his arms to his side.

Andahar's nose was bloody and dripping while Randir spit out a clot of blood. Apparently, the Wood Elf had landed several good punches.

"What is wrong with you two?" Laerwen demanded, her hands on her hips.

"Why is he kissing you?" Andahar demanded.

"He is my betrothed. The man I intend to marry. Or have you forgotten?"

"She's mine." Randir gave him a bloodied smile of triumph.

"You hush." She pointed at him and turned back to Andahar. "I told you before I intend to marry Randir."

"And I told you, Princess, I would fight him for you if I had to." His heated gaze landed on Randir. "I had to. He was kissing you."

"When did he say that?" Randir struggled against Drake but he wouldn't release him. "Let me go you overgrown human."

"No," Laerwen said, answering for Drake. "Sir Drake, please take Lord Randir to his chamber in the palace. I wish to have a word with King Andahar. Alone." She placed particular emphasis on the word king.

"Laerwen—"

"Randir, please. I beg you." She stepped toward him. "Please go with Sir Drake. I will get this all sorted out."

"If he lays a hand on you—"

"He won't." But secretly she hoped he did. A hand and the brush of a lip.

Andahar shrugged off his brother. But Eldrin waited, one hand on the hilt of his sword.

"Leave us," Andahar said.

"Are you certain?" Eldrin asked.

He nodded "Go."

Eldrin and the others filed past, leaving the two of them alone among the trees. Andahar wiped blood off his nose with the back of his hand. They stood there in the quiet of the woods, staring at each other. Now that she had him alone, she wasn't sure what to say to him. All she knew for certain was Randir did not make her feel as Andahar had when he kissed her. She was terrified of that. Terrified she would end up in a loveless, lonely marriage with a man who did nothing for her.

"My apologies, Princess." He had blood on his sleeve as he tried to staunch the flow from his nose. "I saw him kissing you there and I…I don't know what happened. I snapped. All I saw was red. Anger. Jealousy. Emotions I'm not familiar with when it comes to a woman."

"It's been an emotional day for all of us," she said, trying to find an excuse—any excuse—to make for him. "You're weary and not thinking clearly. I'm sure it has nothing to do with me."

"I'm thinking clearly enough," he snapped. "And it has everything to do with you. I didn't like seeing him kiss you."

"Why?"

"Because you belong to me, damn it."

Her heart tripped. Warmth spread through her, making her body tingle with excitement. He wanted her. He thought of her as his. She had never seen such a fierce need or devotion from anyone. Even so, she knew she couldn't allow him to think so.

"But I don't belong to you, Andahar. I belong to Lord Randir. My decision still stands. I intend to go through with the marriage. He is of my clan. He can help me rebuild the Fire Elves."

Andahar charged toward her, his eyes still burning with a hint of fury. But she could see, too, the fiery desire there. "You don't want that. You don't want him."

"I do want him. It's the right thing to do. It is my duty—"

"Duty." He snorted. "You didn't even realize your arms hung by your side the entire time he held you in his. Did you?"

He was right. Laerwen had allowed Randir to hold her close to him, but she couldn't bring herself to do the same. She could only think of Andahar.

"You think you know me so well. Randir is the only man I want."

"No it's not." His tone was critical, harsh, unyielding as he ripped out the three words. A shadow of annoyance crossed his face before he regained his composure, his hands flexing to calm his ragged nerves. "You want me."

"No." When he tried to take another step toward her, she put her hand on his chest. "No, Andahar."

"You cannot deny you feel nothing for me."

Damn him for seeing right through her. Was she so transparent? Pain tightened in her throat, a lump forming there.

She swallowed hard to keep her emotions in check as a flash of wild grief cleaved her. "We cannot do this. And you know why."

Despite her attempt to keep her voice steady, it wobbled.

"Will you stand there and tell me when I kissed you, you did not feel the heat of desire as I did? That you did not feel as though we were made to kiss each other? That you were born for me and only me?" Desire burned bright in his eyes. So bright and so hot, she could almost feel it. He leaned closer to her, his voice a deathly whisper. "Or do I need to kiss you again?"

His words burned her, scorched her exposed skin, making her dizzy and her body threaten to be engulfed in flames. She wanted to fall into his arms, let him kiss her again. Feel those velvety soft lips against hers again. Taste the wild berries and honeywine on his tongue and know that he, too, burned for her.

But it was not to be. She wouldn't—couldn't—allow it.

"Stop." She pushed harder on his chest. He relaxed, allowed her to shove him away. He took a step back, the disappointment clear in his crystalline eyes. "Randir is my future."

"Then tell me the truth. You feel nothing for me?"

"Nothing."

The pain of saying it knifed through her, slicing her from throat to navel. Opening her and making her bleed her guilt, her sorrow, her despair. All made worse to see the crestfallen look collapse the hope in his face. But she had to tell him, didn't she? She had to make him believe she didn't love him. If a little. She had to make him understand she belonged to Randir and she would marry him no matter what. Her duty, loyalty and responsibility to her people was that strong. So strong she was willing to sacrifice her own happiness to make sure her people never suffered again, to make sure their home was once again in the Hin'dar Rhule, to make sure she and Randir would protect it with a never before seen fierceness.

Aye, she had to make Andahar understand and believe that.

He backed away from her. "If that's truly how you feel, then I won't bother you again. You have my word."

He left her there in the woods to return to the palace. The moment he was out of her sight, she crumbled to her knees and put her face in her hands.

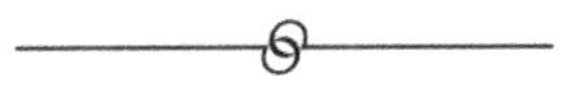

Laerwen didn't know how long she was there alone in the woods. Once she managed to get her emotions under control, she sat back on her heels and looked up at the sky. She could hear the chirping of birds and the swaying of the trees in the slight breeze. The rustle of leaves.

She hated the decision she had to make but knew, deep down, it was the right one. She would forever mourn the loss of Andahar. Would they have been able to make a life together? Talaiel and Eldrin seemed to have figured that out. But a Skye Elf and a Wood Elf were not so different.

She was used to the dry, arid climate of the Hin'dar Rhule. Here, where it was humid and damp most of the time, it was as though she were suffocating. As though she were drowning. She tried to ignore it. But now, as she sat on the blanket of leaves, it pressed all around her. No, she could not live here for the rest of her days.

As she sat there, it had gone eerily quiet. Glancing up, she noticed the birds had all but deserted the treetops. Their song was no more. Where had they gone? She climbed to her feet and strained her ears to listen.

Something was amiss. Laerwen took off at a dead run. As she neared, she could hear screams and shouts. And she could smell smoke. The closer she got, she could see the Woodlands was on fire.

Her heart nearly stopped. Fear burned through her veins like acid. She halted on the edge of the clearing, her muddled brain having a difficult time trying to understand what was happening.

Fomorians. They were here in the Woodlands, attacking what was left of her people and the Wood Elves. And she had no weapons. No way to defend herself. But she had to do something. She had to stop them.

Several trees to her left were ablaze. She could hear screams of fear and panic. She ran toward the fire, saw a woman near it with a soot-streaked face and tears rolling down her cheeks.

"My babies are in there," the woman sobbed.

In there…that must be what's left of her tree home. "I'll get them."

Laerwen started to charge inside, but the woman caught her arm. "It's too hot. The fire spread too fast."

"I can save them."

She shoved the woman off and darted past the flames. Once inside, she pulled her sari over her nose and mouth to block out as much smoke as she could. But her eyes instantly watered. She glanced left and right, trying to find the children. And then she heard the cries coming from somewhere to her right.

Overhead, the dry wood crackled. Laerwen knew it was only a matter of time before the entire roof collapsed. She had to get them and get out as fast as she could. She hurried through the small home, following the cries to a closed door. She kicked it open just as beams collapsed in front of her.

Glancing down, she saw her skin glowed golden. Fire Elves were known for their resistance to fire. But that didn't mean she still couldn't be burned. She would have to hurry. She inched around the burning beam and heard the cries again. She found the children—two golden-haired girls—hiding in a closet. A few minutes later and they would have been burned alive.

Laerwen pulled open the door and beckoned for them to come to her. But they cowered into a corner, clinging to each other.

She waved them toward her. "Come. There's not much time. Your mother is waiting outside."

More creaking and she knew the entire place was about to collapse. They didn't hesitate when they heard their mother waited. They bolted into her arms. Laerwen place the smaller girl on her hip and took the other one by the hand.

"Stay close to me. Okay?"

The little girl nodded, her big blue eyes full of tears and fear. Laerwen inched around the burning beam and back into the hallway. She pushed the girl in front of her and, with one hand on her shoulder, she guided her out.

Just as they stepped through the doorway into the fresh air, the roof buckled. The waiting mother shrieked with relief and took the girl into her arms, hugging her tight. Laerwen handed the smaller girl over.

"Thank you. Oh, thank you so much, lady."

But their relief was short lived. Laerwen saw several Fomorians heading right for them. She picked up the bigger girl and clutched her against her.

"Follow me."

The woman saw the Fomorians heading for them. She asked no

questions as she darted after her. Laerwen had no idea where she was headed, but she had to get them away from those barbarians. Neither she nor the woman would be safe and they would kill the children. She weaved a path through several trees, looking for someplace to hide. She found a door standing open to an empty house and dove inside.

Once the woman was safely inside, Laerwen closed the door and slid the bar into place.

"That won't hold them for long," she said. "We have to find a place to hide you and the girls."

"Who are they?"

"Fomorians." Laerwen gritted out the word between clenched teeth.

"This is Abram's house," the woman said. "He has a cellar."

"Good. You can hide in there. Go."

"What about you, Princess?"

She blinked, surprised the woman knew who she was. "I'll be fine. I have to find my people."

She had to make sure Randir and Hiram were all right.

And Andahar.

She also could not deny she wanted to kill as many Fomorians as possible.

"Go to the cellar. Wait there with your girls until it's safe."

The woman nodded, started to go but stopped to give her one last glance. "Thank you."

"You're welcome."

As the woman left with her daughters, Laerwen glanced around the room looking for something—anything—she could use as a weapon. Sofa, rug, chairs, bookshelves. And then she spied it standing in the corner. The sword looked like an antique, like something that was meant to be kept in a place of honor instead of used as a weapon.

Today it would be used as a weapon. She grabbed it from the stand and opened the door.

Laerwen charged out of the house and into the fray, swinging the sword and killing as many Fomorians as she could in her wake. She took out all her anger and fury on those attacking the Woodlands. She wanted them all dead. Every last one of them.

She cut her way through the men and into the glen. Most of them had converged there, fighting with the Wood Elves and what was left of her people. As she battled her way through, she couldn't help but look for Andahar. Where was he? Was he safe?

And what of Randir? Had Drake made it to his chamber with him as he asked? She made her way to the stairs to the palace, killing anyone who got in her way.

She saw the ugly mage walking toward her in an unhurried gait. He had watery blue eyes and a hook nose. He seemed oblivious to the flurry of activity around him. His eyes were locked on her and she got the distinct feeling he was coming straight for her. With a purpose. She backed up a step, wondering what to do next. If she ran, he would come after her anyway.

The only option she had was to stay and fight. She gripped the hilt tighter in her sweaty hands, widened her stance.

"Bring it on, mage."

His lips peeled back from his rotten teeth in a fierce snarl that also doubled as his smile. He lifted his hands, palms out. She saw the flash of light and reacted with her quick reflexes. She flattened herself against the ground, watching as the light went right over her head. It struck a tree.

He growled his annoyance.

She jumped to her feet and charged him. He was not in the least intimidated by her. He threw another flash of light, trying to hit her with magic. She ducked but it grazed her shoulder, sizzling the skin there. She winced but kept running toward him.

Out of the corner of her eye, she saw the man heading for her but she couldn't react in time. He barreled into her, knocking her off her feet. The sword tumbled from her hand in the skirmish. They collided with the ground, him on top of her and the wind whooshing out of her lungs.

He grabbed a handful of her hair and dragged her to her feet. Tears immediately sprang to her eyes with the pain. Her captor clamped an arm around her body and held her close as the mage advanced on her.

"Hello, Princess. Glad to see you here." Then he looked to the man holding her. "Bring her. Tie her up if you must but we need her alive."

Where were they taking her? Her heart slammed against her chest as the man dragged her away. She struggled against him but he was far stronger than her. There was no way she was getting away from him.

"What do you want?" she demanded.

"You'll find out soon enough, Princess." Lorcann's back was to her and he didn't turn when he answered her. He merely kept walking.

Behind her, she heard running footsteps but couldn't turn her head to see what was happening or who it was. The next thing she knew, her captor grunted and released her. He slumped to the ground. She spun to see Randir had come to her rescue.

"Run," he said in a quiet voice.

She backed away, shaking her head but Randir didn't stick around to see. He charged toward Lorcann, who never saw him coming. But he heard the shuffle of Randir's feet in the leaves and turned just as Randir used the hilt of his sword of punch him in the back of the head. Lorcann went down in a heap.

"Run, damn you, Laerwen!"

She did as he commanded, not waiting around to see what would happen to next.

Chapter 9

The attack had come on so suddenly, there wasn't any way they could have been prepared for it. It started with the fire on the east side of the Woodlands. Several houses had been lit and the blaze spread so quickly, it was hard for his people to react.

But that was the least of Andahar's worries. When the Fomorians charged into his home, his immediate worry was the gates had been breached. He hadn't even heard the warning horn from the gatekeeper. His brother, who would have sounded the horn as soon as he knew something was wrong, had been with him and his siblings at the funeral.

If the warning horn hadn't been sounded then that could only mean the gatekeeper was dead and never saw them coming. The Fomorian mage must have used his magic to get to the gates and break through the wards Lady Talaiel had placed to get inside.

As the enemy poured inside, killing everyone in their path, Navin shouted to Andahar he was going to check the gate. He hadn't seen him since.

Now the newly crowned king fought for his life as well as the life of his people. Eldrin and Talaiel sprang into action. She had called her people from the sky, which was somewhat of a relief to Andahar. The Skye Elves were known for their strength. But would they get there in time?

Half the Woodlands were on fire. His people couldn't work to put it out because they were busy trying to stay alive. The men had come out fighting with everything they had.

Andahar cut down enemy after enemy, trying to make his way to the giant tree with the spiral staircase. He had seen a lot of them ascend toward the palace. He had to make sure his people were safe.

As he fought to get to the tree, Eldrin slashed his way to his side.

"Where is Princess Laerwen?" Eldrin asked.

"I don't know. I left her in the woods."

"You mean you two didn't kiss and make up?"

Andahar gave him a sour look. "Find her. Make sure she's safe."

"As you say, my king." Eldrin spun and stuck his sword in a Fomorian just as he was about to attack Andahar from behind. "Are you sure I shouldn't stay with you? You are king now."

"Find Laerwen."

It was the last thing he said to his brother as he made a dash for the tree. He took the stairs two at a time. Sir Drake, his sister, Randir and Hiram should all be safe inside the palace. That's where they were headed when they left him and Laerwen in the wooded area. He had to get there to warn them.

At the top, he was greeted with several more Fomorians which he did away with instantly. Up here, the rope bridges were littered with the dead. He hadn't found anyone—Wood Elf or Fomorian—alive yet. He pounded his way down the bridge to the palace.

Once inside, he made for the throne room and halted abruptly when he saw someone sitting on his throne. He lounged back in the oversized chair, one ankle propped on his knee as he leaned against the armrest. He held a golden goblet in his free hand and sipped casually as though he were at banquet.

"Ah, good eve. You must be the king of the Wood Elves."

"Who the bloody hell are you?" Andahar advanced with slow steps, holding his sword pointed at the man.

Another Fomorian. But by the looks of this one, though, he seemed rather important. Not as disgusting or ugly as the rest of them. As though he were a leader. He smiled, remaining in the chair as though he belonged there.

"Who am I? My name is Cormac."

Andahar blinked and stared at him. Cormac? The one who had worked with Lord Kieran and the Goddess of War? It couldn't be the one and same. The man had died in the underworld. Andahar had never met him, face to face. He'd only seen him from a distance at the battle at the Stone of Destiny on the Hill of Tara. From what he remembered, this was not the same man. Could this be an imposter? Someone who could have taken on the persona of Cormac?

"Aren't you dead?"

He laughed. A jolly, bellowing laugh as though it was the funniest joke in the Otherworld. "I was, aye." He dropped his foot with a clomp and stood, his boots thumping on the wood floor as he walked toward him. "But thanks to some serious dark magic and a new body…well…I'm quite alive again."

Andahar's sword didn't move. The tip was a breath away from the man's nose. "I should kill you right now."

He lunged but Cormac flashed out of the way. A wide smile spread on his face as he reappeared behind Andahar. "If you can catch me, I suppose you can kill me. Or die trying."

Andahar snarled at the Fomorian. "What do you want? And who are you really? No one escapes the underworld."

"But I did." He smiled, his eyes crinkling at the corners.

"How do I know you are who you say you are?"

"You wish for me to prove it? Very well then. You and I may have never met but we were both on the Hill of Tara. We have a mutual friend. The lovely Princess Elyne."

"*Queen* Elyne," Andahar corrected.

Cormac's brows rose. "Ah, queen now is it? I saved her life. In return, she saved mine when she could have had me executed for my part in the war with the Fae and Lord Kieran."

He continued to detail the battle that had unfolded that fateful day, when Queen Maeve had nearly perished and the Fae Treasured had been lost forever. Andahar stared at him, his sword point never wavering. He had the memories of the Fomorian, it was clear. He had been the only one of his race at that battle.

"How did you escape the underworld?" he asked.

"There was a mage who helped me. Brought me back from the dead," Cormac said.

"Lorcann."

"Ah, so you know of him." He clapped his hands together. "Wonderful. That saves me a lot of time."

"That's where he's been. He disappeared after Marath was killed."

"I've heard all about Marath. Bloody fool if you ask me. But Lorcann is an even bigger fool."

Tired of the verbal volley, Andahar pressed the tip of his sword into Cormac's nose, pricking the flesh and beading blood on the surface. "My people are dying at the hands of the Fomorians. Now I ask again. What do you want?"

He didn't even flinch. "Lorcann wants to destroy the Otherworld. He seems to think he can do it too. I'm here because I wanted you to know who had beaten you. Who had destroyed your clan and your people."

Andahar snarled. "You will never beat us. You will never destroy the Woodlands or the Otherworld."

"Is that so? Who's going to stop us? You?"

Before Andahar could answer, Cormac put his hands up, palm out. The blast hit the king in the chest. He flew backward, his sword clattering to the floor. The force of it was so great, he ended up at the entrance to the throne room. The breath whooshed from his lungs and he gulped, trying to catch it. Cormac advanced on him.

"I don't want to hurt you, truly. But you give me no choice. I have to defend myself."

The pain was almost too much. He crawled toward the door, trying to get to the rope bridge outside. He hoped the Skye Elves would make an appearance soon. They needed their help.

"You don't want to destroy us," Andahar said, his words breathy as he gasped through the pain. He clutched his middle and dragged to a sitting position. "I know you. I saw you on the battlefield at the Stone of Destiny. Even when you were ordered to kill Princess Elyne, you couldn't. And I know you saved her life."

Cormac's lips peeled back in a snarl as he stared down at him with a sort of fierceness Andahar had never seen. Even though he didn't know this Cormac's face, he knew what he said was true. He could read it in his expression. He could read it in his eyes and knew this man truly was who he said.

"You were forced to fight for Lord Kieran and Morrigan. For your family."

"Do not speak of them here to me now!" His hands remained fisted. His lips peeled back from his teeth in an ugly snarl.

But Andahar pressed on. "Morrigan killed them anyway before you could get to them. Before you could save them. Why are you going along with Lorcann now? When you are nothing more than another agent of evil?"

Cormac flashed to stand in front of him before he could react. The man had him by his tunic as he pulled him toward him, their noses only a breath apart. "You dare speak of them to me. You don't know anything about them."

"I know they were killed. I know you mourn them."

Andahar searched his eyes and saw truth in them. He saw the desperation and the grief. He knew deep down, the mage had never recovered from losing them.

"How many children did you have?" Andahar never looked away. He kept his gaze trained on the man in front of him. The man who still held him by the tunic. He could see sweat beading his upper lip as he stared back at him.

"Three. All girls." Cormac shoved him away and stood up. He raked a hand through his hair as he turned away. Andahar could see his back muscles were tight with tension.

"You don't want to hurt us. Not really. Do you?" Andahar asked. He hoped he could talk some sense into the man. Then maybe they could stop the senseless killing.

"No." The admission was a quiet one, his back still turned to Andahar. "But Lorcann is determined."

"It doesn't have to be this way." Andahar got to his feet. He scanned the ground for his fallen sword, saw it within reach. But he didn't want to lunge for it. Not yet. He wanted to talk to Cormac. "Call off the attack."

"I can't."

"Why not?"

"Lorcann has their loyalty."

"And you don't?"

Cormac turned his head to look at him over his shoulder. "That's right."

"Then help me. Help us. You can help us fight against them. We can stop this madness. We can stop all of this killing and banish them back to the Sorrow Lands."

The mage flung around, his face red with anger. "No. I will never allow that to happen again. Never. My people don't deserve that sort of prison again."

Andahar was at a loss. If they didn't banish them back to the Sorrow Lands, then where? What could be done about them? The Fomorians outnumbered them all. They'd killed nearly the entire race of Fire Elves. They'd been defeated twice before but that was prior to their release from their watery prison. And now there were far more of them.

"The Unseelie realm," Cormac said. His normal pallor had returned as he met Andahar's gaze. "They can be moved there."

"But the Barrier has been fully restored. And only Unseelie may enter."

"I can enter. I did once before. Or have you forgotten?"

Andahar shook his head. "I haven't forgotten anything."

"I know how Lord Kieran took it down. I can get past the Barrier. And then the Fomorians can be banished there."

"And you'll help?"

Outside, they could hear a squawk and shouts. Cormac ran past him and to the rope bridge. Andahar heard him swear under his breath before he turned back to him.

"I will contact you again soon."

And then he disappeared in a flash of light.

Andahar stumbled outside. Overhead, he could see the moon dragons as they flew in. The Skye Elves had arrived and already they were fighting against the Fomorians. It took a moment for him to realize they were retreating as fast as they could.

They might be leaving, but they would be back.

He scanned the treetops for his brother, for Laerwen, for anyone. But he found none of them. He started down the rope bridge, stepping over the dead, as he headed for the staircase. He needed to find them. He needed to make sure they were all right.

As he ran toward the stairs, he wondered why Cormac had spared his life. Why he didn't want to kill him.

He hurried down the stairs and came to an abrupt halt the end of it to take in everything he saw. Some trees were nothing but burned out shells that still smoldered. His people worked to put out the flames as best they could with buckets of water. They'd managed to contain most of the fire but it still raged in some areas.

Dead littered the ground. His people, Fire Elves, Skye Elves and Fomorians. He didn't want to know how many were lost this day.

"Andahar, come quickly," Eldrin called. His face and hands were covered in dirt and blood. His clothes were splattered with it. By the look on his face, Andahar knew something was wrong.

"What is it?"

"Navin."

He followed his brother to the main gate, which was Navin's post. When he heard of the attack, he had hurried to find his men and to secure the gate. Navin was on the ground. Andahar had never seen so much blood and knew instantly his brother was mortally wounded. He collapsed to his knees beside him.

"Andahar…brother." He reached for him and fisted his tunic with his bloody hand. "I'm sorry."

"No, don't be. You did your job." The sting of tears pricked his eyes.

"Are the people safe?"

"Aye. Thanks to you."

"I should have…never left my post. I have…failed you."

"No, brother. You have never failed me."

He tried to say something else but couldn't find the strength. His eyes fluttered closed as the life ebbed from his body. He was gone. Eldrin squeezed his shoulder.

Andahar stood and turned to him.

"Cover him. I don't want anyone else to see him like this. Is Allanna safe?"

"Drake is guarding her."

"And Talaiel?"

"I cannot keep her from a fight. Andahar—"

"Did you find Laerwen?"

"Not yet."

"I have to find her." Though he had no idea where to look for her. He'd start where he left her and retrace his steps.

"Be careful."

Laerwen heard the screech of the moon dragons overhead as they arrived with reinforcements from the Skye Elves. It was a relief. As soon as the Fomorians saw them, they retreated back to the gates. It didn't stop Laerwen from killing them. She cut her way through the ones who were foolish enough to stay and fight.

"Laerwen!"

Randir ran toward her from the way she'd come. Relief sputtered through her knowing he was safe. He was there, alive and fighting against the Fomorians. She grinned when she saw him.

"What happened? How did you get away? The mage tried to kidnap me. If you hadn't' come along—"

"I know. I saw. Come on."

He took her by the hand as they started for the stairs to head to the top of the trees. As Randir cut down one Fomorian after another, a sudden flash in front of them halted their progress.

The mage again.

"Fire Elves," he spat. "You should have died in the Hin'dar Rhule."

"But we didn't," Randir said. "You failed."

The mage lunged for Randir and planted his hands on his chest. Light burst from the touch, making Randir's body convulse. His head fell back at a sickly angle. Laerwen screamed. She tried to attack the mage, but he had some sort of protective shield around him. She pounded against the invisible bubble with the edge of the sword but it was to no avail.

When he finally released Randir, he fell to the ground. The mage flashed away.

"Randir!"

Laerwen was blinded by tears as she dropped to her knees. His skin was sickly white as though the mage had drained every ounce of life out of him. He had two charred marks on his tunic where the magic had touched him. There was no pulse.

Randir was dead.

Laerwen covered her face with her hands. Her betrothed was gone and with him, her last hope of rebuilding her race. The sounds of battle dimmed around her. And then a hand landed on her shoulder. She looked up into Andahar's face.

She burst into tears all over again. He said nothing as he knelt beside her and wrapped his arm around her shoulders, pulling him to her.

"Now I've lost everything." Her voice was muffled against his tunic.

No, she did not love Randir but she did respect him. He had wanted her despite everything that had happened.

She couldn't stop the wracking sobs that followed. She pressed her face into Andahar's neck, letting the tears fall. For Randir. For her parents. For her realm. Her people. For everything. She could no long bear the weight of it all. She had crumbled at last, her stoic façade she'd built to protect herself completely shattered. Her life would never be the same. She would never marry Randir. She would not rule with him.

Though she would rule her people. It was time for her to stop pretending nothing had changed and embrace the truth. Her parents were dead. She was queen now. The sole ruler of the Fire

Elves. The only one who could lead them back to the Hin'dar Rhule. The only one who could save her people from total annihilation.

But now she was going to allow Andahar to offer her comfort. To hold her, soothe her, console her. She was going to take this moment to grieve and allow her emotions to run through her and her tears to flow. He stroked her hair as he held her against him. She fisted her hand in his tunic, clutching the fabric in her fingers and wrinkling it against her palm.

His arm tightened around her. "Hiram is here," he said softly into her ear.

It was all she needed to dry her tears in an instant. If Hiram was there, then there were others of her people. She could not allow them to see her as a shattered shell. She sucked in a deep breath, let it shudder out of her as she composed herself. Laerwen wiggled out of his grasp and wiped the tears from her eyes before she turned to face her advisor.

The look of sorrow, shock and grief on his face nearly destroyed her. Nearly rendered her into a mess of sobs once again. But she swallowed the lump in her throat and faced him.

There were several Fire Elves who had joined him, standing behind him. A few of the women shed silent tears while the men looked on with grief-stricken faces.

"Princess....Lord Randir—"

"You will address me as queen now. I am the last of my royal line." She held her head up high. "Lord Randir and others died fighting for us. To save us from the Fomorians. His death is an honorable one."

"Prin—Queen Laerwen, you have my deepest sympathies on your great loss," Hiram said. "Lord Randir was a noble man and one who possessed great honor and fortitude. He will be missed."

He, along with the others, lowered their heads in a silent prayer.

"King Andahar, will you assist us in the burial of our people?" She turned and met his gaze as she spoke. Even he gave her a look of sympathy.

"Aye, of course. Anything you need, you shall have it. Anything I can do to help you, my assistance is yours."

"The Fire Elves believe that for the spirit to pass into the hereafter, the body must be burned in the fires of the Hin'dar Rhule," Hiram said. "Surely you don't mean to travel back there, your majesty?"

"A funeral pyre will have to suffice, Hiram," Laerwen said without shifting her gaze to her advisor. "Is that possible, your majesty?"

Andahar never let his gaze off hers. And somewhere in those crystalline depths, she knew he could see right through her pretense of remaining strong. Mayhap it was because he could sense something inside her had changed, that she had decided to use the title she was born to—queen.

"We can assist you with that," Andahar said. "We can set them up in the meadow on the other side of the loch."

"Thank you. Your help is much appreciated. Come, Hiram. There are preparations you and I must make for the funerals."

She bustled past Andahar, brushing him as she moved away. For a moment, she thought he would reach out to her but he didn't. Even as she passed him, though, she saw the dampness she'd left behind with her tears and the winkles in his tunic from her fists.

No one else seemed to notice. Hiram fell in step next to her. The others went their separate ways to deal with their sadness over the lord's death in their own way.

"Are you all right, Laerwen?" Hiram's voice was soft and tentative next to her.

"I am, Hiram."

"Lord Randir's death is quite a blow. Word will spread quickly to our people."

"I know," she said. "That is why I've decided to take the title of queen. You were right, Hiram. It's time I did that. I should have all along. I should have married Randir sooner. Mayhap this wouldn't have happened."

"You cannot look back, your majesty. It won't bring back Randir or your parents. You must only look to the future now."

"No. Now I will look to today. The present. Now I will harness my anger and hate and destroy those Fomorians once and for all. If it's the last thing I do."

"Laerwen." His hand clamped around her arm as he turned her to face him. "Revenge is not the answer."

"It is. And I will be damned if those Fomorians take another life from the Fire Elves. I will kill every last one of them." *And Andahar will help me if I ask him.*

"There has to be another way."

"There is no other way to fight evil, Hiram. Except with violence. See to the funeral pyres. I will be in seclusion until they're ready."

"As you wish."

She walked away, leaving him there in the woods to head back to her chamber. She could no longer stop the tears from slipping down her cheeks.

Chapter 10

Cormac flashed outside the gate of the Woodlands and looked back at the destruction they'd caused. Trees were still on fire or smoking. They had managed to kill quite a few of the Wood Elves and Fire Elves.

Until the Skye Elves showed up and his people scattered. Fear was a great deterrent. The Fomorians refused to fight against the Skye Elves, knowing it would be a losing battle.

Fools. They were all fools. And weaklings. Not all Fomorians possessed magic—only a few of them could call themselves mage. Like Lorcann and Cormac. Most were nothing more than violent barbarians. Something they proved over and over again every time they attacked.

Lorcann flashed beside him.

"They run scared from the Woodlands," Cormac said.

"It is better to run rather than fight a losing battle. Besides, I managed to kill one of the nobles."

"Which one?"

"One of the Fire Elves. He was to marry the princess. You were supposed to kill the king. Did you?"

Cormac stared at him as he remembered the conversation he'd had with Andahar. He had tried hard to forget his wife and children, but the king hadn't forgotten and he had made a point to remind him. To remind him that he'd been a pawn of evil for both Kieran and Morrigan.

And now Lorcann.

Lorcann wanted him to kill Andahar. But killing the king would only mean another would take his place. Would he then be asked to kill the next sovereign?

"I didn't have a chance before the Skye Elves arrived," Cormac said.

"Then you failed." Lorcann started up the path away from the Woodlands.

Cormac had no choice but to follow him. "What do you intend to do? Punish me? Because you can't. Your magic is failing."

Lorcann halted and rounded on him. "My magic is the only thing that saved you from the underworld."

"Aye, that is true. But when you resurrected me, did you realize how much of your power you gave me? And killing Randir used what precious little you had left."

"You lie."

"Do I?" he taunted. "Prove me wrong them."

In a fit of fury, Lorcann slammed his hands on Cormac's chest. Nothing happened. Not even a flash of light, a glimmer or shimmer. A slow smile spread on Cormac's face. He lifted his hand and placed it on Lorcann's chest.

The mage flew backward as though he'd shoved him. He crashed against the ground and skidded a few feet before coming to a stop. The flash of light had been so bright, it blinded even Cormac. He blinked furiously to get the white spots out of his line of vision.

"You see? I don't lie. Your magic is depleted." He walked toward Lorcann, stopping close enough to kick dirt on him. "From now on, you will answer to me. I lead these people. And I will decide what happens to the princess and the Hin'dar Rhule."

"If you don't allow us to take the power from the lava, then our people will die."

"Then we die. An eventuality we all face one way or another. I've died once already and I'm willing to face it again. Are you?"

His eyes narrowed. "You bastard. I should have left you in the underworld."

"Mayhap." He grinned, well pleased with himself. He held a hand down to Lorcann. After a moment of hesitation, the mage took it and Cormac helped him to his feet.

"I'm returning with the others," Cormac said.

"You expect me to follow you? You bastard. You've taken my people and my woman."

Cormac couldn't hide his surprise.

"You thought I didn't know. But I could smell your filth on her," Lorcann said.

"I took nothing that didn't want to be taken," he retorted. "Gweneth came to me. She gave herself willingly and she belongs to me now."

Lorcann cracked his knuckles in a fit of agitation as he glared at him. Clearly he was missing his power and wishing he could strike back at Cormac.

"Since you cannot flash, I will flash us both."

Lorcann glanced at his outstretched hand in a moment of consideration. He crossed his arms in defiance.

"Fine then. We'll do it the hard way."

Before Lorcann could react, Cormac wrapped his arms around the mage and flashed away back to the Sorrow Lands. As soon as they were back, the mage shoved away from him and then landed a punch on his jaw. Cormac stumbled a few steps back before he could get his bearings. But he wasn't fast enough. Lorcann launched, head down, and hit him in his gut. They flew backward and Cormac lost his footing and they collided with the ground.

As they landed, Lorcann landed punch after punch on his face, the side of his head. The surprise attack made Cormac forget his newfound powers. But only for a moment. He pushed his hand against Lorcann's ribs. The mage was gone in an instant. When Cormac climbed to his feet, Lorcann was on the ground, his tunic smoking.

In that instant, Cormac could have killed him. But he'd taken it easy on him. He noticed the others standing around watching the fight. Cormac wiped blood from his mouth with the back of his hand.

"Lorcann has lost his magic," Cormac announced. "He has agreed to relinquish command to me. Haven't you, Lorcann?"

The mage's response was to cough and spit.

"I'll take that as your agreement." He looked up at those still standing around. "Go and tell the others. Make sure they know," Cormac said. "From now on, you will follow me and my command."

They headed off one by one and Cormac turned on his booted heel toward his tent. Gweneth stood outside his tent, a small smile playing upon her lips. Her long hair cascaded over her shoulders and down her slender form. She wore a gown of pale pink that hugged all her curves.

"Well played, my lord," she said and beckoned him. "Well played. Now come inside for your reward. I will help you relax."

The full force of his fatigue hit him as he shuffled past her. "Not tonight."

Yet she followed him inside. "Do I not please you?"

He looked her over. She was appealing. That he didn't deny. Nor could he deny she reminded him of his lost love. The wife he had tried to forget only to be reminded of her by the king of the Wood Elves. He could see her inherent strength in Gweneth's features. Her very appealing features. Aye, she pleased him. And it pleased him to know he had stolen her from the worthless mage, Lorcann.

"You do."

She kept one hand on his chest as she walked around behind him. She slipped her hands under his tunic and up his back, over the taut muscles. "You are tense."

She massaged his shoulders, working out the knots. He wanted to resist. He tried to resist. But he found he couldn't with her fingers kneading away the stress. He let the tension release as he dropped his shoulders.

"You like this?"

"Aye."

"Then allow me to do more for you."

She moved to his side, taking him by the hand and leading him to the bed. She helped him remove his tunic. He lay face down and the girl straddled him. She poured a scented oil on his back and rubbed it into his pores.

As she did so, the cooling sensation spread throughout his body. His body relaxed, all the tension ebbing away as she massaged the scent into him. It made him drowsy. Dreamy. And it made him want her.

"You are relaxed now, aren't you?"

"Aye."

"And you want me, don't you?" Her voice lilted over him, tingling his exposed skin.

Was she using some form of magic on him? "Aye."

Her weight was gone and a moment later, he heard the rustle of clothing. When he turned his head, she stood naked before him. The only thing she wore was a smile of seduction.

"I want you too, Cormac. Take me. Take me beneath you and make love to me."

He rolled to his back as she moved to him. She climbed on the bed and straddled him again. She reached for the scented oil and poured a small portion into her palm. She massaged it into his chest. It heightened his arousal.

He grabbed her wrists, halting her movement. "What is this?"

"The oil is merely an aphrodisiac," she said. "One I made for you."

"You seduce me with potions?"

"You wanted me to seduce you. Did you not? This merely intensifies all that you feel. All that you want." Gweneth leaned toward him, her nipples brushing his chest. "And you want me."

"Aye."

"And you shall have me."

His fingers slowly uncurled from her wrists and her hands went back to working their magic on his chest. The more she massaged, the harder his shaft. The pain of arousal was nearly unbearable.

As if sensing this, she shimmied her lithe body down his. Her hands landed on the waist of his breeches and tugged. He lifted his hips, allowing her to free him. His shaft stood at rigid attention. With a small smile, her hand closed around him and pumped up and down several times before she bent over him.

Her small luscious mouth engulfed him, sucking his hardened length to the back of her throat. He groaned, his hips pushing upward. When she pulled him out of her mouth, her tongue licked him from base to tip in one long stroke of such eroticism he thought he might lose consciousness.

As she held him tight in her grasp, her tongue did a swift dance over the tip in a tight circle. She didn't stop with one. She swirled her tongue over him again and again before taking him once more into her mouth. Her glorious, wet hot mouth knew exactly how to suck him and how he wanted to be sucked.

And then she nudged his legs apart as she took his shaft out her mouth and bent between his legs. Her velvet-soft hands cupped him and the next thing he knew, she licked his sac, taking her time to explore every part of him. The tip of her tongue moved along his ridge.

Pleasure exploded behind his closed eyes as he bucked upward. Her hand closed around his shaft and she pumped him while continuing the onslaught of her tongue. His hands fisted in her hair, pulling at her scalp and urging her onward. He knew he was seconds away from releasing his seed and would have if she hadn't stopped.

Before he could protest she straddled his hips and pushed him inside her warm wet body. Filling her. She rode him hard as she rocked her hips over him. He could only look at her through half-lidded eyes, watching her as she fondled her breasts and pinched her nipples. Her head fell back, exposing the long column of her throat. She moaned with the sheer pleasure of it all.

He wanted to come. He wanted to feel that release inside her. But he wanted to lick her more. And he wanted to take her from behind.

Cormac pushed to a sitting position, grabbing her around the waist and flipping her to her back in one swift movement. She gasped a breath and giggled as he pushed her into the mattress.

"I wasn't finished," she breathed.

"Neither am I."

He crushed a fierce kiss against her lips, sucking her tongue into his mouth. He didn't linger there long as he made his way down her body, pausing only long enough to suckle one nipple—one perfect hard bud. He rolled his tongue over it for a quick moment before he moved downward.

Her hips opened with eagerness as she anticipated his next move. Her knees fell open exposing the beauty between her legs. He swiped two fingers down her wet slit, feeling her hot damp core. He had to taste her.

Cormac met her gaze as he licked her sweetness off his fingers. Desire flooded her gaze as she pinched her nipples.

"Let me feel you, Cormac. I need to feel you."

He bent, gently pulling apart her lips, and slid his tongue inside her. Her gasp of pleasure vibrated throughout her entire body. He lapped up her arousal as though he were a starving man. As though he had never tasted a woman before. And he hadn't tasted this one before. Not like this. He'd taken her once before, but it had been a swift coupling. He hadn't had a chance to taste her, explore her, memorize her body with his hands and his mouth.

Gweneth rolled her hips to and fro against the rhythm of his tongue as he licked her. When she came against his mouth, he had never tasted anything as sweet.

Before her climax had even ended, he moved on top of her and plunged his shaft inside her. She gasped with her pleasure and together they found their rhythm. Their climax came together and he knew in that instance he would never release her back to Lorcann.

In the afterglow of their lovemaking, Cormac held Gweneth in his arms and listened to her rhythmic breathing.

He had returned from the fires of the underworld. He lived once again. The Wood Elves and the Fire Elves? The Hin'dar Rhule? Would he allow Lorcann to capture the Fire princess and use her to harness the power of the lava?

He knew the answer to all of these questions. He knew he couldn't do any of that. He wouldn't. He had allowed Lord Kieran to pressure him into following him because he had captured his family and hidden them away. The location of them had died with Kieran.

So when Morrigan had offered him the same thing, he had jumped at the chance to find them again. To be with his wife again. To see his children once more. He had intended to go north. To escape all of them and live in peace.

A part of him felt he could still do that—escape. Only this time, he would take the girl with him. He couldn't let her go.

He had told Andahar he wanted to see the Fomorians banished to the Unseelie realm. To the Darkness. Now that he had most of his power back, he could use what magic he had to go through the Barrier. He knew how Kieran did it.

Aye, he would escape. He would take all the Fomorians with him to the Unseelie realm. The only question was how. How would he be able to do that? He would have to use some form of trickery. Some way to get them there without Lorcann or the others knowing.

And then it occurred to him he could contact Andahar for help. He could tell him what his plan was and the Wood Elf would help him. He and the Fae queen. Elyne had promised him she would help him find his family once. Mayhap she would help him once again. This time, though, he would take his rule to the Unseelie realm. It was without a king. He could rule them there.

The final battle would happen on the charred plains of the Hin'dar Rhule. This was where Lorcann wanted to make his last stand. Where he intended to take the magic from the fires using the princess of the Fire Elves.

"Your thoughts are loud, my lord." Gweneth's sleep-laced words wafted to him. She lifted her head and propped her chin on her hand to look up at him. "What troubles you?"

"Don't you know already?"

"You intend to go to the king of the Woodlands," she said. "And tell him of the plan at the volcano."

"I do," he said with a nod. There was no denying it when she clearly heard what he'd thought. "Do you intend to stop me?"

"No." She rolled to her side and sat up, tucking her legs under her. "You are meant for more than this." She waved her hand around the tent. "If you intend to rule the Unseelie realm, then I intend to be by your side as your queen."

"How do I know I can trust you?"

"Trust isn't a tangible thing. You can't see or touch it. But you can feel it." She took his hand and put it against her chest. Her heart beat slow and steady. "You have my trust and my heart. From the moment I saw you."

He looked at her. Really looked and thought for a brief moment he saw the flicker of his wife's face in hers. "You remind me of someone." He brushed her hair from her face. "Someone I once loved."

"I know." She smiled. "You are powerful, as am I. Together we can rule the Fomorians. I will help you get the Fomorians to the Unseelie realm. The Barrier is closed but there is a way to open a portal to the Darkness."

"You know how to do this?"

"I do."

"And you'll help me?"

"I will."

"Then tell me your plan."

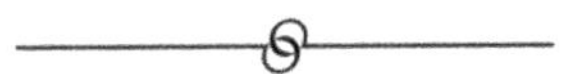

The sun was beginning to set. Laerwen dressed all in black as she sat on the floor, her knees curved under her. She pressed the palms of her hands together in front of her heart, her eyes closed. She prayed for forgiveness from the gods.

She'd watched Randir die by the hand of that awful Fomorian. And there was nothing she could have done to stop it, even though she had tried.

Guilt swarmed her. She had, only before he had died, faced Andahar and told him she would marry the lord despite her feelings for the prince. Now king. Randir may not have loved her—nor she him—but they could have built a life together. They could have rebuilt the Hin'dar Rhule together.

Now what was to become of them? Of her people? Her realm? Would it be forever lost to the Fomorians?

She didn't know. So she prayed for forgiveness and strength to be able to go on. To face what was to come. She didn't know if she had any more strength left in her.

A knock sounded on her door before it opened. She knew without looking, Hiram had come for her.

"Your majesty, they are ready."

Laerwen pushed to her feet and turned to face her advisor. He waited in the doorway dressed all in black. Together they made their way out of the palace, down the stairs and to the meadow where the funeral pyres had been erected. Four of her people had died. One of them Lord Randir.

The Wood Elves, as well as her people, gathered to pay their final respects to those who had fallen. It seemed all eyes fell on her waiting for her to say something. She was queen, after all, she should have something profound to say, but all she could think to do was stand there, numb to it all.

"Your majesty, a few words?" Hiram whispered. She knew he was trying to urge her on.

"Aye, of course." She stepped away from the group, letting her gaze touch each of the bodies that had been so carefully placed upon the pyres. Randir was in the middle dressed in his finery. "It is with a heavy heart today that we say farewell to our friends and loved ones. They fought against the Fomorians not once, but twice. They gave their lives to protect us. To make sure we could go on living. For that, we shall never forget them. They will live on in our memories for all eternity."

Hiram and three others stepped forward to light the funeral pyres. Laerwen took the torch from one of her people to light the one under Randir herself. She placed the fire against the wood and watched as it spread upward.

She didn't know how long she stood there watching the fires. All she knew was darkness had descended and the only light in the area was that of the flames reaching upward to lick the sky. Hiram had tried to pull her away but she refused. She remained, waiting until they were nothing more than embers.

One by one her people and the others filed away leaving her there alone.

But she wasn't alone. She sensed rather than saw the presence as he moved to stand beside her. He fixed his gaze ahead on the flames before her. She knew Andahar stood by her side for a long moment before slipping an arm around her shoulders. She let him. She drew his strength into her, refusing to cry when all she wanted to do was break down.

"It wasn't your fault, you know," he said.

But she couldn't help but blame herself. Randir had saved her from the attack. From being captured. Something Andahar didn't even know yet.

"There wasn't anything you could have done."

"I am still responsible for him and his death."

"No, Laerwen."

"If it hadn't been for me, he wouldn't have been killed. But he came for me. When the Fomorian mage tried to capture me, Randir stopped them. He killed them and knocked out the mage. The mage must have followed me when he came to. He found us so easily. He got his revenge by killing Randir." She didn't know why the words bubbled out of her but she couldn't stop them. "They were after me, Andahar. Me."

"But they didn't capture you," he said. "And I will protect you."

"You can't. Randir couldn't. No one can. They breached the gate and the wards Lady Talaiel put in place. They can do it again."

"We will find another way to stop them." He sounded so confident it was hard not to believe him.

"I don't know if there is another way. Mayhap I should surrender to them."

"Laerwen, no. They'll kill you."

"We don't know that. If I give myself up to them, mayhap they'll leave my people alone. Me for the Hin'dar Rhule. I could negotiate with them. Give them what they want."

Andahar stepped in front of her, the firelight flickering over in his face. She could see the concern in his eyes as he gripped her by the shoulders. "That is suicide and you and I both know it. I've sent for Queen Elyne and the Skye Elves are here. They will help us. We will get the Hin'dar Rhule back without you having to sacrifice yourself."

"Isn't that what a ruler is supposed to do?"

He shook his head. "No. I won't let you do it."

Laerwen resisted the urge to shrug away his hands. She wanted to step away from him. To tell him he couldn't stop her. Her mind was made up. She was going to surrender to the Fomorians. She believed, deep down, it was the only way to save her people.

"Are you going to stop me?"

"Aye, I am."

"You can't."

"I will."

"How? By chaining me up in my chamber?"

"No, by chaining you up in mine." In the darkness, she saw the sliver of a smile. He was toying with her and it did nothing but make her angry.

She pushed him away. "I'm not jesting, Andahar."

"Neither am I. I'm not going to let you go. Not after everything that's happened. Your people have lost so much already. They shouldn't have to lose you too."

Andahar may be right in that but she was still stubborn as they came. "I—"

A flash of light stopped her. It was so bright, it blinded her. She blinked furiously, trying to get rid of the flash in her eyes.

"Cormac. What do you want?" Andahar stood in front of her now, so close she could feel his body heat radiating over her.

"I told you I would return, did I not? I've come to warn you. There will be another attempt on the princess's life."

She finally got her vision clear enough to see the man standing before Andahar. She peered over the king's shoulder. "I surrender."

"Laerwen—"

"That's not necessary," Cormac said. "At least not yet. Lorcann is planning a final battle at the volcanoes of the Hin'dar Rhule when the sun and moon align."

"The night of the eclipse?" she asked. "Why?"

"It is believed the volcanoes are scheduled to erupt then," he said.

"That's merely folklore," Laerwen said. "They haven't erupted in thousands of years. They're dormant."

"For now," he agreed with a nod. "But not on the eclipse. They will erupt and Lorcann believes there is some magic that can be harnessed from the lava."

"Is that true?" Andahar asked, looking at Laerwen.

"Folklore. Nothing more. All Fire Elves grew up with the stories of the magic in the lava, how it could be harnessed. It would take a sacrifice to…" Her words trailed off, the sudden realization smacking into her. Her stomach cramped. "That's why he wanted to capture me, isn't it?"

"It is," Cormac said. "He intends to use your blood, Princess. When the lava flows, he will sacrifice you to release the magic within."

Andahar was right. The Fomorians were going to kill her. She had been naïve enough to believe they would let her people live if she turned herself over to them as a prisoner. How wrong she was.

Andahar moved to stand closer to her, slipping an arm around her and pulling her to him. "I'm not going to let you take her."

"I'm not here to take her," Cormac said. "I'm here to warn you. And…offer you a truce."

"What sort of truce?" Andahar asked.

"I thought about what you said before. And you're right. I don't want to hurt you or the Fire Elves."

Laerwen glanced up at Andahar, the question on the tip of her tongue. But she didn't get a chance to answer when he said, "But Lorcann does."

"I will handle the mage myself," Cormac said. "He is of no consequence to you."

"He killed Randir," Laerwen said. "I will see him dead for it."

"Leave him to me, dearie. He's not worth your trouble." He looked back to Andahar. "If you help me, your realm will be free of all Fomorians."

"What do you want?"

"The Unseelie realm is without a king. I intend to fill that void." He thumbed at his chest.

"You?"

"Aye. Is that so hard to believe?"

"Well…no. But the question of the Barrier remains."

"I have a solution for that. There is a sorceress who is willing to help me. I have her trust and her assurance she will not betray me. Once the volcanoes erupt, we can use that as a distraction to open a portal to the Unseelie realm. With our combined magic, the two of us can banish all the Fomorians there."

"But if the volcanoes erupt then we're all dead anyway," she said. "We Fire Elves can withstand the heat of the fire but not the lava."

"We will plan out battle locale accordingly," Cormac said.

Andahar glanced down at Laerwen. Her heart had kicked into overdrive at the thought of seeing her beloved realm once again. If the volcanoes did erupt, the land would be destroyed but it was nothing she and her people couldn't overcome.

The Woodland king looked back at Cormac. "And you're certain it will work?"

"No. But the sorceress and I have a plan in mind."

"I'd rather you discuss it when Queen Elyne and her husband have arrived. They are due here soon."

"I don't have time to wait. I need to go back. I will return, though, with the final battle plan."

Before Andahar could reply, Cormac flashed away. They stood there a long moment, his arm still around Laerwen's shoulders, as her eyes re-adjusted to the darkness after the flash of light. She finally stepped away from him.

"Do you believe him?" she asked.

"I believe he truly wants to help us."

"Why?"

"Because he was forced to help Lord Kieran and Morrigan before. They held his family hostage and the Goddess of War killed them anyway."

She turned to him but his face was difficult to. "But he could want revenge." Like her. Revenge on the Fomorians that wiped out her realm and murdered her parents and Lord Randir.

"I don't think so. What he told us tonight makes him a traitor to the Fomorians. They could kill him for that." He moved toward her, his feet crunching in the bracken. "Let me take you back to your chamber, Laerwen. The night air turns chilly. Tomorrow Queen Elyne and King Derron arrive. We can reconvene then."

After a moment's hesitation, she nodded. "All right."

He took her hand and led her away from the embers of the funeral pyres. The walk back up the winding staircase, through the palace and to her chamber door was a silent one. Neither of them spoke. She didn't know what to say to him. She still harbored some guilt for Randir's death. Mayhap Andahar knew that. When the halted at her door, he gave her a chaste kiss on the cheek before leaving.

Chapter 11

The king of the Wood Elves prepared his younger brother for burial. He, like his father, laid in state, the burial shroud over his body. The people of the Woodlands filed by, one by one, to pay their last respects.

King Andahar, Lord Eldrin, Princess Allanna and their spouses joined together once again to say farewell to their brother, Lord Navin. Though Allanna didn't take her brother's death as hard as their father's, she was still inconsolable. Sir Drake held her close to him as she wept while they entombed Navin next to their father. It had been a difficult time for all of them, including their people.

Two funerals in two days did not bode well for his rule. And he wasn't even counting the deaths of the Fire Elves.

He couldn't help but think of Laerwen. Leaving her the previous night had been as painful as pulling a dagger out of his heart. All he wanted to do was take her in his arms, hold her, comfort her. But she had pushed him away. She had kept him at arm's length. And he knew why—she blamed herself for Randir's death.

None of them spoke as they headed through the woods back to the palace. Andahar intended to visit her once they left the tomb. To let her know she was still not alone and that he would do all he could to help her. But on their way back, he saw Leopold walking at a fast clip toward them. Andahar came to a halt as Eldrin and the others.

"My king, their majesties the queen and king of the Fae have arrived," Leopold announced. His chest heaved as he tried to catch his breath.

"Oh, thank the gods," Allanna muttered.

"Please show them to a guest chamber in the palace, Leopold."

"Queen Elyne has asked to speak with you immediately, your majesty."

"Show her to my private chamber then. Lord Eldrin, will you

join me?"

He turned to his wife, kissed her cheek. "I'll see you after."

"I think I should check on Laerwen. No one has seen her emerge from her chamber yet today," she said.

"Please let me know how she's doing," Andahar said.

She smiled. "You'll be the first to know."

They met Elyne and Derron in the king's private chamber. When she saw Andahar, she came forward and clasped him by the hand, kissing him on either cheek.

"Andahar, it's good to see you again. My condolences to your family. I was very sorry to hear about the king and your brother, Lord Navin," she said.

"Thank you, your majesty."

"Please call me Elyne. We've known each other well. It seems silly to call each other by title."

He'd always had a soft spot for the princess, now queen, of the Otherworld. He would never forget the day she came to the Wood Elves asking for help with the war they'd fought at the Stone of Destiny. A hard won battle between the Fae and Kieran's Unseelie army.

Derron clasped his hand and shook it.

"Thank you both for coming," Andahar said. He poured tankards of honeywine and passed them to his brother and the Fae monarchs.

"We could not refuse your call," Elyne said. She beamed at Eldrin then. "I understand congratulations on your recent nuptials are in order for you, Lord Eldrin."

"Aye, they are. Thank you."

"I should very much like to meet your new bride."

"You will. All in good time." Andahar waved them all to a seat. "As well as the queen of the Fire Elves."

"So it's true then?" Elyne took a sip of her honeywine as she perched on the edge of her chair between Derron and Eldrin. "I'd heard the realm was utterly destroyed."

"The Fomorians left no survivors. Those Fire Elves who remain are here in the Woodlands."

"How are they faring?" Derron asked. "I would think they have a hard time adapting to the humidity."

Andahar nodded. "There are some who have trouble with the thicker air here. But all in all, they have adapted quite well. It is my intention to help the Fire Elves rebuild the Hin'dar Rhule since I feel somewhat responsible for the destruction."

"What happened with Lord Marath was not your fault," Eldrin put in. "It wasn't anyone's fault we had a rogue hell-bent on reinstating the Treaty of Separation."

"I have to agree," Elyne said. "Lord Marath was a ruthless killer."

"And just a wee bit crazy," Eldrin added.

Though they shared a chuckle, Andahar knew it was all too true.

"I believe I also speak for Elyne as well when I say you have the Fae pledge to assist in the rebuilding. We will do whatever we can," Derron said.

Andahar nodded. "I was going to ask, but I'm glad you offered. I will pass along your offer to Queen Laerwen." He cleared his throat and turned serious. "I have asked you here for another reason, Elyne. Primarily to ask your assistance in battle against the Fomorians."

"Of course. Anything you need. We're happy to help you." She reached for Derron, clasped his hand. "Derron and I have already rallied the troops. All you need to do is say the word and they will be dispatched immediately."

"I thank you." Andahar sipped his honeywine, considering his next words carefully. "Also, I have been visited by a certain Fomorian…named Cormac."

Both Derron and Elyne stared at him as though he'd grown a second head. Finally it was Derron who broke the silence.

"Cormac was left for dead in the underworld. We all saw his broken body there."

"Aye, I know. I remember hearing the tales of Maeve's rescue. However, I believe he has been somehow resurrected by a powerful mage, Lorcann. He was Marath's right-hand man during that whole debacle." Andahar took another sip of his honeywine to calm his ragged nerves. "But you will likely not recognize him. He's taken another body."

"Another body?" Elyne asked.

"Aye. I remember what he looked like at the Stone of Destiny. This is not the same man, physically. However, his spirit has been somehow transferred into another body," Andahar said. "He lives. I assure you."

"Cormac is a dangerous man," Derron said. "Again I say we

should have killed him when we had the chance."

"Lot of good it would have done," Elyne retorted. "He's alive once again. What did he want?" She directed her last question to Andahar.

"He wants to become the Unseelie king."

Silence again. Elyne chewed on her lower lip. Derron ran his hand over his chin. Eldrin took a long quaff of his honeywine.

"That is interesting," Eldrin said at last. "He intends to take over the throne as Dark King?"

"And rule the Unseelie realm," Andahar said with a nod. "I'm inclined to allow him."

"What does he hope to gain?" Elyne asked. "There is nothing there. The Barrier has been restored along with the walls between the human realm and the Otherworld. There are no portals open either."

"He claims he has the help of a powerful sorceress. He told me the Fomorians plan to make their final stand at the volcanoes of the Hin'dar Rhule."

"Can you trust him?" Derron asked.

"I don't know. I was hoping you could give me some insight."

"He saved my life when Lord Kieran's tent was set on fire," Elyne said. "I would have burned alive in that tent had it not been for Cormac."

"But this is not the same man," Derron said. "He could be more deranged. More dangerous."

"He did tell me Lorcann's plan, though, was to harbor the magic in the lava of the volcanoes. The only way the magic can be drawn out is by spilling the blood of a royal Fire Elf."

"Queen Laerwen?" Elyne asked.

Andahar nodded.

"Why would he tell you this?"

"Because he wants us to help him stop Lorcann and get to the Unseelie realm. He believes he can banish the entire race of Fomorians there and seal the Barrier once more." Andahar leaned back in his chair and expelled a breath. "I know it sounds farfetched. I'm not sure I believe it myself. But the Fomorians attacked us and tried to capture Laerwen. Cormac had every opportunity to kill me but he didn't. I believe there is some truth to his story."

"So we go along with this," Eldrin said. "Then what?"

"We make our final stand in the Hin'dar Rhule against the Fomorians. Our people, the Skye Elves, the Fae. Cormac said the volcanoes will erupt on the day of the eclipse."

"That doesn't leave us much time," Elyne said.

"We should mobilize the troops at once," Derron added. "Send them directly to the Hin'dar Rhule."

"That was my thinking as well," Andahar said. "I had hoped you would agree to this plan."

"How does this sorceress intend to break the Barrier?" Elyne asked.

"Cormac didn't say. I suspect he didn't want to reveal all his plans at once."

"I don't like this." Derron got to his feet and prowled the room. "It seems too easy. What if Cormac is leading us into a trap?"

A flash of light and then, "I assure you I am not."

Derron halted mid-step. Elyne jumped to her feet, sloshing some of her honeywine over the rim of her cup. Andahar and Eldrin stood too. Cormac was on the other side of the room, leaning casually against the wall, his ankles crossed. He dug under his fingernails with the tip of a dagger.

"What I told Andahar was the truth. I intend to rip the Barrier and send the Fomorians there. Along with myself and my sorceress."

"Why should we believe you?" Derron moved to stand in front of his wife, keeping her behind him as though a protective shield.

"Because if you don't then the Fomorians will kill the Fire princess and destroy the Hin'dar Rhule once and for all. I'm not making this up, I swear to you."

"How did you get in here?" Andahar asked. "The walls are warded."

"Not very well. At least not well enough to keep me out." Cormac shoved off the wall and put the dagger away. "The eclipse happens in less than a fortnight. You and your armies will set up on the easternmost ridge. Princess Laerwen knows the landscape well. She will be able to show you. Lorcann intends to march on the volcano."

"And when the volcano erupts?"

"That's where you come in," Cormac said. "Once the lava starts to flow, Lorcann will want to find the princess. You must guard her with your life. She cannot be captured by him. We only have a matter of minutes before it makes it down the mountain. Gweneth and I will rip open a portal through the Barrier and push the Fomorians inside. Once we're all there, she'll close it and I will proclaim myself Unseelie king."

"You think it's that simple?" Elyne asked, shaking her head. "You don't know what sort of chaos will be happening when that volcano erupts or when the Barrier opens."

"No, but I will do what I can to contain the Fomorians to one general location. It is up to you and your armies to keep them from leaving the Hin'dar Rhule."

"I don't like this plan," Derron said. "There are too many holes in it."

"I will do what I can to keep the Fomorians from killing too many of your Elves and Fae but I cannot make any promises."

Before anyone could protest or reply, Cormac flashed away. They all stood stunned for a brief moment until Andahar sank into his chair. "That, as they say, is that."

"I hope you know what you're doing, brother," Eldrin said.

"As do I, Eldrin. As do I."

A knock on her door. Laerwen ignored it. She didn't want to see anyone right now. She didn't want to see anyone ever. She wanted to wallow in her misery and self-pity. Her guilt. She wanted to be alone. She was alone. And it was her fault.

Randir was dead. Her parents had been murdered. Her people left in her realm had been massacred. What sort of queen was she?

She'd locked herself in her chamber, refusing to see anyone. Even Hiram. She wanted to be alone, as was her right. She only ventured out for food and drink when she knew the palace slept. She hadn't spoken to another since the night Cormac visited and Andahar walked her to her chamber.

Another knock. A persistent one.

She sighed. She'd have to face someone eventually.

"Laerwen? It's Lady Talaiel."

"Pox," she cursed. She couldn't ignore the Lady of the Skye, could she?

It took all her strength to peel herself off the bed and pad to the door. She pulled it open wide and ushered Talaiel inside. When she was in, Laerwen closed the door.

"How can I help you, my lady?"

"I came to see how you were faring."

Laerwen trudged to the window and peered out. It was mid-afternoon. Somewhere in the palace, they would be having their noon meal. And below the treetops, they would be doing their normal daily activities. What was normal? Laerwen didn't know anymore.

"I'm fine."

"We haven't seen you at any of the meals."

"No, you haven't," Laerwen replied. She was unwilling to give up any more information. She wasn't in the mood to chat.

"Laerwen, I know what you must be going through—"

"No, you don't." Her head swiveled in the lady's direction and she pinned her with her fierce gaze. "No one knows what I'm going through."

The lady clasped her hands together in front of her and remained unflustered. She gave her a small smile. "You are a strong woman, Laerwen. We all know that. And we're worried about you."

"I'm really fine." She turned back to the window but she could hear Lady Talaiel take a few steps toward her.

"No. You're not. You're grieving. And you have every right to. Laerwen, you are not alone. You know that. Lord Eldrin and I, as well as the king, are here for you. To stand by your side no matter what comes to pass."

The burn of tears threatened and she blinked them away. She was strong. But she was tired of being strong. She was tired of holding her head high. She was tired of pretending nothing was wrong. She was just tired.

"The king, in particular, is concerned about you." Lady Talaiel's voice was low and soft and close. She had moved toward Laerwen and stood behind her.

"Is he?" Her voice cracked, much to her dismay.

"Aye, he is. What can I do for you?"

Laerwen shook her head before the Lady of the Skye finished. "Nothing. There is nothing anyone can do for me. Randir's death is on my head."

"No, it's not. You shouldn't carry the guilt or the blame for that. He did his duty to you and you to him. You brought him here from the Hin'dar Rhule, to safety—"

"Only to have him killed!" She reeled on Lady Talaiel, unable to stop the shed of tears. "Aye, he died because of me."

"He died protecting you." Her voice remained steady and calm. "You have to know that."

Laerwen slumped against the window edge. She leaned her head against the cool surface and closed her eyes, allowing the tears to flow freely.

"I know he did. Yet I still cannot stop from feeling guilty."

"That will pass. And you have the rest of us to help you. Even the king of the Wood Elves. He cares for you a great deal."

Laerwen flushed and turned away, not wanting Talaiel to see her reaction. She knew he cared for her. She'd developed feelings for him. Feelings she wasn't yet prepared to acknowledge.

"We all saw the way he reacted when he found Randir kissing you." There was a humorous lilt in her voice.

Laerwen would never forget the way Andahar looked. The rage and jealousy in his face. The way he punched Randir and the way the two of them fought.

"It is not possible," Laerwen said, ever the stubborn woman. "We are too different. I don't know how it would work between us."

"But it's worked for me and Eldrin. And we are of two different realms."

Suspicion settled over her then and she turned to face the lady. "Did the king send you here?"

"No. He did not. I came because I'm concerned about you. I want you to think about these things before you make your final decision. I've seen the way you look at each other. You care for him, too."

"Aye." The word slipped out of her on a whisper. "But the Hin'dar Rhule—"

"Has a ruler. You. You are queen now. Where you go, what you choose, your people will follow. They've been here in the Woodlands long enough to know Andahar. To see how he treats you. They will approve of the match."

Laewren chewed her lower lip, knowing the Lady of the Skye had the right of it. She *was* queen now, whether she liked it or not. No, there hadn't been a formal coronation for her but she her duty was bound to her people and her realm. She was a royal of the Fire

Elves. She needed to accept her role as queen.

Hiram, she knew, would be ecstatic she had finally embraced her title. But would he be ecstatic about embracing the king of the Wood Elves as her king? Should they marry, what would it do to the Hin'dar Rhule and the Woodlands?

"And what of the Wood Elves? Would they approve of the match with their king?" she asked.

"They would, I'm sure. They have so far accepted your presence here in the Woodlands without objection," Talaeil said.

Laerwen, though, was aware of the sideways glances they gave her. She preferred to wear her Fire Elven traditional garb. Not the gowns of this realm. That could change, though. She'd been presented with an entire wardrobe of clothes handpicked by the princess but up until now Laerwen had shied away from them. Mayhap now was the time to embrace what the Woodlands had to offer if she were to allow herself to be courted by the king.

She blinked, surprised by her own thinking that she was ready to be courted by the king so soon after Randir's death. Though, she amended, she had never loved Randir as she should. Their relationship was one of arrangement. It didn't stop the grief from spearing her over his death, but it also released her from any romantic feelings she may have considered for Randir. She was free to love whom she wished.

And so was the king of the Wood Elves.

"I will consider your words, Lady Talaiel."

"Good. That's all I can hope for. Now I shall take my leave of you." She turned headed toward the door.

"My lady, one more question." Talaiel paused, her hand on the latch. "Has the Fae queen arrived?"

"Oh, aye, she has. She and her husband. I'm sure King Andahar will want to introduce you to her soon enough."

Laerwen chewed her lower lip. Mayhap it was time for her to get out of this stuffy chamber and make herself presentable again. She'd lingered her far too long. And she really wanted to meet the queen of the Fae.

"Do you know where they are?" she asked.

"In the king's private receiving chamber, I believe."

When the Lady of the Skye was gone, Laerwen decided it was time to make an appearance.

She changed into a gown from this realm. It was royal blue in crushed velvet with a high collar, long flowing sleeves, belted at the waist. She had opted for this more traditional dress of the Wood Elves rather than her sari and her head veil. She let her hair flow freely over her shoulders and down her back. To give the appearance that she had accepted their culture. She could not get Lady Talaiel's words out of her head. *He cares for you a great deal.*

She splashed cold water on her face, hoping to wash away the tear streaks. She didn't want them to see she'd been racked by emotion. She wanted to appear as she always was—strong and confident.

Once dressed, she pulled open the door and stepped into the drafty hallway. Sentries were still posted at her door but she paid them no mind. She knew where the king's private chamber was and headed there directly. She would meet the queen and king of the Fae with her head held high.

She garnered a few curious glances as she made her way through the halls. These nobles likely hadn't seen her dressed this way before. As she passed, she acknowledged them with a nod.

A guard and Leopold stood outside the king's private chamber. Leopold snapped to attention and greeted her with a smile and a bow.

"Your majesty, how may I serve you?"

"I understand the king and queen of the Fae have arrived. I should like to meet them."

"The king has been in conference with them along with Lord Eldrin. I shall announce you."

Leopold opened the door, swinging it wide enough for her to see inside. He announced her arrival and everyone got to their feet. Andahar approached her, his hand out to her.

"Princess Laerwen, I'm glad you've come."

"I am queen now," she said, gently correcting him, embracing the title at last.

"Aye, of course. Queen Laerwen, allow me to introduce you to Queen Elyne and her husband, King Derron, rulers of the Fae."

Elyne stepped forward first, a bright smile on her face. She was tall and lithe with golden blonde hair and cornflower blue eyes. She extended her hand to Laerwen.

"How delightful to meet you at last." She shook her hand and turned to Andahar. "She's quite lovely, Andahar. She reminds me of an Indian princess."

"An Indian princess?" Laerwen's brows drew together as she looked to Andahar for clarification.

"Queen Elyne has spent quite some time in the human realm. I'm certain she refers to something of a human trait."

"Oh, aye. Forgive me. I forgot that not all Otherworlders have been to the human realm as much as I have. Or Derron for that matter. But that's a tale for another time. The Fae would like to extend our deepest sympathies on your loss, your majesty."

"I appreciate that, thank you."

Derron stepped beside his wife and extended his hand. When Laerwen reached for her, instead of shaking her hand, he brought it to his lips and kissed it. "A pleasure to meet you, your majesty."

"We were discussing the battle plan at the Hin'dar Rhule," Andahar said. "I consulted with Elyne since she and Derron are familiar with Cormac. They have agreed to lend their troops to ours as well as help rebuild the Hin'dar Rhule."

"I'm grateful." Laerwen couldn't stop the lump that formed in her throat.

She was overwhelmed. She didn't understand how all these royals were so willing to help her—someone they hardly knew— fight her war and rebuild her home. She glanced at Andahar and didn't miss the adoring look he gave her. She knew he did all this for her. Her and her people.

"Thank you."

"You've arrived in time for a feast," Andahar said. Though she was sure he was talking to the Fae queen and king, his gaze never left her face. "Shall we move to the dining hall?"

"Sounds delightful," Elyne piped. "I'm famished. Come along, Derron. Lord Eldrin, I should like to hear all about your latest ranger exploits."

They filed out of the room, leaving Laerwen alone with the king. An uncomfortable silence settled between them. She couldn't hide from his adoring looks then. Not that she wanted to. He studied her features in an unhurried way that made all her senses stand up and take notice. Her skin prickled sensual sensations she couldn't deny.

"You look quite beautiful in that gown."

She blushed like a young girl receiving her first compliment from her latest crush. "I...I thought it would be appropriate to wear to meet the rulers of the Fae."

"You can wear whatever you wish." His gaze trickled down her and then back to her face. Then he cocked a grin. "Or don't wish." Then he cleared his throat and extended his arm. "Shall we join the others?"

She hooked her arm in his and they walked toward the dining hall.

"I'm glad to see you, Laerwen."

"I apologize for being such a recluse."

"I understand why you were."

"I may not have been in love with Randir, but he was my friend."

"There is no need to explain."

He smiled down at her. A warming smile that said he understood with perfect clarity. It caused a curious swooping deep in her womb and made her weak in the knees. All she could think of at that moment was how much she wanted to kiss him. Their last kiss marched back into her mind and she found she could not forget the way his velvet lips brushed against hers or the way he tasted of wild berries and honeywine.

She licked her lips as if in anticipation of that kiss. She didn't miss the way his gaze flickered there and then back up again before he turned away.

"Do you still taste like brown sugar?"

Her pulse throbbed at the base of her neck. Did she? She didn't know. "Do you wish to find out?"

He halted in the middle of the corridor and turned to her, his hands on her shoulders. His pale green eyes—so mesmerizing—locked on hers. Her breath hitched in her throat as he cupped her face in his warm hands.

"I do wish it. If you will permit me."

She blinked, slow and languorously, and nodded. Then everything went into super slow motion as she waited, not breathing, as his lips descended to hers. When they met, it was a tentative kiss at first. Not unlike the first one they'd shared on horseback. His lips were indeed still velvet soft and he still tasted like wild berries and honeywine, which she found so curious.

His tongue dipped inside her mouth and he took his time exploring. Tasting her, teasing her, making her want more than his kisses. Her hands moved up his chest and around his neck, pulling him to her. It had turned into a kiss of longing, of wanting, of needing. She blocked out any other thoughts about her future, her kingdom, the men and women she'd lost. All she could think about right then was Andahar and kissing him.

Their romantic interlude was cut short by someone clearing his throat nearby. They broke apart, though reluctantly. Leopold waited patiently, his hands clasped in front of him.

"Your guests await, your majesties."

"Right." Andahar took her arm again and led her away, following Leopold into the dining hall. He gave her a sideways glance full of mischief. "If you were wondering, you do still taste of brown sugar."

Heat throbbed through her body right down to her feminine core. "Do I?" She couldn't bring the words to her throat to tell him he still tasted of honeywine and wild berries. She didn't know why. For whatever reason, they were frozen there and unwilling to come out.

"You do. Would it be too forward of me to say I'm not finished with you?"

Laerwen giggled but couldn't force herself to answer a question she didn't know how to answer. She hadn't fully committed to him yet and hadn't wanted to admit to herself that she wanted Andahar with a ferocious need that would only be assuaged by being with him in the most intimate way.

Deep down, she knew she wanted to be with him. If things were different, if there wasn't a war to be fought or lives to be saved, mayhap she could allow herself to have that.

"I too have guilt over Randir's death," Andahar said. "I told you once I would fight him for you. And I meant that. I never wanted him dead, though."

Her gaze fluttered to the floor in front of them. She fixed on the shiny wood planks, trying hard to not allow the tears that threatened fall. She'd cried enough, hadn't she?

"Andahar—"

"It's something I wanted you to know."

Their arrival in the dining hall stopped any response she might have had. She and the king greeted the guests.

Chapter 12

It had been a gay feast. For that short time, they all forgot about the Fomorians and the impending battle. All that mattered was spending time with each other. They regaled Laerwen with fanciful tales. The Queen of the Fae was quite fun-loving and told how she once turned back the hands of time to save Derron from certain death. Laerwen was mesmerized by the idea that the Fae could alter time.

"How does that work exactly?" she asked.

"Fae magic," Elyne said with a smile that crinkled her blue eyes. "It's easy to do in the human realm where time is more linear."

"I thought time was linear everywhere," she said.

"It is but isn't," Derron said with a grin. "Time in the Otherworld moves at a different pace than that of the human realm. With our magic, we can sift to any place and any time we wish. In this realm or any other."

"Sift?" Laerwen's brows drew together in question. "Is that what Cormac does?"

"No," Elyne said. "But it's similar. We alter the sands of time to get where and when we want. He merely thinks of a place he wants to go and flashes there. He can only flash within the Otherworld and no other realm."

Hearing this gave Laerwen an idea. Hope bloomed in her breast. "Why can't you just alter time to before the attack on the Hin'dar Rhule? Then I can stop the massacre before it happens and save lives." She could save her parents and Randir. None of them would have to go through this tragedy. It seemed the perfect solution.

"Oh I'm afraid it's quite forbidden. It's against the Laws of Fae. I should have never done it in the first place," Elyne said, glancing at Derron. "But I was a desperate, angry woman."

"And you paid the price for breaking that law too." Derron's hand landed on hers and held it. He brought her fingertips to his lips and kissed them. "Yet I love you for it. For all you did for me."

They told her how Elyne had gone back in time to save Derron from dying at a jousting tournament—something he used to do before the Otherworld came under attack. Before Maeve relinquished the throne to her daughter.

Laerwen sat back in her chair, trying not to feel deflated. If she had the power to alter time, would she? She thought she might. She was an angry, desperate woman too. She wanted her parents back, by the gods. She wanted the Hin'dar Rhule to be safe once again.

But, alas, none of that was meant to be. And she had to face the true reality of her life.

"How did the Treaty of Separation come to be abolished?" Laerwen asked.

It was known in the Elven realms the Wood Elves and the Fae didn't get along due the death of the former Fae king. His murder was blamed on the Elves and the then-queen, Maeve, was determined to exact her revenge. That was why the Treaty of Separation had been enacted but later abolished. Laerwen was never quite certain how they came to that point of removing it.

Andahar took a sip of his honeywine. "That is another tale for another day."

"Aye. A very long tale, indeed," Derron agreed. "And we're fatigued." He pushed back from the table and Elyne followed. She took his hand.

They bid them goodnight. Laerwen watched them leave the table.

"On the morrow, I will assemble the rangers," Eldrin said.

"Good." Andahar gave a nod of his head. "I'm glad to hear it."

Eldrin and Lady Talaiel rose wishing them both good night. That left her alone with Andahar, save for a few servants still wandering around and cleaning up after the feast. She sat across from him, watching him watch her. He raised his goblet and extended it in a high toast.

She raised hers. They clinked together.

"To victory," he said and drank.

"A little early for that, isn't it?" she chided.

"I'm optimistic." He winked.

It sent her heart tumbling to her feet. She downed the rest of her honeywine but found the taste soured in her mouth.

"I should like some ale, I think," she announced and rose,

scanning the room for a pitcher of ale or something a bit stronger.

"How about whiskey?"

Andahar stood and turned away from the table, walking across the dining hall to a high table on the other side. He grabbed two small cups and filled them with a pale amber liquid then walked back to her.

"I've never had whiskey."

"Nor I. Shall we try it together?" He handed her the cup.

She held it between her palms and looked down into the liquid, smelling the sharp tang and smiling. "It smells delicious. And strong. Like I might get drunk on one sip." She glanced up at him, her brows raised in question. "Or is that what you're trying to do, your majesty?"

"Get you drunk? Why I never."

She laughed. Together the two of them downed the drink in the same instance. It burned all the way down to her toes, giving her a lovely warming feeling and making her head thick. As though she'd suddenly grown fur between her earlobes. She laughed again. A hearty laugh that come from the belly up her throat. She held out her cup.

"Another."

"Are you sure, your majesty?"

She wiggled the cup at him. "Another!"

He went back to the table, grabbed the decanter and returned to fill her cup and his. They clinked cups and then downed the drink together.

"How wonderful this is. I haven't been this happy in ages." She giggled.

"Did you know it's the color of your eyes?" He held up the decanter, the amber liquid winking in the candlelight making it sparkle. "I've always thought so."

"Have you?"

"I have."

He set aside his cup and advanced around the table, walking in slow, silent steps like a big cat. As though he were on the prowl. Indeed, his mesmerizing green eyes sparked with desire and need. Everything she'd been feeling since the moment she saw him. She turned her back to the table and watched him approach. Her heart beat so hard, she was sure he heard it.

Andahar pried the cup from her fingers and placed it on the

table next to her. He pinned her between the table and his wall of muscle. She'd only noticed that for the first time. Gods, he was handsome. With that fall of silvery hair and those pale green eyes. She couldn't stop from reaching up to brush away the locks from his forehead, letting her fingers glide through the strands and over his scalp.

His eyes fluttered closed as though he had never experienced something so wonderful. He pressed against her, pushing her hips against the table. Laerwen lost her balance and fell back. She only had time to put her hands back to halt her descent but in the next instance, he was on top of her.

She wasn't opposed to his weight pressing against her. The weight of him against her body made her weak and light-headed. Or mayhap that was merely the whiskey making her feel that way.

"Laerwen."

"Aye?"

"You are beautiful."

His gaze searched her face then flickered lower over her upper body. With him on top of her and the way the gown pressed against her bosom, it made all the flesh come together and push upward, heaving out of the edge of the gown. He dragged his finger across her, his pale skin a contrast to that of her bronzed flesh.

"Andahar?"

"Shh. Let me look at you."

It occurred to her they were in plain view of all the servants. They could be walked in on any moment. But the more he touched her, the more she found she didn't care. Her head fell back, landing with a quiet thud on the table while his hands roamed over her breasts.

"Touching you is like touching heaven."

A mewl escaped her as the heat flooded her core. Her legs opened and wrapped around his waist. He settled there and she could feel the hard length of his shaft nestling between her legs. The damn skirt was in the way.

His head dipped to her earlobe and he licked her there. It sent more heat pouring into her.

"I have never wanted anyone as I want you."

"Nor I." She surprised herself with the admission.

His mouth, so hot, landed on her neck as he kissed her. He

kissed his way to the back of her ear and back down again. He kissed his way across her breasts that she so desperately wanted to be freed yet the damn dress held them right in place. He kissed his way up her chin to—finally—her lips.

And oh, gods, what a kiss that was. His searing mouth did not take his time as he had before. He took what he wanted, his mouth pillaging her. His tongue dueling with hers. She noticed then that he did not taste like wild berries and honeywine. He tasted like whiskey. Strong, sharp, tangy. Much like the taste in the back of her throat. They had shared the drink and now shared the kiss of passion.

Laerwen pulled him to her, all the sharp angles of his body thrusting against her. She was aware of his hips bones and his hard shaft as he rocked his hips against her. And her body responded in like as a moan bubbled up her throat.

Gods, what were they doing? This was insane and she had to stop.

But she couldn't stop any more than she wanted to stop.

Finally, she broke her mouth away from his demanding one and turned her head. "Andahar." His name came out a breathy whisper.

But his mouth continued to taste her and kiss her and make her mind frazzled so much so she couldn't think or form a coherent thought.

"I want you. I want to make love to you here, Laerwen."

Her heart burst inside her chest, making little starbursts against her closed eyes. Oh, gods, and he would too. Right here on the dining hall table. If she let him.

She gripped him by the shoulders and shoved with all her might, pushing him up and away from her.

"Not here. Not like this."

Even though her body wept with need and desire and she wanted to say yes. She wanted him to take her here, right now.

Clarity seemed to come into his eyes as he blinked. He pushed off her and stood, smoothing his hands over his tunic and then his hair. As if he had been so swept away, he'd lost control of where and who he was.

"My apologies, your majesty." He held out a hand and helped her to stand. "I was overcome."

Then he gave her a quick bow. "I bid thee good night."

And just like that, the magic was broken and he was gone.

"Well how about that," she said to no one in particular.

She plopped down on the chair she'd vacated only moments before and poured herself another whiskey. Mayhap the drink would numb her and she wouldn't feel the flood of disappointment and hurt that pressed against her chest.

He'd left her in the dining hall alone. As though screwing her against the table had been his only option. What about screwing her in his bed, by the gods? What about that? Wasn't she good enough for that?

She slammed the empty cup on the table, the sound resonating throughout the room. But there was no one to hear. And no one to care. After some time of sitting alone, she peeled herself from the chair and headed to bed.

But as she walked toward her chamber, she became enraged he had the nerve to leave her like that. She was not going to allow him to do that because it was clear he wanted her and she wanted him. And hadn't they wasted enough time already?

When she reached her chamber, she quickly changed into one of her more revealing outfits. Not one of the gowns of this realm, but a low cut blouse with short sleeves, the voluminous skirt and a sari she had commissioned from the royal dressmaker. The color was a deep garnet trimmed with silver thread. As she threw the sari over her shoulder, she reached for her veil and carefully concealed her hair.

Now let him resist her if he could.

What was he thinking? Had he lost his ever-loving mind? How could he have allowed the drink to cloud his judgment so? Laerwen deserved better than that. She deserved to be taken to his bed. Not taken against the table.

He slammed the door to his chamber and leaned against it, wiping the sweat of embarrassment off his brow. He had at least saved face that time.

By the time he'd reached his royal chamber, he had lost his nerve and the drink had fizzled from his veins. It was just as well. He vowed never to touch the stuff again.

As he pulled off his tunic, preparing for bed, there was a sharp knock on his door. He paused and stared at the door with wide eyes. Who could that be at this hour? Surely not the princess—or queen rather. As he hesitated, there was another knock on his door. This one more persistent and louder. He dropped his tunic to the floor and pulled open the door.

And halted, his heart in his throat.

Laerwen stood in the doorway. His body reacted at the sight of her dressed in that fiery red sari, her head covered with the veil. He could only see her face and her hands and nothing more. The opaque material covered her from head to toe. His senses went reeling.

Gods, he wanted her. He wanted to run his hands over all that soft skin. He wanted to kiss every inch of her, explore her, memorize her, know her. She was exquisite and perfect and he wanted her.

He had never wanted another woman like her. Not in his entire life. And the last thing he had thought of was marriage now, even as he sat the throne. Something about her made him want marriage and children and an eternal life. With her.

"I hope I'm not disturbing you." Her voice was soft and melodious, hardening his shaft. Her gaze slipped over his naked torso and desire clouded her eyes. "We have unfinished business."

"We do not," he said, matter-of-factly. "If this is about the dining hall—"

"You know it is."

She shoved her way inside and kicked the door closed with her heel. The bang reverberated around the walls. He flinched, hoping she hadn't awakened anyone in the palace. He backed up as she advanced on him, the intent clearly written on her face. She'd come here with seduction on her mind. And he'd be a damn fool to reject her now. When she so clearly wanted him.

His shafted had hardened to a painful length. But, alas, he couldn't allow it to happen. He would never take advantage of her.

"You're still overcome with the whiskey," he said. "I cannot allow you to do this."

"I assure you, your majesty, I am quite lucid. Do you think I would have come here dressed like this if I wasn't? I knew what I was doing the moment I slipped into these clothes. Just as I know what I'm doing here. Now. With you. Alone."

Oh, gods. She was killing him.

She stepped toward him again, gently tugging the veil from

around her neck. It fell open, revealing her low-cut tightly fitting blouse that stopped just below her breasts and was low cut enough to show off ample cleavage. He tried hard not to look at her but he failed. He had to look. He had to see all that brown sugar skin, her breasts pushed together and up, showing the perfect roundness of them. Not to mention her flat abdomen and all those womanly curves his fingers itched to touch. He wondered if her skin was as soft as it looked. The jeweled waistband of her pants hugged her hips low, revealing her bellybutton and giving him a hint at what was below.

Exquisite perfection.

"I wish to thank you for all that you have done for me and my people. Your assistance and that of the Skye Elves and the Fae have been…humbling."

"There is no need to thank me, Laerwen. I did it because I wanted to help you. They did it because it's the right thing to do."

"Aye, I know. But none of it would be possible without your help and I know that. As do my people. I am eternally grateful."

"Laerwen—"

She'd reached him and placed two fingers over his lips. As their gazes locked, she pulled away the remaining veil, letting it flutter to the floor in a whisper. Her dark hair fell about her face in soft waves. His fingers itched to touch her. To run his fingers through all those silken strands.

"I wish to give myself to you." Her words came out in a breathy whisper as her hands landed on his bare chest. "And not for any reason other than I have allowed myself to fall in love with you, Andahar. I want you."

He was stunned to silence as he looked at her. His hands moved up her arms and he cupped her face. Gods, did he hear her right? She loved him? She wanted him?

When did she change her mind? She had been so hell-bent on marrying one of her kind, she had rejected him time and time again. She had never allowed him to get any closer. And after Randir died, she had become somewhat of a recluse.

"I realize what you must think," she continued, as though hearing his inner thoughts. "That it seems strange I should change my mind, but in all honesty, I have wanted you from day I came to the Woodlands."

"It is the same for me. I've always wanted you, Laerwen." His thumb brushed across her cheek.

"I admit Randir's death was difficult for me. You were right. I did blame myself. I know now it wasn't my fault and I've tried not to harbor any guilt over it." She paused and tugged her lower lip.

"But you do."

She nodded.

"You are allowed to grieve for all that you've lost, Laerwen."

"I know. But I wanted to be strong."

"You are strong. The strongest woman I have ever known." He kissed her forehead. "I want you to be sure, though."

"I am sure."

It was clear to him now that she'd planned the entire thing. It only made his shaft harder. It only made him want her more.

"What changed your mind?" he asked.

"Lady Talaiel and I had a conversation."

"Ah, she can be quite persuasive when she wants to be." He smiled, grateful for his brother's wife.

"If we survive this—"

"When," he corrected. "When we survive this. Because we will. We are not going to allow the Fomorians to beat us."

She smiled and fluttered her lashes. Gods, he loved that about her. Did she know what she was doing to him? "When we survive this, I hope you are still willing to help rebuild the Hin'dar Rhule."

He considered this for a moment as he looked at her, his hands still on her face. She was lovely. Quite possibly the most beautiful woman he'd ever seen. Help her rebuild the Hin'dar Rhule? Nay. He would do more than that.

"I will. I intend to be by your side. As your husband, if you'll have me."

Her cheeks flooded with color as she looked down, away from him. He could see her chest rising and falling in quick breaths and it did nothing but wonderful things to her breasts.

"I love you, Laerwen. I think I always have since that first moment I saw you."

"Andahar…" She placed her cool hands on his chest, right over the wild beating of his heart. She glanced up, those whiskey-colored eyes meeting his and her mouth curving into a smile. "Do you? Love me?"

"Not a moment goes by that you are not in my thoughts. I would give my life to save yours. I would do anything to see you smile. To make you happy. So, aye, I love you. More than I could ever tell you."

She lowered her eyes but he could see the flush creeping into her cheeks, turning her skin a beautiful shade of pink. How could she have taken his heart so completely so quickly? He didn't know the answer to that. He didn't care. All he cared about was that she loved him back and that she would become his wife.

"I'll marry you." Slowly her eyes lifted to his. "I'll marry you now or after the battle. I'll marry you whenever you want. I just want to marry you. Belong to you. Be with you. I love you as you love me."

His heart turned over and dropped to his boots. He had not intended to profess his love for her nor ask for her hand in marriage. But he had been overcome with emotion and could no longer stand the thought of her not being in his life. He could not let her go back to the Hin'dar Rhule alone.

He kissed her then, their lips meeting softly at first and then as the kiss intensified, their passion increased. She'd agreed to be his wife. He had never had more joy than he did right then.

He led her to his bed. She remained silent as she helped him undress her. Removing each piece one at a time. Sliding the tunic from her upper body to reveal her perfect breasts, the raspberry-colored nipples peaked and ready for his mouth to taste.

Andahar took a moment to run the pads of his thumbs over her hard peaks. Her eyes fluttered closed again as she tilted her head back, as though it was the most erotic thing that had ever happened to her. But he was far from finished with her. He dipped his head, flicked his tongue over one. A breath of delight shuddered out of her.

Her hands threaded through the locks of his hair, her nails scraping over his scalp, making it tingle. It delighted him. It excited him. When he sucked her nipple between his teeth and gently nipped, she sucked in a sharp breath. He did the same with her other breast and her fingers tightened on his hair.

Laerwen stepped out of his arms and away from him. He watched as she shimmied out of the skirt, letting the material land at her feet in a shimmering pool of fiery color. Beneath the skirt, she wore nothing and stood delightfully naked before him.

Her skin looked soft and supple. Her waist curved inward, giving her the perfect hour-glass figure. The V at the apex of her rounded thighs was completely devoid of the thatch of curls he expected. She was bare and blissfully beautiful. She had long legs he couldn't wait to have wrapped around his waist while he slid inside her. She flicked the length of her hair over her shoulder and gave him a delicious smile.

"You approve, my king?"

Oh, aye, both his brain and his shaft approved.

"Now your turn," she urged. "I wish to see you."

Gods, he loved how brazen and demanding she was. He loved how she ordered him to remove his clothes, to bare himself to her. Wasting no time, he toed off his boots and stripped out of his breeches, shoving them down to his ankles and kicking them out of the way. His manhood stood at reckless attention, pointing right at her.

But she didn't look there. She kept her gaze trained on him as she approached him, stepping over the discarded clothing. The fire of desire flickered in her eyes, or mayhap that was the braziers blazing brightly in his chamber. He didn't know. He didn't care.

Laerwen's hand landed on his chest, her fingers trailing over the muscle and the sprinkling of hair as she circled behind him. She stepped away from him and then he heard her breath exhale as half the chamber was plunged into darkness. Only a few candles remained, the glow flickering across the coverlet of the bed.

Her body pressed against his back, her breasts crushing into him. His eyes fluttered closed as her hands slipped around from behind him. She flattened one hand in the curve of his chest. Her other hand wrapped around his hardened length, her long slender fingers closing over his shaft in a gentle grip.

"I wish to feel you." She must have stood on tiptoe as she whispered it, for her breath tickled his ear.

Her thumb roved over his dampened tip, heightening his arousal more than he could comprehend. His head could very well explode before he could bury himself deep inside her.

"Laerwen—"

"Let me touch you."

Her hand pumped back and forth several times before moving lower and cupping his sac. His eyes closed and he bit his lip, using all his strength to remain standing and perfectly still while she worked her seductive magic. She petted him in a way he never thought would arouse him. When her hand closed over his shaft again, she pumped several more times.

"You torture me, your majesty," he said.

"My torture is not yet finished." She released him and moved to stand in front of him. He could see the mischief in her eyes. "There is more in store for you."

She said it as she dropped to her knees and before he could protest, she took his long length between her lips and sucked him to the back of her throat. The groan of pleasure ripped from his lungs as his head fell back on his shoulders. It was a most unexpected pleasure as she licked him.

Andahar let his fingers tangle in the length of her hair, threading his way through the soft locks as she continued her oral onslaught. He watched her beautiful mouth do sinful things to him. Things he had only imagined a woman could and would do. When she stopped, she looked up at him with desire flooding her eyes. He gripped her hair close to her scalp and gave a little tug, pulling her up to her full height.

"Did you like it?" Her eyes glinted with lust. The peaks of her perfectly dusty pink nipples brushed against his naked chest.

Like it? He had never experienced anything so divine. "Where did you learn something like that?"

"It is known by our people." She gave him a slow seductive smile.

He dropped one hand from the tangles of her hair and slid his fingers between her bare female lips, sliding into the damp heat. Her eyes closed, her head tilted to one side as he stroked her.

"You are a most beautiful woman."

She only hummed her response as she stepped her feet apart to allow him more access. He had never felt anything quite as divine as her. He'd had women before—certainly—but none like her. He had never experienced a woman who was devoid of the curls hiding her sex.

His fingers moved out of her and over her lips, touching her, outlining her, feeling every luscious curve from the top of her thighs and back again. He licked his lips. He had to taste her.

"Move to the bed."

Her eyes popped open, the lashes fluttering with the pulse racing in her throat. His voice was huskier than he intended. But she complied. Taking one slow step after another backward to the bed. When her knees hit the edge of the feather mattress, she sank to her bottom.

"Command me, your majesty. Tell me what you wish of me."

"Lean back. Open your legs to me."

When she did as he asked, his heart thunked a rapid beat. He had never seen a more beautiful woman lain out before him. He moved to the bed, sank to his knees and parted her nether lips with a gentle touch. When his tongue slid between the folds, she gasped. She lifted her legs, letting them rest on his shoulders. Her back arched as she opened more for him. Giving him more of her to taste, to tease, to pleasure.

As Andahar licked her, tasting her sweetness, he slid a finger inside the warm core. It did nothing but excite him more than he already was. She mewled her encouragement and her hips rocked against him. She didn't seem like a dewy-eyed virgin. No, she seemed like an experienced lover who knew exactly what she wanted and how she wanted it.

It was exhilarating.

She cried out his name as her body moved against his, the core of her so hot and damp, he lapped it up.

When he stood, he looked down at her naked body. Her eyes were closed. She gripped two fistfuls of the coverlet, her hair splayed out around her head and her breasts peaked to hard little nubs. Her sex still glistened—with both his onslaught and her arousal. She inhaled and exhaled with deep breaths.

"Look at me," he said, his voice still gravelly.

Laerwen fluttered her eyes open to meet his gaze. And he could see there the love, the yearning, and the want staring back at him. And then her gaze traveled down to his hard shaft standing at attention.

"Take me, Andahar."

He could no longer resist her. She slid backward to give him room when he climbed onto the bed between her legs. She opened to him as he slid home, pushing inside her as she emitted a little gasp of pleasure. Their bodies collided, thrusting against each other, the friction heating them.

She was perfect.

She was divine.

She was heaven.

She was his everything at that moment. He slid his arms around her, pulled her to him as he thrust in and out of her. One arm wrapped around his waist while her free hand tangled in the locks of his hair. Their mouths met in a fiery kiss, as though they both could not get enough. As though they could not taste enough.

When he came inside her a moment later, she shuddered with him. Their tongues never stopped dueling even as their bodies slowly descended from the height of arousal. He could still taste her sex on his lips and he wondered if she, too, could taste it.

He finally broke from her, lifted up to look down at her. He brushed hair from her face as she smiled that slow seductive smile.

"I love you, Laerwen."

She kissed his chin. "I love you back."

It was the best four words he'd ever heard her speak.

Chapter 13

Laerwen burrowed deep within the blankets of Andahar's bed as she curled next to him, her head on his chest. He held her, his hand brushing her hair. Her fingers trailed through the fine hairs on his chest, slipping over the muscles there and back again.

For the first time since that horrible day when her realm was destroyed, a sense of safety and security came over her. But she'd always felt that way with Andahar. The loneliness she'd experienced seemed to finally abate. And it seemed as though she could face all the terrors of the world with him at her side.

"What are you thinking of, princess?"

"I am queen now," she teased. "Or have you forgotten?"

"I forget nothing. You will always be a princess to me."

She grinned in the warm glow of the room though he couldn't see her. "I'm wishing this night would last forever and never end."

"I wish that too."

Alas, it must end and they both knew that. She rolled toward him and looked up at him. "I'm also thinking I don't feel so alone anymore now that I know your true feelings."

He brushed a lock of hair from her face. "Nor I. Though you were never truly alone."

"I know that now." She smiled. "You have always been there for me."

"And will continue to be."

She rested her head once more against his chest. "When should we announce our engagement?"

"Whenever you wish. Today. Tomorrow. It doesn't matter to me."

"And when will we marry?"

"Today. Tomorrow." She could hear the smile in his voice.

She giggled. "It's a fair question."

"It matters not to me when we marry, so long as we marry."

"I wish to marry you today."

"That will take some doing."

She rose sat next to him, pulling her fingers through her tangled hair. "All we need is an officiant. You have a High Druid in the realm, I assume? I don't want anything elaborate or boastful. Not in a time like this, when we are about to go to war. Can we not just…marry?"

He reached for her and pulled her down to him, his hands on either side of her face as he placed a gentle kiss on her lips. "Is that truly what you wish?"

"It is."

He nudged her out of his arms and slipped from the bed, reaching for his breeches. She watched in stunned silence as he dressed.

"What are you doing?"

"Dressing. Let's go now." He picked up her clothes and tossed them to her. "Before you change your mind." There was a playful smile tugging at his lips.

"I'll not change my mind," she said. "You're going to wake the High Druid now to marry us?"

"Indeed I am. We will greet the dawn as husband and wife."

She slid to the edge of the bed and stood, still naked, her hands on her hips as she thrust out her breasts. "Are you certain you don't wish to ravish me again?"

His gaze raked over her as he smiled. "Tease." He moved to her in one step and pulled her to him. "I shall next ravish you when you are my wife." He planted a kiss on her lips before releasing her.

With her heart beating rapidly, she pulled on her skirt and top, and then wrapped the sari around her, tossing the end over her shoulder. She placed her mother's veil over her hair, hiding the long lengths.

They paused and he fingered the veil, his thumb running over the lacy edge.

"It was my mother's," she confessed. "All that is left of her."

"It's as lovely as you."

He took her by the hand and led her from his chamber. They crept down the deserted hallways while the rest of the palace still slept. It was quiet and peaceful and no one was about. Not even the guards. As though they had all gone off to their own chamber to slumber away the wee hours of the morn. And it seemed to her as if they were two young lovers sneaking away for a romantic rendezvous. When really, this was so much more…quixotic. So delightfully wonderful, she thought her heart might burst from joy.

They arrived at a door and the king knocked, his knuckles rapping on the solid oak like a demand. It took several long, silent moments before it finally opened and a rumpled man appeared on the other side. He held a candlestick in one hand, the yellowish glow casting wavering shadows across his aged face. He squinted into the hallway at the king and then, realizing who stood before him, straightened and bowed.

"Your majesty. Your presence is most unexpected at this time of the night. Is there something amiss?"

"Eran, the queen of the Fire Elves and I wish to be married at once," he announced, his voice strong and sure.

The High Druid blinked surprise before casting his eyes at her, giving her a quick once over. His brows knit with question as he looked back at his king. "Your majesty?"

"I believe I made myself perfectly clear. Marry us." Andahar's hand tightened on hers as he pulled her closer and wrapped his arm around her. "We wish to be wed at once."

"Aye, of course."

He stepped aside and welcomed them into his chamber.

The ceremony only lasted a short time. Merely long enough for the High Druid to perform the ritual handfasting and for them to exchange their vows. They sealed it with a kiss. Her pulse was aflutter as they left the High Druid's chamber and headed back to their own.

They hadn't discussed how their rule would work. Would he return with her to the Hin'dar Rhule to help her rebuild? She knew she could not stay here and leave her realm to ruin. Marrying Andahar also meant she would have to spend a fair amount of time here in the humidity of the Woodlands, something that seemed not to have bothered her. In fact, she'd never even thought about the humidity of the Woodlands. Mayhap because she'd been so distracted with other things.

At any rate, she wasn't ready to discuss that yet. For now, she only wanted to revel in the bliss.

When they reached his chamber door, he opened it. As she took a step to go in, he caught her arm. She gave him a questioning look. He swept her into his arms and carried her across the threshold. She giggled as he kicked the door closed.

He set her to her feet. "And now, my wife, about that ravishing you requested…"

Cormac knew the ranks of the Fomorians were divided. Some swore allegiance to Lorcann and others to him. He knew this because Gweneth had become his spy.

One of her powers was that she could remove her consciousness from her body. She called it removing herself to the First Sphere. She described it as taking her mind out of her body so she could go anywhere, anytime. She willingly did this for him and learned many secrets among them.

He waited for her mind to return from the First Sphere. She lay on the bed, her hands folded over her chest and her eyes still closed. He had made the mistake once of opening an eyelid and saw nothing but the white of her eye. No color there. Just a void. It had shaken him to his core and he vowed he would never do that again.

But Gweneth insisted he be there when she performed this spell. She needed someone to bring her out of her trance if she had not returned before the black candle burned down to the last mark on the wax.

He could see movement behind her lids and knew she was close to coming out of it. She inhaled sharply as her eyes fluttered open and she sat up. She looked at him, met his gaze, and then leaned over to blow out the candle. It plunged the tent into near darkness. Several candelabras still burned on the other side of the tent.

"What did you learn?"

"Lorcann has worked his men into a frenzy. They hate you."

"Not unexpected. I took Lorcann's powers from him."

"Aye you did. And most of his men. And his woman." She grinned as her eyes glinted in the half-light and then turned serious. "Be warned. They intend to kill you."

"Let them try." He ground his teeth until they ached.

"They will try." She swung her legs off the side of the bed. "Lorcann will not carry the deed out himself. He's convinced his men to attack you."

"How many?"

"Twenty. They intend to ambush you."

"When?"

"Dawn tomorrow. When you go for your morning exercises."

"I will be ready."

"As will I."

"You're not helping me."

"I am. I will. No matter how strong you are, you cannot think to defeat so many. You will be outnumbered." She stood and moved to him, sliding her hands up his chest. "I am to be your queen. I stand beside you no matter what."

Cormac peeled his lips back from his teeth in a snarl before nodded. "All right. What does Lorcann hope to gain by killing me?"

"He thinks he can get his power back. He is mistaken."

"You know this?"

She nodded. "Once the power has been removed as you took it, it cannot be returned. Not ever. He also thinks with you dead, he will be able to lead the attack at the Hin'dar Rhule."

Cormac laughed. "The fool."

"Once you defeat his men, then you will show the rest of them you are the rightful leader." She placed her hands on either side of his face. "You will win this fight."

"Just as I will win the Unseelie realm."

She smiled. "Aye, my love. And just as I will be by your side."

He slipped his arms around her waist and pulled her to him. "Tell me your plan to defeat these brigands."

The following morning, Cormac emerged from his tent, his senses on high alert. He knew Lorcann's men were waiting for him on the edge of the encampment. Before he left, Gweneth had given him an enchanted dagger, one that would make him all-powerful in the coming battle. She was proving to be more and more of an asset. And more and more he knew he could not live without her.

As he left the row of tents, one of the men stepped in front of him blocking his path.

"Good morrow, Cormac."

He opened his palm and let the dagger slid into it. His fingers closed around the hilt as he gave the man a nod of greeting.

The next thing Cormac knew, he was hit from behind. He went

to his knees, the dagger falling out of his hand. Someone punched him in the back of the head while someone else punched him in the kidneys. Another kicked him in the side, he was on the ground then, face in the dirt. He couldn't find the dagger.

Get up and fight! Don't let them defeat you.

It was Gweneth's voice in his head. He lifted his head enough to see the dagger just out of reach. But there were too many punching and kicking him. The next thing he felt was a sharp stabbing pain in the shoulder.

He dove for the dagger, knowing he'd been stabbed by one of them. His hand closed on the hilt and suddenly, a surge of power spread throughout him. Something he hadn't experienced before.

Strength poured through his arms, giving him what he needed to break free of his attackers. He turned and lunged, stabbing the first one in the gut.

That's it, my love. You can do it. Kill them. Kill them all.

He wasn't sure if Gweneth was projecting herself into his head, if she was on the First Sphere or what. But it didn't matter. All that mattered was he had the strength and the power to kill all of these men. Dark shadows pressed into his vision, giving him one thought and one thought only. He saw nothing else. Heard nothing else. Knew nothing else. All he knew was he killed them, one by one. He wasn't even sure how he managed to do it, his actions had become such a blur.

By the time he stopped, his chest heaving from exertion and sweat trickling down his face, the men were in a heap at his feet. Even the one who'd blocked his path was dead. He recalled him trying to get away but he wouldn't let him.

When his vision cleared and the power had dwindled inside him, he blinked and saw the crowd had gathered before him. Staring at him. Gaping at the dead on the ground. His gaze landed on their faces, picking them out one by one. Making sure they all saw he knew they were there.

"Let this be a lesson to you all. I am in command here. Not Lorcann."

No one replied. Slowly the crowd dissipated, leaving only Lorcann there.

"What sort of trickery did you perform to kill my men?" he asked.

"No trickery."

"Liar. I saw you. No one possesses that kind of strength or power. Not even the highest wizard."

"I do. I have that kind of strength. And power."

"They will never follow you out of loyalty. Only fear."

"Fear is all I need." Cormac gave him a wide smile.

Lorcann said nothing as he turned and walked away.

Gweneth emerged from her hiding place and stood next to Cormac.

"He will not stop," she said. "He's still desperate to kill the princess of the Fire Elves."

"I didn't think he would. He's desperate to get his magic back and he'll do whatever it takes to do that." He glanced at her, took her hand and held it. "You know this for certain?"

"When I was in the First Sphere, I saw him conspiring with the others. If this did not work out, he has another plan for her. He will take her on the battlefield in the Hin'dar Rhule. He is merely biding his time until the final fight."

"Then my lady sorceress, it's time we pay a visit to the Woodlands."

She smiled. "By your command, my lord."

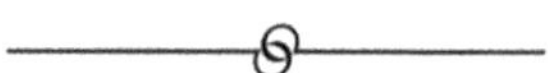

They agreed to tell no one of their nuptials. Laerwen wasn't ready to break the news to Hiram, though Andahar didn't see how it mattered. He honored her wishes, though, to keep the marriage secret until after the battle was over.

Andahar left her alone in his chamber so she could prepare for the day. He headed to the dining hall to break his fast. There he found his brother and the Lady of the Skye.

"Your majesty arrives late for your morning meal," Eldrin said. "Would that have anything to do with the lovely Queen of the Fire Elves."

"That would be none of your concern," Andahar said.

Eldrin snickered. "You were the last two here when we all retired. We hoped there would be some…development."

"Development?"

"It's quite obvious the lady fancies you," Lady Talaiel said with a smile. "She's quite smitten actually."

Andahar knew that. They'd professed their love for each other only hours ago. He shifted in his chair as the servants brought a heaping bowl of porridge. "There is a week left before the eclipse. We must begin moving toward the Hin'dar Rhule."

"Changing the subject, brother?" Eldrin smirked.

Andahar gave him a pointed look. "Aye, I am."

Talaiel rested her hand on Eldrin's arm as if in warning to keep him quiet. Eldrin pressed his lips together and Andahar could tell he resisted another barb about Laerwen. "I believe you'll find everything in order," he said. "Queen Elyne said she is ready to move her troops as soon as you are. She has offered to sift us all there to make the journey less labor intensive."

"Did you agree to that?" Andahar asked.

"I thought it might save the troops from unnecessary exhaustion. If she can sift us there, then we should allow her to do so."

"I will speak to the queen about her plans for that."

"As you wish."

At that moment, Laerwen made her entrance. Andahar and Eldrin stood as she approached the table dressed in her traditional Fire Elven clothes—the trousers that billowed around her legs but were tight at the ankle, the long tunic and the sari over her shoulder. She also wore the veil over her head, hiding her silken locks of hair. He knew now how precious that veil was to her.

"Good morrow, Queen Laerwen." Eldrin bowed with his greeting.

"I'm glad you could join us."

Andahar couldn't suppress the smile that erupted over his face. He held his hand out to her and she came to him, her gaze pinned on him and not looking at anyone else in the room. When her fingers slid against his palm, a zing of happiness jolted through him.

Her cheeks held a rosy pallor, something he'd not seen in her before but he suspected was the look of delight at being near him again. At least that's what he hoped for. He couldn't help but look at her differently now that she was his wife. His heart.

"I hope I'm not interrupting," she said.

"Not at all. We were just discussing our journey to the volcanoes."

"Oh." Her eyes lit up at that and he could see the hope and anticipation in them. "We're planning to go soon then?"

"Soon." He kissed her hand. He was aware Eldrin and his lady observed the intimacy they shared. Somehow, he didn't care if they saw. He wanted to shout to the world she was forever his but she had forbidden it. He understood her need for secrecy but he didn't have to like it.

They returned to their seats. The servants came by with a large bowl of porridge for Laerwen. She wasted no time digging into it.

"I hope you know the Skye Elves are ready to assist," Talaiel said. "I've also added more wards around the Woodlands. I don't know if it will keep the Fomorians out for good should they decide to attack again, but it will deter them."

"Thank you, my lady. Cormac seems to have become quite powerful. He may be able to punch through those wards no matter how good they are."

"You are quite right, King Andahar."

At the sound of Cormac's voice, everyone jumped to their feet. Eldrin pulled his sword. No one had seen him flash into the room. He was getting entirely too good at that and it disturbed Andahar. Laerwen took a step behind him, peering around him at the Fomorian mage who had made his presence known.

Cormac leaned against one of the far walls, his ankles crossed and his arms folded over his chest. A woman none of them knew stood next to him. Her black eyes alighted on everyone in the room, pausing on each face is if to memorize them. Her sleek black hair fell over her shoulders. She exuded power and confidence and Andahar knew this was not a woman to be taken lightly.

Cormac, however, looked as though he'd just been in a tavern fight. He had an oozing cut above his left eye, which was black. His knuckles were raw and red. His lip was split. He held up his hands in surrender.

"Stand down, ranger. I assure you I come unarmed."

"Shall I search you to find out?" Eldrin said.

"Put the sword down, brother. We can trust him."

"I'm not so sure about that." Eldrin eyed him suspiciously.

Andahar placed his hand on his brother's wrist and pushed down his hand. "I'm sure. Who's your friend?"

"May I present to you Gweneth? My lady sorceress."

So this was his woman. The one who had agreed to help him through the Barrier to the Unseelie realm.

"She stands beside me and is my future dark queen."

Elyne and Derron chose that moment to enter the dining hall and stopped short at the sight of Cormac. She didn't hide the look of surprise on her face. Nor did Derron hide the scowl.

"Cormac, what are you doing here?" Andahar snarled.

He pushed off the wall and walked toward them, his hands still up and visible. "I'm glad you could join us. I've so looked forward to this reunion. Your mother fares well, Princess?"

His gaze landed on Elyne. Derron slipped a protective arm around her shoulders. "Queen. She is queen now," he said. "As I am king."

"Ah, queen. Forgive my insolence. You both have my congratulations on your coronation as rulers of the Otherworld."

Andahar saw the smirk cross his face before he managed to hide it. For all his intent, Cormac sounded less than happy about Elyne and Derron as rulers.

"My mother is fine, Cormac. You're looking well for a dead man. In fact, you look like a new person altogether."

To that he laughed. "No longer dead. My spirit was put into another's body so that I may live again."

Her eyes narrowed, suspicion evident on her pretty features. "Is that so? Then tell me something only Cormac would know."

"I released you from Kieran's burning tent and took you on the back of Nero to the Stone of Destiny."

One thin blonde eyebrow raised. "And what did you say to me?"

"That I was taking you to meet your fate."

Relief passed over her features as she smiled and blew out a breath. "Aye. You really are Cormac."

"Then we can get on with business." His gaze flickered to Andahar. "I've come to discuss our truce."

"You realize you are now a traitor to the Fomorians. And to Lorcann."

"Lorcann has no power. But he still intends to steal the princess—forgive me, the queen of the Fire Elves—to sacrifice in the fires of the Hin'dar Rhule. He has not given up that quest."

Behind him, Andahar could feel Laerwen shift with her unease. Her hand landed on the small of his back.

"He can't have her."

"No, he can't." Cormac nodded in agreement. "However, I have a plan I'd like to propose."

Andahar glanced around at the expectant faces of the others. "We're listening."

"Since Lorcann is determined to see this through, we can use it to our advantage. She can lure the mage to her while Gweneth and I open the portal to the Unseelie realm."

"As bait?" Andahar shook his head. "No. I forbid it."

"Come now. You haven't even asked her yet." He looked at her then and smiled. "Your majesty?"

"No," Andahar said again.

"I'll do it." Laerwen stepped out from behind Andahar. She held up her head, as though ready to take on the world. Ready to take on the dangerous mage.

"Laerwen—"

"Andahar, I want to do this. If it means getting back my realm and my home, then I'm all in."

"It's too dangerous. I won't allow it."

"You can't forbid me," she challenged.

"I can. I'm—" He halted, clamped his mouth shut when he realized he was about to announce he was her husband. He would forbid her because it was his duty to protect her. "I don't want to see anything happen to you."

She softened, knowing what he was about to say. She placed her hand on his chest. "I know."

Cormac cleared his throat loudly. "I appreciate the affectionate moment but we have plans to make. Can we resume? If her majesty is willing to act as bait, then we have a chance to make this work. My lady Gweneth will explain."

She had remained where she flashed in with Cormac. Now she came toward them and paused beside him. Her glittering dark gaze landed on each and every one of them before resting on Laerwen.

"Cormac commands the Fomorians but there are still those opposed to him. Those loyal to Lorcann. Though they will never show it, their allegiance is divided."

"How do you know that?" It was Eldrin who spoke. That heated gaze of hers landed on him.

She narrowed her eyes. "I have my ways of knowing these things."

"We can trust what she says as the truth," Cormac put in. "She is more powerful than any of us put together and she knows Lorcann's plan."

"Once we are in the Hin'dar Rhule, they plan to alter the attack," she continued. "Their first order of business is to get the Fire Queen. They will do whatever it takes to capture her. Even kill each other. You do not yet understand how desperate Lorcann is to have his power back."

"I think I have an idea," Laerwen said, her tone flat.

"We will position Queen Laerwen in the middle of the field. This will allow those loyal to Lorcann to show themselves," Cormac said.

"Out in the open? She'll be an easy target," Andahar said. "I don't like that idea at all."

"Aye, she'll be an easy target. Which is exactly what we want." Cormac nodded agreement.

"You expect her stand there waiting to be attacked?"

This time Derron spoke up. He stepped around Elyne and positioned himself near the other two men and edged toward Laerwen. As though they were a wall of muscle. Andahar was well pleased with that show of solidarity.

"Once the traitors show themselves, they will be killed immediately," Cormac said.

"That's how you intend to cull the herd, so to speak?" Andahar asked.

"Indeed. Once the traitors are dealt with, then we can proceed with opening the Barrier to the Unseelie realm."

"How many Fomorians are left?"

"Five thousand. Though I expect that number to go down," Cormac said. "When they realize what we intend to do, most won't be willing to go into the Unseelie realm."

"But we will force them," Gweneth added. She had the air of confidence in her tone.

Andahar didn't like this plan. Too many things could go wrong. What if there was a revolt and they turned on Cormac and his sorceress? "And the eruption? You're sure it will happen?"

"Aye, I'm sure," Gweneth said.

"How can you be?" Laerwen asked. "They haven't erupted in thousands of years. Why now?"

"It has always been said the next eruption of all the volcanoes in the Hin'dar Rhule will happen when there is no day and no night. The eclipse is coming," the sorceress replied.

Andahar gave Laerwen a questioning look as if to ask her

silently if the sorceress was telling the truth. She nodded. "I've heard the myths. Though it hasn't occurred in my lifetime, I know it is a possibility."

"All right." Andahar looked back at Cormac. "I'm not entirely sure I'm in agreement with this plan but if you think it'll work then who am I to stand in anyone's way? We will begin mobilizing soon to travel to the Hin'dar Rhule."

"Leave the traveling to me," Elyne put in.

Derron cut a glance to her but she gave him a stiff shake of her head, as if to silence him.

Andahar knew the queen of the Fae could sift them all there. He appreciated the help. It would save days of travel and keep the troops from being weary by the time they got there.

"Then it's settled. We will meet again in the Hin'dar Rhule," Cormac said.

He took a step toward Laerwen and every one of the men stiffened. Andahar saw Eldrin reach for his sword, his hand on the hilt. Derron did the same. The Fomorian mage glanced at each of them before taking Laerwen's hand and kissing it.

"Until we meet again, your majesty."

And then he and the sorceress flashed away. Silence descended on them and none of them seemed to know what to say or do.

"It's settled then," Laerwen announced. "I will soon see my homeland again."

Andahar didn't miss her faint smile of anticipation. A cold knot formed in the pit of his stomach. If anything went wrong, she could die.

"As soon as you're ready, King Andahar, I can sift the troops to the battlefield," Elyne said.

Derron moved to stand beside his wife. But Andahar wasn't sure he was ready.

"How many days until the eclipse?" he asked, turning to Laerwen.

"Less than a week. Sifting may be the only way. It took us several days to traverse the realm. But we were trying to avoid the Fomorians."

"Very well." He turned to the queen of the Fae. "How many can you move at one time?"

"Several hundred, I should think."

"We'll need horses and equipment as well."

But she was nodding before he finished. "I can move that as well. Whatever you need."

"We can move that," Derron said. "She forgets I can also sift."

"And Lady Talaiel?"

"Our sky dragons can fly my people there whenever you give the word."

Andahar reached for Laerwen's hand and laced their fingers. He looked at the expectant faces of his friends and spoke four words that would begin the final battle between them and the Fomorians and rid the realm of them forever. The four words that would seal all of their fates.

"The word is given."

Chapter 14

Laerwen and Andahar didn't talk about the battle plan in the Hin'dar Rhule or her part in it. Nor did they talk about their secret nuptials. Nor did they discuss anything related to anything else. In fact, things had gone frigid between them. Quiet and frigid.

Deep down, Laerwen knew Andahar was unhappy with her agreement to the plan. But she knew it was something she had to do. For her people, her parents and Randir. She also knew this was her one chance to get the revenge she'd been after since the beginning.

When Cormac proposed the plan, she had decided then and there she would be the one to kill Lorcann. She would be the one who made sure he paid with his life for all those lives he and his fellow Fomorians took. She'd sharpened her blade, ready to deal him his death blow. She planned to tell no one of this, especially Andahar. For she knew he would try to talk her out of it. If he had his way, he would try to talk her out of the whole plan and she simply couldn't allow that to happen.

She had packed her things—the beautiful clothes the royal dressmaker had made for her as well as her mother's veil. That she didn't want damaged in the fight, so she'd carefully put it away until the battle was over. She decided not to wear the traditional garb of her people. Once she had everything packed, she made her way to the shops in the Woodlands and bought leather armor—a padded leather vest, chainmail, leather gauntlets, a steel helm, padded pants and tall boots. She would be dressed as the others. She would blend in, which is exactly what she wanted.

She next intended to seek out the queen of the Fae to ask her to sift her to her home realm as soon as possible. But before she left, she knew she needed to find Hiram and tell him her decision to leave. She needed to be one of the first there to stake out the battlefield, to plan her steps carefully to carry out the assassination. She found him in his chamber, readying for the trip back to their realm.

"Your majesty, do come in." He ushered her inside with a wave of his hand. "I've not seen you in many days. I was beginning to think you'd deserted me." Despite the jab, he grinned.

"No, Hiram. I haven't quite been myself lately." She'd been rash and impulsive and married the king of the Woodlands without telling him. She'd agreed to become the decoy in the battle for their realm. Two things her advisor would not like nor with which he would agree.

"You've had a lot on your mind with the death of Randir. The people still believe in you and look to you for guidance."

"Aye, I know. That's why I wanted to talk to you before we return."

"I know of the battle," he said. "I've heard the talk." He folded his arms over his chest. "I wondered when you were going to come tell me."

Her brows drew together in question. "How much do you know?"

"I know you plan to sacrifice yourself."

"I'm not sacrificing myself. I'm merely going to lure the mage and his loyalists from hiding."

"A dangerous plan. Do you know what you risk?" He reached for her, his hand clamping around her wrist. "Don't do it, majesty. You are the last royal Fire Elf alive. There is no one left to take your place."

"I'm well aware of that, Hiram." She pulled her wrist free. "But if we can flush out the man who killed our people, then I intend to do it. You can't stop me."

His eyes widened as if he understood then what she'd intended to do all along. "Oh, gods. You're going to kill him yourself, aren't you?"

She spun away, pacing in the small confines of his room. How could he know? He always read her so well. She could never hide anything from him. Even now. Curse the man.

"That is what you intend to do, isn't it?" he asked.

"He's responsible for the deaths of our people," she said as she paced. "I intend to cut out his heart."

"Laerwen, it's too dangerous. I must insist—"

"No, Hiram." She halted and turned to look at him, her gaze fixed on his face. "I've waited for this chance. It's within my grasp.

I'll not squander it."

"But—"

"I have a plan for the realm. The Hin'dar Rhule will not be without a ruler should I die."

"I don't understand." He shook his head, his eyes so wide and bright, she thought he might break down any moment.

And for a moment, guilt slashed through her. He and her people had been through so much. How could she even think of putting him through this too? Was she that selfish? That hell-bent on revenge she would risk her life? She knew the answer to that even before she thought it. Of course she'd risk her life. Lorcann had murdered Randir. Lorcann orchestrated the deaths of her people and she would not let that go. Not ever.

"If anything happens to me on the battlefield, Hiram, I want you to go to King Andahar. I want you to give him the Hin'dar Rhule to govern. The people have grown to like and respect him as I have. He will be fair and just. He will take care of all of you and the Fire realm."

But Hiram was shaking his head before she even finished. "No. I will not allow it. I simply cannot agree to that."

"There is no other way," she said. "It's my final wish should anything happen to me. And as my advisor, I expect you to see it through." She gripped his shoulders to press her point. "Will you do that for me?"

He pursed his lips together in a thin line. "It's against my better judgment."

She smiled. "I know. So will you do it?"

He nodded and dropped his head, looking away from her. She suspected he was trying to hide his emotions so she wouldn't see the pain she'd caused him. She pulled him into a fierce hug, squeezing him.

"Thank you, Hiram."

He hugged her back then held her at arm's length. "I do not wish to tell the king of the Woodlands the Fire realm is his." He pointed his index finger in her face. "You are not allowed to die."

"I don't plan on it. I intend to live. And rule."

"Good. Now, when do we leave?"

"I'm leaving as soon as possible. You'll follow with everyone else."

"You're leaving now?"

"If I can convince the Fae queen to sift me there, aye. I am."

"I'm coming with you."

She recognized the hard edge of his voice. He was a stubborn man and she knew he would never take no for an answer. "Hiram—"

"No. I'm coming. That's final."

The only way out of this was if she agreed. She nodded. "Fine then. Let's go."

She didn't look back as she left his chamber, Hiram on her heels. She would never look back again.

Things had become chaotic. Andahar wasn't quite sure how it had gotten so out of hand. When word spread of the coming battle, men and even some women volunteered. He took anyone and everyone willing to fight. They would need the strength in numbers.

With the Fae, the Skye Elves, the remaining Fire Elves and the Wood Elves, he estimated they would be at least six thousand strong by the time they were all assembled and ready to fight. And double that since the Skye Elves were so much stronger than anyone else. If Cormac's estimate was correct, they would definitely outnumber the Fomorians. Mayhap their chance of winning the battle and pushing them into the Unseelie realm were better than he thought. One could hope.

In all the confusion, he looked for Laerwen but hadn't found her. She wasn't in her chamber, nor had she returned to his since their discussion with Cormac and the others. She knew he was against the plan. He also knew she didn't want him to talk her out of it. She'd been avoiding him as though he had some deathly illness.

He ended up in his own chamber where Leopold bustled about with several other servants. They were preparing for the journey.

"Leo, a word alone if you please."

Leopold shooed everyone out and gave him his full attention. Andahar told him of the upcoming conflict and his role in it.

"Are you sure it's wise, my king? In lieu of recent events, I think it might be best if you remained here out of harm's way."

He wasn't about let Laerwen go through with it alone. He

needed to be there with her. For her.

"No," he said, his voice stern. "I have to go. I cannot allow my brother and the others to fight the battle without me." Nor could he leave his wife alone in the Hin'dar Rhule. "Princess Allanna will remain here as regent while I'm gone."

"Is she prepared for that, sire?"

"She is. I spoke with her earlier. Sir Drake has agreed to remain behind as well."

"Very well."

"I'd like you to stay here, too, Leopold."

He blinked surprise, as though he hadn't expected that. "Sire, I thought I should accompany you—"

"You know me best. You know what decisions I would make for the realm, should it come to that. I trust you, Leo." He clapped the man on the shoulder. "Allanna is smart but young and still not prepared to rule." He paused, not wanting to say the words aloud. To speak the truth that it was a possibility he wouldn't come back alive. Because he was going to do everything he could to protect Laerwen even if that meant sacrificing himself. He swallowed hard and met Leopold's bright gaze. "I know you'll guide Allanna with your wisdom."

"Of course I will, sire. But you will be coming back. You and your lady."

Andahar cocked his head to the side, pretending not to understand. "My lady?"

"Queen Laerwen. It seems a foregone conclusion that she will return with you."

"She intends to stay and rebuild the Hin'dar Rhule," Andahar said. "I doubt she'll come back with me."

A pang of sadness shifted through him. He'd never thought of it before. Married or not, he knew the truth. He knew she wanted to rebuild her realm and he would never stop her from doing that. But the real possibility remained he would have to return here without her.

"She will." Leopold gave him a confident smile. "She fancies you too much not to."

"It's obvious, is it?"

"Indeed, sire." He stuck out his hand. "May the gods protect you, your majesty. Come back safe, aye?"

He shook the man's hand. "I intend to."

Andahar left Leopold to find Laerwen. He looked again in her chamber, but found it empty. Her room looked sparse and empty. He couldn't find her clothes anywhere and it struck him. He knew she'd packed her things and was gone.

She'd left him.

He cursed under his breath.

She must have asked Elyne to sift her to the Hin'dar Rhule already. His blood pumped hot with anger, with fear, with desperation to get to Laerwen. He hurried through the palace looking for the queen of the Fae. When he didn't find her, he took the winding staircase down to the ground.

There, Elyne was busy directing a group of elves on where to meet for the next time she sifted. She spotted him and smiled and waved but Andahar was far from feeling friendly.

"Where is she?"

"She? Laerwen?"

"Aye. Where the bloody hell is she? Is she there already? Did you sift her there?"

Elyne flushed, as if knowing exactly what he meant. "She…she asked me to take her there early this morning. She was one of the first to go."

Anger flared through him. He spun away from her, pushing his fingers through his hair. "Damn her. She didn't even tell me goodbye."

"Andahar, I'm sorry. I don't know what to say."

"What's the problem?" Derron must have heard the commotion and came over. Ever the protective king and husband.

Before she could answer, Andahar spun back toward her. "Take me there. Now."

"I…" She glanced around the group of men and women and faltered. She looked at Derron, as though he might rescue her from her current dilemma. "I promised they would be next."

"They can wait. Take me to her now, Elyne. Please."

She hesitated, clearly unsure what to say or do.

"I'll take him," Derron volunteered. "You need to rest anyway. All this sifting back and forth is starting to take its toll on you. These people can wait. They'll understand."

She blew out a breath, as though she'd been holding it. "All right."

Derron stepped next to Andahar. "Come on."

They walked a few feet away from the group toward the loch. "I'll not have you upsetting my wife."

"I'm sorry. I'm only worried for Laerwen and her safety."

"Elyne is pregnant."

Andahar took a step back, surprised at the sudden announcement.

"She hasn't told anyone yet," Derron continued. "I keep trying to talk her out of doing all this sifting but she's a stubborn woman."

He was well aware of Elyne's personality traits. "Then I suppose congratulations are in order."

"I want her nowhere near the fight with the Fomorians. She knows this. That's why she's going to stay. Once everyone is there, she will return here where she's safe."

"But you intend to fight."

The king of the Fae grinned. "Of course I do."

"I understand how you feel about keeping her safe. And she will be here in the Woodlands as well as in good company. My sister will remain with Sir Drake. I'm afraid she quite hasn't recovered from our father's death."

Derron nodded understand. "Good then. I'm glad Elyne will have the girl to stay with her. Now, shall we?"

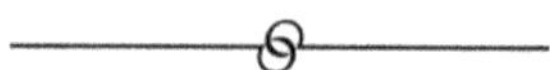

Laerwen took a horse and rode away from the encampment. She needed some time alone to survey the landscape in front of her. She had never seen it this way and it broke her heart. The land was charred. No homes were left. All who had stayed behind were dead, the ground still littered with their corpses. The Fomorians hadn't bothered to bury them nor had they cared. They'd looted whatever was left.

She intended to make sure all the dead received a proper burial. She would speak with Hiram about it when next she saw him.

When she'd first come upon the scene, she dismounted, crumbled to her knees, put her face in her hands and wept. Now she'd recovered from the initial shock and stood to take in the sight, her hand gripping the reins. The horse nuzzled her, sensing the treat she had in her pocket. She pulled out the apple and held it out to her. The mare nibbled it, then took it and crunched it.

Laerwen patted her neck, still staring out at the scene before her.

She wanted to remember this day. To remember how she felt so that it would never happen again. To remember the way it looked, because she would never allow it to be this way again.

It would be an impossible task to rebuild this realm. And should the volcanoes truly erupt? It would wipe out all that remained.

Laerwen heard the galloping horse behind her and knew someone approached. She could guess who it was. She stood stiff, waiting, listening as the rider halted and then dismounted.

"You left without saying goodbye. Why?"

Andahar. His voice was demanding yet gentle. He had ridden out to find her.

She closed her eyes, not wanting to turn around and see him. She knew he would follow her as soon as he discovered she was gone. But she didn't want to face him. Even now. She wasn't prepared for that.

"I had to. I'm sorry."

There was a pause of silence and her hair blew across her face. She tucked it behind her ear.

"I thought I might find you here." His feet crunched on the ground as he approached her, pausing next to her. He looked out at the ruined realm as she did. "I was worried about you."

"There's nothing to worry about," she said, her voice hard yet full of emotion. "I was quite safe here. I even helped build the encampment."

Indeed it had been good to work. She had helped erect several tents, including her own. One she hadn't intended on sharing with Andahar, despite the fact he was her husband. She needed this time to be alone, to plan her moves. She'd been gathering weapons since before she left the Woodlands. Something Elyne knew but no one else.

"You're armed to the teeth," the queen had said. She eyed the dagger at her waist, the one strapped to her thigh and the scabbard holding the short sword on her back. What the queen couldn't see was that Laerwen had also stashed two dirks—one in each boot.

"Aye, I am. And I intend to stay that way. Are you going to take me or not?"

She'd nodded. "Of course. Just don't stab me with one of those blades."

Laerwen knew she jested and laughed. That was moments

before she'd sifted her here and Elyne had nearly fainted. It had scared Laerwen how pale she'd looked. She'd led her to a nearby seat and offered her some water but Elyne insisted she was fine.

"Is Queen Elyne all right?" she asked then.

"Why do you ask?"

"She seemed unsteady when she brought me here. I worried about her return."

"King Derron told me she's pregnant."

Joy shifted through her. That explained why the queen was so pale and unsteady on her feet. All the sifting must be exhausting for her, though she didn't want to admit it. She wanted to help as much as Laerwen did.

"She's going to remain in the Woodlands," Andahar continued. He stepped in front of her then, took her by the shoulders. "Laerwen, are you quite certain about this?"

She knew what he meant. He'd changed the subject back to her acting as bait for Lorcann. "I am."

"And nothing I can say will change your mind?"

"No, Andahar."

"Stubborn woman! Almost as stubborn at the queen of the Fae."

"Aye, I am."

He released her and turned away, shoving his hands deep into the pockets of his trousers. Something she had never seen him do. He was agitated, she knew. She couldn't help but admire the strength in his back and the way his long silvery hair fluttered in the wind.

"Andahar, I have to do this. It's the last chance I have at saving my realm."

"I know." His voice was flat and unemotional. "I don't have to like it though."

She stepped next to him, slipping her hand in the crook of his elbow. "Please don't be angry with me."

"I don't know what makes me more unhappy. The fact I can't change your mind or…" He turned to her, those pale green eyes piercing right through her. "The fact you left me without a word."

Guilt pressed through her bones. She hadn't wanted to face him because she was a coward. She could face the menacing Fomorian mage, Lorcann, without fear, yet she couldn't face Andahar. Her husband. The man to whom she'd professed her love. The man she had spent the night with and did things she would never even considering doing with another man.

Gods, what had she done? She should have never married him. What would Hiram think when he learned of their secret wedding? Would he force her to forsake those vows for her to marry one of the remaining Fire Elves? She had no idea what his reaction would be and it scared her. Being married to Andahar scared her just as much.

"You regret our vows." He said it matter-of-factly, as though he'd read her emotions on her face.

She never was very good at hiding her feelings, was what she thought. She wore her heart on her sleeve. "Andahar…"

He pulled away from her and stalked off. It nearly killed her to see him walk away like that. To know she had hurt him so deeply. She could see it in his eyes. He halted by the horses, his hands back in his pockets as he lifted his face to the sky.

Laerwen saw the movement overhead. There in the distance, the moon dragons were making their way to the encampment. Lady Talaiel really had called them to assist. Hope sprang in her chest. They had a chance to defeat these Fomorians once and for all with the might of the Skye Elves behind them.

"The Skye Elves are coming," he said but his words were nearly lost on the wind. He turned and walked past her. "I must see to them."

"Andahar—"

"No." He whirled back to her. "Do not offer me your apologies or your sorrow, your majesty."

He hadn't called her by her given name and the use of her formal title stung. And with that, he mounted his horse and rode away, leaving her alone, standing in the ruination that was once the Hin'dar Rhule.

Had she made a grave mistake? Had she lost him for good? She didn't know what else to do. She had no idea how or if she could make it up to him. Would he demand an annulment? She was so confused. So bloody confused she didn't know what she wanted any more.

Other than revenge.

As she stood there, trying to decide what to do, the first tremors of the ground vibrated beneath her feet. Her gaze immediately went to the volcano in the distance. But it was still quiet and seemed to be dormant. From this distance, it looked the same as it always had with the peak reaching for the sky.

The ground rumbled again. Judging by the activity beneath her feet, she guessed the volcano could be waking.

She had to see for herself. She had to know if it would truly come to pass. But it was too far to ride—the volcano was at least a hundred miles away. It'd take her too long to get there by horse. And even if she got there, it would take too long to climb—even though she knew every nook and cranny, every handhold and foothold. She'd spent days in the mountains and climbed the volcanoes as a child.

But if she had a dragon…

A plan formed. She mounted her horse and galloped back to the camp. When she arrived at the makeshift stables, she yielded her mount and went in search of Lady Talaiel or Lord Eldrin. She found the Lady of the Skye talking with Andahar. He was clearly happy the lady had arrived as he smiled and greeted her with a hug.

Laerwen wished she didn't have to have the conversation in front of him—he would try to talk her out of it—but time was of the essence and the day was waning. Twilight would be upon them soon enough and she needed to see the volcano for herself.

"Lady Talaiel, forgive the intrusion," Laerwen said, bursting into the conversation. "Can one of your dragons take me to the volcano?"

The lady's eyes widened in surprise and she hesitated a moment. "Aye, of course, but—"

"Why?" Andahar demanded.

"Because I need to see it." She gave him a pointed look, refusing to be intimidated by him. "When I was away from the camp, the ground trembled."

"I thought I felt something," Talaiel said. "Is that what it was? The volcano?"

"I believe it's the first sign it's close to erupting."

"The moon dragons are at your disposal, your majesty," Talaiel said.

"I'm coming with you," Andahar said.

"Andahar, I'm perfectly capable—"

"Do not try to stop me."

The hard edge in his voice and the determined glint in his eye told her he was not going to back down. Just as she wasn't going to back down. He was going and she couldn't stop him. She nodded.

Talaiel led them from the camp away from the tents. She used whatever silent magic she had to draw down two of the moon dragons. They landed near them on a whisper. All the moon dragons were equipped with an Elven saddle as well as reins to help guide them. Talaiel gripped the reins of one.

"I'm coming as well," she announced as she mounted one of the dragons.

That meant Laerwen and Andahar had to ride together. He climbed up first and held his hand down to her. She grasped it, his warm, wonderful hand, and he pulled her up. She settled in front of him, his legs curving behind hers. He reached for the reins, his arms pressing against her sides. His whole body pressed against her, making her keenly aware of him.

They took off and flew toward the volcano as the sun began to set on the horizon, turning the sky a deep indigo. As they neared, a puff of smoke plumed from the peak of the mountain. As soon as she saw it, she had a sinking feeling in her stomach.

Talaiel and her dragon skirted the edge, keeping a safe distance away. Andahar steered the dragon away, following Talaiel's. But Laerwen wanted closer. She had to see the top of it. She had to know.

She turned her head so he could hear her. "Closer."

"It's too dangerous."

Her hands landed on his. "Closer, please. And cover your mouth and nose."

He reluctantly navigated toward it. Her skin could withstand the extreme heat and the smell. Even so, the stench of sulfur filled her nose. The noxious fumes nearly choked her and she pulled her tunic up to cover her mouth and nose, wishing she had her mother's veil.

As they flew over it, the smoke thickened and plumed higher. Andahar banked, giving her a view of the top of the mountain. There she could see the fractures spreading like a spider web from the peak down the side of the mountain. There she could see the small crater that had formed in the summit, indicating it was preparing to crack and break. Under the fractures, it seemed to bulge, as though the fiery depths were preparing to purge to the surface.

Oh, gods.

The eclipse was still two days away but already the volcano was awakening. The sorceress had been right. The legends had been right. Which meant in two days' time, the volcano would erupt and utterly destroy what was left of her homeland.

Something on the west side of the mountain caught her eye. She could make out what looked like a camp with tents much like the ones they were inhabiting. She motioned to Andahar and he saw it too. They banked and headed for it while Lady Talaiel headed back to camp.

As they flew away from the putrid smoke of the mountain, they neared the group and she could better make out who they were. She could see the woman with coal black hair and the man next to her. Laerwen knew immediately these were the Fomorians making their way toward the battlefield. She glanced over her shoulder to Andahar who nodded understanding. They were already in the Hin'dar Rhule, ready and waiting for the battle to begin.

Andahar circled the dragon one more time before returning to the camp. Talaiel and her dragon hovered in the air, waiting for them. When she saw them, she turned and they followed her back, landing outside of camp. They dismounted and Talaiel patted each beast on the snout before they flew away. No one spoke as they stood there, staring back at the steaming mountain.

"So it will come to pass," Talaiel said quietly. She was unaware of what they'd seen on the other side of the mountain. "What will happen when the volcano erupts?"

"The entire realm will be destroyed," Laerwen said, never taking her eyes off it.

Andahar slipped a comforting arm around her shoulders. "Mayhap not."

"It will," she insisted. "You saw it yourself. It is coming. And there's nothing we can do to stop it."

"We cannot stay here," Talaiel said. "What of the battle?"

"The battle will happen anyway," Andahar said. "Eruption or not."

"I cannot allow my people to be killed," she said. "Fighting is one thing. An eruption is quite another."

"Will you desert us in our time of need, Lady Talaiel?" Laerwen couldn't keep the acid out of her tone. The woman looked at her, a cool anger sparking in her emerald eyes.

"You can't seriously think to fight the Fomorians anyway. Not with this eruption imminent."

"The sorceress told us it would happen," Laerwen said. "I admit I didn't believe her either. Now I do. And I intend to stay and fight."

"Andahar?" Talaiel looked at him, as though he were the one to make the final decision.

Laerwen glanced up at him. "You can't back out now. Not when we're so close to…victory." She clamped her mouth shut. She had intended to say not when she was so close to getting the revenge she so wanted.

"I'll speak to Derron. We don't need to endanger any more people than we already have here. It will take too much time to sift everyone back to the Woodlands."

Prickling heat went over her skin. She pushed away from him. "You intend to retreat?"

"Laerwen, when the volcano erupts, it will kill most of the Fomorians anyway. You saw their camp."

But what if Lorcann managed to live? "I'm not leaving. And anyway, we have the dragons. They can help us. We can call upon the other dragons in the realm."

"The Fomorians are already here?" Talaiel asked.

"They camp west of the mountain," Laerwen said. "We saw them. They are merely biding their time until the battle."

Andahar looked at Lady Talaiel. "Mayhap we should discuss this with the rest of the council. I believe we can alter our plan, defeat the Fomorians, and still live through the eruption."

Dawning flickered through Laerwen and she suppressed a smile. "You already have something in mind, don't you?"

He nodded. "I do. I'll gather the others. Let's meet in my tent."

Talaiel sighed. "Very well. My husband and I will see you then."

As she walked away, Andahar gave Laerwen one more glance before he, too, left. She knew their relationship was damaged. She didn't know how she would repair it. Or even if she could.

Chapter 15

Andahar made his way back to the camp and sought out King Derron. He found him along with his brother and ushered them all to his tent. Shortly after they arrived, Lady Talaiel made an appearance and last, Laerwen. They stared at each other a long silent moment. He could see the heat in those whiskey-colored eyes, knew she was still angry with him. He was aware of the small group around them, curiosity in their gazes. He ignored them and focused on his wife. For she was still his woman, whether she accepted it or not. He was not going to lose her so easily.

Eldrin cleared his throat to get his attention. "You called this meeting, brother."

"Right. Laerwen and I confirmed the volcano is going to erupt." As he spoke, Andahar's gaze remained on her angry face. He finally looked away and focused on Derron. "Do you think there's any way to get a message to Cormac?"

His brows knit in confusion. "Cormac already knew of the eruption. His sorceress said as much. Why do you need to get a message to him?"

"Because I have a new plan I want to propose."

"What's the new plan?" It was Eldrin who spoke up.

"I would like it to be known I am against fighting in a place where a natural disaster such as this can occur," Talaiel said. Eldrin gave her a questioning glance but some silent communication between them made him nod in agreement.

"Your objection is duly noted," Andahar said. "I'd like to get a message to Cormac. Tell him we've convened on the field early to fight."

"Why?" Laerwen asked. "What will that accomplish?"

"We get them here sooner. If Cormac agrees, we get them to the Unseelie realm before the eruption."

"You mean to start the war sooner," Laerwen said.

"Aye."

"Even if we could get a message to him," Derron said, "they would likely not make it here in time."

"The Fomorians camp to the west of the great mountain," Laerwen announced. "I will volunteer to take the message."

"You will not." Andahar's words were sharp as a blade.

She glared at him. "I will."

Eldrin put his hands up as though in surrender. "Mayhap the best person to take the message is neither one of you. You both are royalty. You should remain here."

"Mayhap a message is what's not needed at all," Derron put in. He ran his hand over his chin, looking thoughtful. "If the camp is so close, all we need to do is get their attention sooner rather than later."

"You mean to attack them," Andahar said.

"A surprise attack," Derron said with a nod.

"That will void our truce with Cormac." Andahar shook his head. "We can't risk that."

"Then what?" Laerwen folded her arms over her chest.

"I like the surprise attack but we owe it to Cormac to tell him. We must let him know what we intend to do, that we intend to attack before the volcano erupts. That way he and his sorceress are prepared."

"Even though that will ruin Lorcann's plan to sacrifice the princess. Your pardon, I mean queen," Eldrin said with a stiff bow.

Laerwen dropped her arms, her expression pinched and tension-filled. The frustration wafted off her like a bad stench. "I object to this plan. Why can't we keep it as is?"

"You wish to stay here and die with the lava flows?" Talaiel shook her head. "I do not."

"The sooner we attack them, the sooner we get them into the Unseelie realm," Andahar said as he looked at Laerwen. "I'd rather not have Laerwen used as bait."

"And when do you want this attack to happen?" his brother asked.

"Tomorrow night at dusk. We'll use the cover of darkness to our advantage." He glanced at Derron, Eldrin, Talaiel and Laerwen. "What say you all?"

"I'm in," Eldrin announced.

"As am I," his wife agreed.

Derron hesitated only a moment. "Fine. I'm in. But I'll be the one taking the message."

Everyone looked to Laerwen then. By the pinched look on her face, it was clear she was unhappy with the decision. But since she was outvoted, she could only nod. "All right."

They made the final arrangements for Derron's flight across enemy lines to seek out Cormac. Laerwen had enough of them all and left the tent in a huff. Andahar watched her stalk out of the tent, her hands still in fists. He wanted to go after her but remained to finalize the details. He'd find her later and, hopefully, talk some sense into her.

Laerwen prowled through the camp, looking for someone who had a stronger drink than honeywine or ale. What she wanted was whiskey. She needed it after the change in battle tactics. What was Andahar trying to do to her? He was taking away her one chance to kill Lorcann. He was taking away her revenge.

With this new plan, she would not be the lure to bring him out of hiding. There would be no lava to which he'd want to sacrifice her. How would she get to him? Andahar was determined to keep her out of harm's way but she was determined to kill the mage.

She halted, pushed her fingers through her hair. A strong drink was not the answer. The last thing she needed was to get into her cups. She needed a clear head and to maintain her wits. Boisterous laughter rolled out of one of the tents, luring her.

Mayhap what she truly needed was a bit of fun. Something to take her mind off everything including Andahar.

She found a tent of revelers who also happened to be Elven rangers. One of them was Lord Eldrin who sat at a table with three others playing cards, coins in front of them. When he saw her, he waved her over with a smile. When the others saw her, they stood so quickly their chairs tipped over and the table rattled.

"Queen Laerwen, won't you join us?"

"I'm out," one of the rangers said. "I'm broke anyway." He scooped up what remaining coins he had and left the tent on a stagger.

Laerwen watched him go and then peered at the remaining faces before her, the men who had come to fight for her realm and her people. How could she say no?

"Gentlemen, have a seat," she ordered as she walked toward the table. There was one vacant chair next to Eldrin. "What is this game?"

"Five card stud," the ranger said. "My friend, Maggie, taught us how to play."

"Maggie? The human girl?"

She recalled the story of the girl who went back in time to save Derron and fell in love with the Scottish knight. Laerwen scooted up to the table and peered over at Eldrin's cards. They had symbols and numbers on them. She had never seen anything like it.

"Aye, the human girl. Shall we teach you?"

She glanced around the table of expectant faces, noticed several tankards and tried hard not to think of whiskey. Or the way it made her feel when she drank it with Andahar. That night in the dining hall, they had imbibed together. He had pressed her against the table, kissing her with such a ferocious passion—

"Your majesty?" Eldrin interrupted her thoughts. "Are you quite well? You look flushed."

Damn her vivid memories. "Aye, I'm fine. Bring on the cards."

He laughed as they finished their hand. One of the rangers happily scooped the coins toward him with his winning cards.

"First, a quick lesson. Have you ever seen cards before?" She shook her head. "Then, let me show you. There are two red and two black suits. Clubs, spades, hearts and diamonds." He held out an example of each to her. "These are the face cards. Jack, queen, king. Ace is the highest card."

The next hand dealt her in. She received one card face down and one card face up, as did the other players.

"Bets?" Eldrin asked.

Laerwen eyed the empty place before her, wondering how she would bet with no coins. The rangers leaned over and dropped a handful in front of her with a wink. "To get you started."

They placed their bets and another face-up card was dealt. More bets, another card and so on. Laerwen quickly realized she was not very good at Five Card Stud and immediately lost her hand.

"Don't worry about that," Eldrin said with a grin. "You'll get the hang of it."

They dealt another hand and this time she came out the winner. They cheered with her. One of them handed her a tankard of whiskey. One celebratory drink wouldn't hurt, would it? She took a sip as the men took a healthy quaff from their tankards as Eldrin dealt another hand. Another hand she managed to win again, though she began to suspect they were letting her win since she was royalty.

"You know who's good at cards? Queen Elyne. It must be a queen thing," Eldrin said. But he was smiling at Laerwen.

"Is she?"

"She used to frequent the gambling tents when she was at tournament in the human realm."

"I had no idea she could play cards. Mayhap sometime I will play a game with her," she said as she scraped her latest winnings in front of her.

Eldrin chuckled. She drained her cup one last time and then stood. They all stood with her.

"Gentlemen, I thank you for the drink and the game but I think it's time for me to retire."

"So soon? You haven't cleaned me out yet," Eldrin said.

She looked at the pile of glittering coins in front of her place at the table. It was a paltry sum. One that wouldn't even buy a decent destrier. She ignored the despair pressing into her regarding the state of her realm. Would she have to rely on the kindness of the Wood Elves forever? Would she even be able to rebuild the Hin'dar Rhule to its former glory?

I'll think about that tomorrow.

She pushed all the coins to the center.

"You divvy them up, Eldrin."

And then she bid them goodnight. As soon as her back was turned, she heard the jingle of gold as they fell on the pile of coins. She giggled, well pleased with the thought of the men clamoring over the gold.

As she headed back to her tent, exhausted and high on her last win, she caught sight of Andahar. When he saw her, she halted mid-step. They stared at each other a long moment before he started toward her. She stood her ground, her heart pounding a wild tattoo.

At the sight of him walking toward her, her drunkenness was forgotten. The elation of winning at cards or drinking whiskey fizzled.

"We must talk," he said.

She wanted to be defiant. She wanted to fold her arms over her chest and tell him no, that there was nothing to talk about. But she couldn't. She couldn't hurt him like that. She'd already hurt him enough. So she nodded agreement.

"Come with me."

He headed down the path and she fell into step beside him, her nerves a jangled mess. They didn't speak as they made their way through the encampment. They stopped near the opening of one tent and he motioned for her to go inside ahead of him. He followed her in, but she couldn't face him. Instead, she focused on the candelabras placed around the large tent.

The orange-yellow glow warmed the small space, making flickering shadows dance over the canvas walls. There was a small desk littered with maps and notes on parchment, an inkwell, a writing implement, a stick of wax, his royal seal, a candle burning brightly. A stool was pushed neatly under the desk. Next to that was his bed, which was nothing more than a frame with a feather mattress she knew had been carried in by servants.

"Tell me truthfully, Laerwen. Do you regret our marriage?"

Oh, gods, why did he have to ask her that? Her eyes closed against the pain it caused her to hear him ask her. She wrapped her arms around her middle and stood there a long moment, not wanting to answer.

In her solace, she had come to a decision. She knew she had to leave him. It would never work out between the two of them. Looking at the Hin'dar Rhule earlier made her question everything she had done and believed in. They were too far apart in their lives, their realms. He had the Woodlands and she was determined to see her realm returned to its former glory. Did she regret marrying him? No. Did she regret the consequences of that marriage? Aye, she did.

"Do you?" he asked, this time more firm.

"No, Andahar."

"If you do, I'll go to the High Druid at once and have our marriage annulled, if that's what you wish."

She spun to face him. "Is that what you wish?"

"No." He took a step toward her. "I regret nothing. But you do, don't you?"

"I don't know."

It frightened her how easily he could read her, sense her thoughts. She did know but she was too afraid to admit the truth aloud. She knew what her mind wanted but what her heart wanted was something completely different. She had never intended to fall in love with Andahar, nor had she intended to marry him. Yet she had on both counts.

He took another step, closing the gap between them. "I connected with you, Laerwen, from the first moment you came to me in the Woodlands."

"And I with you." She reached for him, placed her hand on his chest. The slow steady beat of his heart pulsed beneath her fingers. "But I don't know if marrying you was the right thing for my realm or my people."

He clasped her hand, holding her in place. "But was it the right thing for you?"

Laerwen couldn't meet his gaze. She focused on their twined fingers, the way his skin brushed against hers.

"What does your heart say?" he asked, his voice soft. Like a caress over her skin.

"My heart says I love you. That has never changed." She looked up at him, met that gorgeous green gaze. Again, how was it he could read her so well? How was it they had become so in tune over the short amount of time they'd known each other?

"What did change?"

The battle plan. The way he treated her. The way he insisted she be kept out of harm's way. But she couldn't tell him she planned to kill the mage herself. She couldn't tell him she had a burning need to avenge the deaths of her parents and Lord Randir. She owed them that. They had given their lives for her.

"I can make my own decisions, Andahar. I decided to go through with Cormac's plan to lure Lorcann into the open. I'm willing to live with whatever consequences that presents."

"Even if you're killed?"

She nodded.

"I'm not willing to live with those consequences. You are my wife."

"That changes nothing."

"It changes *everything*."

They stared at each other in a long silent moment. Laerwen realized he would never back down. She couldn't change his mind any more than he could change hers…if he knew the truth. Which he didn't and he never would.

"Do you believe this plan will work?" she asked. "Truly?"

"It has to." He lifted her fingers to his lips and kissed the tips. "I don't want to lose you. If anything happened to you I couldn't bear it."

Her heart dipped to her toes. Gods, she didn't want to lose him either. If everything else was stripped away, that was the bare truth. "I know."

"I don't wish to fight with you. Especially on the eve of battle. You'll stay with me tonight?"

Her resolve melted at her feet. She had intended to remain in her own tent, alone, while she brooded and plotted. He was right—she didn't want to fight with him either. She found herself nodding.

Andahar pulled her into his arms and kissed her with a fiery passion. He'd not kissed her like that before. It was a passion he no longer suppressed. She kissed him back, the fire inside her suddenly ignited. She no more thought about what she was doing. She only thought about what she was feeling and right now, she wanted him. She wanted him to make love to her all night. For on the morrow, things could change. When Andahar learned of her plan, he might never speak to her again. Or, worse, she could be dead.

So intent on each other, neither heard the tent flap or the intruder.

"Andahar, I— Oh, my pardon."

The sudden interruption made them pull apart as though they'd been caught doing something they shouldn't. Eldrin looked everywhere but at them.

"I'll just, um, go then." He backed toward the tent flap.

"What is it? You have news?" Andahar pulled her against him, holding her, as if he might be afraid she would bolt.

"We've had word from King Derron. He has successfully delivered the message to Cormac." Eldrin smiled, well pleased.

"And he agreed with our plan?"

"He did. He and his lady sorceress are willing to alter their plan for opening the Barrier and getting the Fomorians into the Unseelie realm."

"Good. Anything else?"

Eldrin glanced from her back to Andahar. "It was nice playing cards with you, your majesty. I'll, ah, leave you two alone now. Good night."

As soon as he was gone Andahar looked at her, the surprise

evident in his face. "Cards? You played cards with him?"

"I did. With Eldrin and his rangers. And won nearly every hand." She grinned.

"I thought you tasted like whiskey. I'm disappointed you enjoyed the drink without me."

"You are king, are you not? I'm sure you could snap your fingers and have it delivered to your tent right away." She was teasing him and he knew it.

He grinned and slipped his arms around her waist. "I'd rather snap my fingers and have you delivered to my tent." His lips brushed hers. "You are the only thing I wish to get drunk on."

The heat of desire washed over her as all the blood drained from her head, leaving her lightheaded. She couldn't disagree. She liked feeling that way too when she was in his arms.

"Let's get you out of all these weapons." He slid the straps for the scabbard off her shoulders and dropped the short sword to the ground. He knelt to untie the dagger strapped to her thigh. Through her pants, her skin tingled. "What are you planning?"

"I like to be prepared."

He looked up at her, his gaze piercing with question. "You're planning to fight."

"Aye." That was all she was prepared to admit.

"I can't talk you out of it?"

"No."

He rose to his full height, his lips parting to object. She placed her fingers over them. "No more talking, Andahar."

As he dropped the dagger to the floor with the short sword, she removed the one at her waist. Then she bent and removed the dirks from her boots. He raised an eyebrow in question and mayhap even a little admiration as she blushed with her chagrin.

"Gods, I love you," he whispered.

His lips met hers as he shoved off the padded vest then pulled the tunic over her head. She stepped out of his arms and finished undressing, watching as he did the same. They fell together on the bed, his mouth leaving a searing trail from her lips down her throat. He paused to pay homage to each breast, dropping a soft kiss on each taut nipple.

Her breath shuddered out of her as her hands wound into the silky locks of his silvery hair. Something she had come to love to do. The way his hair slipped through her fingers was like water sluicing over flesh.

Andahar kissed his way down her body, his lips leaving a hot trail and making gooseflesh bloom over her exposed skin. She had not intended to fall into his bed again but here she was. Letting him caress her. Kiss her. Love her.

His tongue swirled over her bellybutton before he moved lower, placing one kiss on each hipbone and then pushing her legs apart. He lifted his body up to look at her, meeting her gaze. In that look she saw all the love he had for her.

Her body reacted with a flood of heat right to her core. Without taking his eyes off hers, he slid two fingers down her wet slit. She couldn't stop the whimper from escaping.

"More?" he asked.

"Aye, more. Touch me there again."

He flattened his palm over her mons, his thumb sliding between her wet folds over her swollen nub. He moved back and forth. She opened her legs to him and lifted her hips, allowing him more access. When she rocked from side to side in a silent plea, he pushed two fingers inside her.

Laerwen gasped, arched her back and pushed her body into him. He thrust in and out of her, all the while his eyes never leaving her face. And then he removed his hand and bent over her. Before she could mourn the loss of his touch, his tongue slid between her lips.

She moaned her appreciation. The sensation was nearly more than she could handle and it wasn't long before she came against his mouth. As she did, he slipped his fingers back inside her and her muscles contracted around him while he rocked them back and forth.

When she stilled, he removed his hand. His body landed on hers as his mouth overtook hers. She kissed him hard.

"I hope that's not all." The words purred through her throat.

"Fear not, my queen. I'm not finished yet."

To prove his point, his hard shaft entered her, filling her. It didn't take long for her body to respond to his thrusts. He held her close, kissed her as he moved in and out. She rocked against him, matching him thrust for thrust. Their bodies synced and they came together moments later.

There was no denying she would never love another. If she died tomorrow, she was glad she stayed tonight with Andahar.

Chapter 16

She awoke the next morning curled against his side, his arm around her as he held her to him. As she always did with Andahar, he gave her a sense of safety.

From the moment she had met him, he gave her that comfort. She hadn't quite decided what it was about him that made her feel that way. Not that it mattered that she didn't know the answer. Even after being with him all night, she knew she had to leave him. Thought she would always love him no matter what, she could see no way for them to be together.

Aye, Lady Talaiel and Lord Eldrin seemed to make things work just fine. But he was not a king. Andahar was.

He stirred, shifting behind her. His hand slipped over her ribs and up to cup her breast. He gave it a gentle squeeze.

"Good morrow." His words were sleep-thickened in her ear.

She rolled to her back to face him. He propped up on one elbow and gazed down at her. "Did you sleep well?"

"When I slept I did." He had a mischievous glint in his eyes. "Did you?"

Warmth cascaded through her. "I didn't sleep much, thanks to you."

"My apologies, my queen." He kissed the tip of her nose. "I found you quite irresistible."

Her finger traced the outline of his pointed ear. "Do not mistake that for a complaint, your majesty. It was far from it."

"Are you hungry?"

As if on cue, her stomach rumbled in response. "I guess I am a little. I seemed to have expended a lot of energy last night."

"You were quite demanding, if I say so myself."

She punched him in the shoulder. "And you weren't?"

"I never said I wasn't." He grinned, giving her a wink. He slid out of the bed and pulled on his trousers.

Laerwen scooted to the edge and slipped out of the bed. She

walked, naked, to her clothes, making sure he saw every inch of her. He stared longingly after her.

"If you don't wish to be back in the bed flat on your back, I suggest you get dressed quickly."

"As appealing as that sounds, I'm afraid food wins over lust, my king."

He laughed as she grinned and the two of them dressed. She replaced every weapon she'd come in with.

"I have to say, an armed woman is a sexy one." He pulled her into his arms, holding her close and making it obvious he wasn't going to let her go so easily. "I find it difficult to believe you aren't planning anything. Some coup or something."

"No, Andahar. As I told you, I intend to fight alongside you and Eldrin and everyone else. This is my realm." She swallowed the lie and it left a bitter aftertaste in her mouth.

He kissed her nose. "I worry."

"I know." She pushed out of his arms, using the necessary force to put distance between them. "There is no need."

And how would he react when she told him she wanted that annulment? Would he hate her? Never speak to her again? Thinking of this sent pain lancing through her heart. She shoved it aside and turned away, not wanting him to see it in her face. He would be able to read it in her expression. He would know.

His warm hands landed on her shoulders. She couldn't stop from leaning into him, closing her eyes and relishing that moment.

"When all this is over, I intend to take you on a proper honeymoon. Just you and me and nothing else to worry about, to think about, to plan. We could visit the Skye Realm if you like. Or even see the Fae kingdom."

Oh, gods, why did he have to say that? "I'd like that." She nearly choked on the words as they clotted in her throat. Tears suddenly burned the backs of her eyes and she squeezed them, willing them to go away.

"Andahar, are you in there?"

It was Lord Eldrin, calling from outside the tent. Thankfully, she didn't have to face Andahar as he released her and stepped outside. It gave her the necessary minutes to compose herself. She could hear the low murmurs of their voices. After taking a cleansing breath, she stepped out to join them.

"See that they're cared for," Andahar was saying. "Ask Lady

Talaiel where she's keeping her dragons."

"I intended to but I wanted you to know first," Eldrin said. He noticed her then and gave her a nod in greeting. "Good morrow, your majesty."

Andahar took her hand, held it, as they both watched him walk away.

"What was that about?" she asked.

"Queen Elyne called the other dragons to help us. Aura, Ambrielle, Luna and Nero arrived this morning."

"They're going to fight with us?"

"They'll be a great asset. Especially because they can see in the dark."

An idea formed. If she could take one of them, mayhap she could find Lorcann from the sky.

"Four dragons. The only ones I've seen have been Lady Talaiel's Skye dragons and only from afar. Never close up."

He looked at her, grinning. "Then come. I'll introduce you."

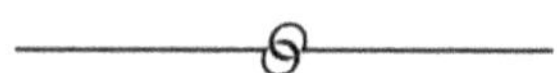

The dragons were amazing. Andahar had taken her to greet them along with Lord Eldrin and Lady Talaiel. The Lady of the Skye seemed to have a way with the large beasts. She knew how to communicate with them—apparently they could mind speak. Something Laerwen didn't know about them either.

She expected them to be nothing more than giant, fire-breathing beasts that hoarded treasure and had no personality. She was so wrong. While they were giant, indeed, they didn't breath fire unless they wanted to or hoard treasure and they had more personality than most people she'd met.

Luna was silvery like the moon dragons of the Skye realm. Only her wings were not silent or translucent like them. She had blue eyes and was the smallest of the four dragons. Laerwen loved her on sight and patted her nose affectionately. She was playful and sniffed Laerwen and then head-butted her as if in greeting. As if she were a giant feline who wanted nothing more than to be petted. Luna mindspoke to her and told her she belonged to Derron and that he was her chosen rider.

The emerald dragon was Ambrielle. She was sleeping, curled into a ball, her tail wrapped around her. When Laerwen approached, she lifted her head and peered at her with big tawny eyes. Ambrielle obviously gave Laerwen no more thought as she put her head back down and went right back to sleep. She had belonged to Queen Maeve at one time but now was riderless. Lady Talaiel said she was here on behest of the new Queen of the Fae. Once her services were no longer needed, she intended to return to wherever it was she'd come from.

The most impressive dragon was Nero. The largest of the four and the color of night, he blinked red eyes at her, smoke curling from his nose. She wasn't so sure he wouldn't breathe fire at her at any moment so she kept her distance. His size was quite intimidating.

"He may be big," Andahar said, "but he can fly so silently you'd never hear him coming."

And that scared Laerwen. "It's a good thing he's on our side."

Next came Aura, the great blue dragon. Her scales were such a deep blue they were almost purple. When the morning light caught them just right, they sparkled. When Andahar introduced her, Aura blinked her giant gold eyes and lowered her head in silent greeting. She was bigger than Luna but still not the largest of the four. She lowered to the ground to allow Laerwen to pet her neck. When she did, the great dragon seemed to purr which sounded more like a gravely growl deep in her throat.

"She's beautiful," Laerwen remarked.

I belong to Queen Elyne.

The voice burst through her head with such clarity Laerwen looked around to make sure no one was talking to her. "Did you hear that?"

"Hear what?" Andahar asked.

"That voice."

"That's Aura speaking to you," Lady Talaiel said. "She has connected to you. Talk to her."

Laerwen turned back to Aura, who blinked her giant eyes and gave her a quick nod in agreement.

You remind me much of her. You have the same inner strength.

"Thanks." She placed her hand on Aura's snout.

I will allow you to ride with me for the coming battle. I am at your command.

"Oh, I couldn't do that."

The queen will not mind. In fact, she insisted.

"Are you quite sure?"

Quite sure, my friend.

"Thank you," Laerwen whispered.

"What is it?" Andahar's hand landed on her shoulder as he looked between her and the dragon.

"Queen Elyne has offered Aura to me for the coming battle."

"That's quite an honor," Lady Talaiel said. "To ride with a dragon that has chosen you means you are special."

"I always knew she was," Andahar said, smiling at her.

Hope prickled her. Now she knew she could face whatever was coming. She could hunt down Lorcann and avenge the death of Randir and her parents.

Now she had a dragon on her side. Lorcann didn't have a prayer.

It was later that day when silence descended on the camp. There was no more merrymaking, no more revelry, no more laughter. It was as though everyone had turned serious and focused on the upcoming task at hand. Tensions ran high and she knew everyone waited for the sun to set. Waited for the battle to begin.

Even though Laerwen now had the dragon on her side, her nerves were a jangled mess. She had no idea how she was going to pull off her attack without Andahar knowing. He would likely stay by her side the entire time. All she needed was a brief moment of distraction.

They started their march late in the day so they could be near the Fomorians by sundown. Lady Talaiel stayed behind at the camp. She would command the moon dragons and send them when the battle was nearing an end—when the Barrier would open. It seemed to take an eternity to get in place. Now they gathered so close to the enemy she could see the curling smoke from their campfires.

There was no fear of discovery because Derron had used his Fae magic to hide them behind a glamour. Laerwen had never realized how powerful the Fae were until now. Having the element of surprise would be the difference between victory and defeat.

They were ready to march. Prepared to attack. Some on horseback. Most on foot. Swords gripped and gleaming. Arrows nocked against bows. Dragons waiting patiently to take flight.

They were as ready as they could be.

In her heard, she heard Aura's voice.

When you have need of me, call me. I will come to you.

You can hear my thoughts? Laerwen mindspoke back.

Aye, I can. I am now attuned to you as I am the Queen of the Otherworld.

Laerwen smiled. *Good. Then when we head for the Fomorians, I want you to pick me up. There is one man in particular I'm looking for. One I intend to kill.*

There was a pause of hesitation and then the voice rumbled through her mind. *As you wish.*

The sun kissed the horizon, changing the shade of the sky from the pale pink to a pale indigo.

"Don't leave my side," Andahar said. It sounded more like a command than a request.

She looked up at him knowing she couldn't make him that promise. He met her level gaze.

"Promise me that."

She loved he was so determined to keep her safe but she had other plans. So she did what she could only do—she nodded and lied to him.

"Now, let's get back your homeland."

Andahar made a motion, some silent hand signal to Lord Eldrin who did the same. Torches throughout the group of men and women lit here and there. Just enough to give them light enough to see the terrain ahead.

But Laerwen didn't need to see. She knew this terrain better than anyone.

Another few moments passed and then the land was plunged into twilight. The sun had finally disappeared.

Overhead, Laerwen could hear the distinct *whomp whomp* of dragon's wings and glanced up. She could see the dragon, Luna. Her silver scales were illuminated by the faint torchlight. She and the other two glided overhead with ease. And then she saw the shadow moving at the same speed. She only picked out Nero by the red glow of his eyes. He was silent on the wind, something she had never expected out of something so large.

Andahar gave another signal. With the world plunged into darkness, they headed for the Fomorians and crossed the enemy lines.

The surprise attack didn't remain a surprise for long. Once they were discovered, the alarm was sounded. She wasn't sure what role the dragons played in this assault. For now, it seemed as though they were flying in circles overhead, as though waiting for a signal.

As she ran next to Andahar, killing Fomorians with her short sword, she saw the flaming arrow arch through the sky. It left a blazing trail as it landed on a tent and set it afire.

That's when she heard the screech of the dragons overhead. And the next thing she knew they were diving low and spitting their fire, setting the camp ablaze.

Chaos reigned then. Somewhere in the confusion, she lost track of Andahar. He had stepped away from her, shouted an order and then he was gone in the crowd. This was her chance to get to Lorcann.

She called Aura and the great azure dragon cleared a path. She landed not far from Laerwen who grabbed up the reins and leapt on her back just as she took flight again. Several Fomorians shot arrows at Aura, but the points bounced off her hard scaly hide as though they were made of nothing more than cotton.

Aura burst upward through the sky. The cool wind hit Laerwen in the face as she looked into the inky blackness and the stars twinkling there. And for a moment, she could forget everything and have the dragon take her away.

But only for a moment.

Get closer to the camp, she said to the dragon.

Aura dove so fast it made Laerwen's heart leap into her throat. She clutched the reins with one hand and the short sword with the other, scanning the crowd for the mage. She spied him running into the pandemonium.

"There!" She pointed at the man.

Aura dove toward him, making Fomorians and Elves alike scatter to get out of her way. She landed hard on the ground, causing it to shake. Laerwen slid out of the saddle and headed right for Lorcann. But as she ran across the scorched earth, it rumbled beneath her feet. It was not the dragon who make the ground shake—it was the volcano. She halted and looked up at the mountain as a great gray cloud of smoke plumed from the top.

It was a moment that cost her precious seconds. In the time she had taken her eyes off Lorcann, he had taken advantage of the situation. He hit her in the back of the head with something.

Starbursts clouded her vision. She sprawled forward, landing in the dirt. The sword fell from her hand.

Aura emitted a high-pitched screech. She took a step toward Lorcann. Laerwen could smell the fire bubbling up in her snout.

No, Aura. He is mine to kill.

It would have been easy to let the dragon fry him like an animal on a skewer. But that would have taken away the satisfaction of killing him.

"And I thought I'd have to search for you," Lorcann said. "Here you are. Delivered to me by a dragon." He grabbed her hair and jerked her head back. "How fortuitous."

"I will kill you." She bit the words out between her teeth.

He laughed. "You seem to be in no position to do that, oh mighty queen of the Hin'dar Rhule. Not so mighty now, are you? I've taken everything from you. Now I will take your life." He pulled her up by her hair, put a knife to her throat. "We'll be riding the great beast to the top of the volcano. That's where you'll die and I'll get my magic back."

Aura screeched again.

"What about the magic for your people?" she asked. "Or do you plan to take it all for yourself?"

His hot breath wafted over her ear. "I like that idea quite a lot. Aye, that's what I'll do. Those peasants aren't worth it anyway."

Laerwen said nothing as she slipped the dagger from her waist listening to him ramble. She clutched it in her hand and jammed it in his thigh until she hit bone. The jarring had been such a horrible feeling, her stomach twisted in a knot and she thought she might retch. Somehow, she managed to keep her hand on that dagger long enough for him to release her and shove her away.

His scream still echoed in her ear as he yanked out the blade and tossed it away. Blood ran down his leg, soaking his pants and turning them into a shiny black. It was the time she needed to grab her short sword. As she spun back to face him, his face was bright red with pain. She could see this in the flickering firelight that blazed all around them.

She wasn't scared of fire. She never was. She never would be. Because she was a Fire Elf, her skin was resistant to the heat. Laerwen could take a lot, but she knew if she stayed around it too long, eventually she would burn like the others.

He was ready for her when she faced him again. Her sword

clashed against his. She'd had a few lessons in sword play when she was younger, all of which came back to her as she fought against Lorcann. But she still lacked exceptional skills.

The mage was far better. He swung at her wrist, smacking the blade against it, cutting her and making her drop her sword. She yelped and cradled her now-bleeding wrist against her chest to staunch the flow.

Lorcann pointed the blade at her. "Get on the dragon. Now."

Laerwen had no choice but to obey. He followed her and climbed behind her, grabbing the reins.

But Aura wasn't feeling so generous. She jerked her head from side to side and screeched again.

"Control your dragon, bitch, or I stick you right here and now. I only need your blood in the fire. And you don't have to be alive for that."

The tip of a blade jabbed her kidneys. *It's all right, Aura. Do as he says.*

Aura lifted off and flew into the night toward the top of the volcano.

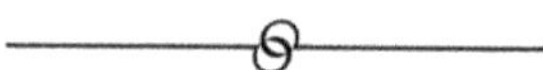

Andahar heard the screeching dragon. When he looked in the direction of the beast, though, he couldn't see much of anything except for Aura on the ground screaming at whatever it was in front of her. There was something down there she didn't like. Something that was clearly agitating her. Could she have been injured? Captured? Or was something else wrong?

And where was Laerwen? He'd lost track of her in the battle. He hadn't seen her in the last few minutes and his heart raced with fear as he tried to look for her in the ensuing melee.

At the moment, he had bigger problems. Like where the bloody hell was Cormac and his sorceress? He had agreed the attack at night would work and now he was missing. Andahar hacked and slashed his way through the Fomorians trying to find the all-powerful mage but he couldn't. Why hadn't he opened the Barrier yet?

He caught sight of his brother then. "Where is Cormac?" He had to shout over the din of clanging swords and dying men.

"I don't know."

Andahar saw him then as he bobbed out of one of the tents, the girl right behind him. Blood streaked down his face. His tunic was coated in it too. He looked as though he'd had the life beat out of him.

"Over there!" Andahar pointed with the tip of his sword.

He and Eldrin made their way through the fighting men to get to Cormac and Gweneth. The Fomorian mage looked as though he might pass out any moment. His face was ashen and he wobbled on his feet. Gweneth had her arm around his waist, helping him stay upright.

"What's happened? Why haven't you opened the Barrier yet?" Andahar couldn't keep the hard edge of out his voice.

"Lorcann's men overpowered him," Gweneth said.

"I thought he was powerful," Eldrin said. "His magic didn't save him?"

"When your men attacked, Lorcann knew something was awry. Those loyal to him assaulted us. There was no warning. No way to avoid them," she said. She sounded as though she blamed them for the attack on Cormac. "I can't open the Barrier with him weak like this. We need a healer."

But Andahar was already shaking his head. "There's no time for a healer."

To punctuate his words, the ground rumbled beneath their feet. The earthquake wasn't enough to make them fall but it was definitely enough to get their attention. Andahar looked up in the night sky at the top of the mountain. He could see the smoke curling.

That's when he saw the dragon flying toward it, her glittery azure scales reflecting the fire that raged all around them. He could barely make out two shapes riding on her back.

"Oh, gods. Laerwen."

Eldrin looked up too and saw them. "Did Lorcann capture her?"

He turned back to his brother. "Find a healer. Do whatever it takes. Just get that Barrier open."

"Where are you going?"

"I'm going after Laerwen."

He didn't even have to call the black dragon before Nero appeared over him, landed and gave him a nod with his giant head. Andahar reached for the reins and hoisted up on his back. A second later, Nero was in the sky chasing after Aura.

Andahar hoped he could get to her before it was too late.

"Can you catch them, Nero?" He didn't know if the dragon could understand him or not.

Nero snorted then opened his snout as a ball of fire puffed from his mouth.

Andahar grinned, patted his neck. "Let's get my girl back."

Chapter 17

Aball of fire illuminated the night sky behind them. Laerwen turned her head to see the dark shadow racing to catch up to them. She knew Andahar would be on the back of Nero.

Lorcann kept the dagger pointed in her kidneys so she didn't dare move another muscle. Her wrist had been bleeding profusely and soaked through her vest and tunic. She could feel the stickiness of it on her skin beneath the material. She was starting to feel lightheaded from the loss of blood. Lorcann had significantly injured her, handicapping her to the point she didn't think she could fight back.

She didn't know how she was going to get out of this but she hoped Aura—and now Andahar and Nero—could help her.

I can kill him for you.

Aura's voice boomed in her head. She was aware the dragon could simply fry the mage to a crisp and it would be done and over with. She could easily agree to that but then she wouldn't have avenged the deaths of her parents or Randir if she allowed that to happen. And she really wanted to kill that bastard.

No. I need to be the one to do it.

By your command.

"Land here," Lorcann commanded.

Aura, do as he says.

The dragon alighted on the top of the mountain just as a puff of noxious smoke emitted through the top. Laerwen covered her mouth and nose with the edge of her vest.

Lorcann clamped a hand around her upper arm and pulled her off.

"Tell your dragon to fly away."

Laerwen hesitated for a moment. If she did, she could simply call her back again. The mage pressed the tip into her back again.

"Tell it!"

"Go, Aura."

Aura's eyes blinked and she snorted smoke as if to say she wouldn't leave.

"Go. It will be fine." *And I will call you if I need you.*

That seemed to appease her and she lifted off, flapping her giant wings on the wind and disappearing in the night sky. Laerwen could see the encampment below them. It was ablaze, lighting up the ground as though it were a beacon. She could hear the screams and yells of men as they fought and killed each other.

"Are you ready to die, Princess?" he asked.

"I guess you didn't get the royal decree," she said. "I am queen now."

"Doesn't matter to me. You'll be dead either way." He grinned, showing off those yellow, stumpy teeth.

She held up her bloody wrist. "You have what you need. I'm bleeding. Just take my blood."

He shook his head. "No. I need your blood in the molten rock of the mountain."

"What do you intend to do? Throw me in the pit of lava? If the volcano erupts, you'll be killed too. Then what?"

"I need you dead."

She wasn't sure if he was thinking clearly. Nor was she sure he wanted her dead because he wanted to wipe out her entire race or if he truly believed the power of her blood in the lava.

Another belch of steam from the mountain. He took her arm again, his fingers biting into her flesh. "Come along, dearie."

Lorcann dragged her along the edge of the mountain toward a fissure. It was as though he knew exactly where he was going and mayhap he did. He may have already scoped out the volcano while they were off planning a war.

Overhead, she thought she heard something—a flap of a wing. She glanced up in time to see the darkness move across the sky blotting out the stars. She knew Nero was overhead. She saw the talons extend in time for her to jerk her hand out of Lorcann's grasp and duck.

It wasn't clear to her if Nero was trying to claw the man to death or if he was merely trying to scare him. Whatever his intent, he managed to knock Lorcann off his feet just as Andahar leapt from the saddle. He landed close to her and put himself between her and Lorcann, his blood-stained sword at the ready.

"Andahar…" His name came out on a breath when she'd

meant it to be anything but reverent.

"What happened to you? Are you all right? How badly are you hurt?" He fired off the questions so fast she couldn't reply. "Never mind all that. Let's get you out of here."

Before she could respond, Lorcann launched from the ground at Andahar. It had taken the king by surprise and they both tumbled backward to the ground. She saw his sword fall from his hand as the mage put the dagger up to his neck ready to slice. Laerwen reached for her own dagger at her waist—why had she only just now remembered it?—and clutched it, trying to make her mind work and decide what to do.

She hesitated long enough to have Nero fly by with a screech, clawing at the man and shoving him off the king. His claws shredded Lorcann's back. Lorcann tumbled to the side as Andahar snatched up his sword and got to his feet. The mage was slower to get up, though, and stumbled.

Laerwen didn't wait another minute for her chance to attack. She ran at Lorcann and managed to stab him in the shoulder. He shrieked and reared back, his dagger hand slashing at air. She'd lost her grip on her dagger and it now stuck out of his shoulder. Good thing she'd come with extra. She snatched the one out of the holder strapped to her thigh.

"Laerwen, what are you doing?"

"I'm killing him!"

She went for him again but this time Lorcann was ready. They tumbled together and she was so close to his disgusting face she wanted to gag. He grabbed her around the waist, holding her close.

He licked her cheek.

It had taken her by such surprise, she froze.

He reached for her hair and grabbed a handful, yanking her head back and putting the dagger to her throat.

"You wish to die now?"

"Let her go."

Overhead, Aura screeched her unhappiness. Laerwen heard the flapping of her wings as she flew by. Nero was nothing but a black blob in the sky. But she knew he was there too, circling.

"Or what?" Lorcann taunted Andahar as he backed up, step by step. He headed for the fissure. "You cannot hope to save her. She will die this night as will so many of your men. You too if I'm lucky."

Oh, she hated him. He pulled and tugged on the strands of her hair as he carefully backed away from Andahar. But as he took another step, the steam from the volcano puffed up again. Laerwen held her breath but Lorcann coughed and let her go.

The mountain rocked under their feet so violently she lost her footing. They all did. She knew she was falling and tried to turn her body so she would land on her good arm, not the injured one. As she landed, her body jarred and pain lanced through her.

She looked up to see Andahar also on the ground. He pushed to his hands and knees, shaking his head to clear it. Lorcann was on his side, writhing as though he were in pain.

The ground rumbled again followed by a cracking sound. She scrambled to her feet and stumbled to Andahar just as he stood. They wobbled together, falling into each other. He held onto her to keep her steady.

Behind them, the mountain had started to cave in. The fissure widened, opening a large chasm. Lorcann was on his feet now, stumbling to get away from the rift.

"What's happening?" Andahar shouted it so he could be heard over the din.

"The volcano—"

It was all she got out. A flash below caught their attention and they looked down to see a bright white light growing bigger and brighter.

"Cormac opened the Barrier. We have to get out of here," Andahar said.

"But Lorcann—"

"Will die here. We're leaving."

"No." She pushed away from him. "I'm not going until he's dead. Until I kill him."

Andahar stared at her as dawning came over his features. "That's what this is about, isn't it? Your revenge. That's why you wanted to be the bait for Lorcann in the first place. You intended to kill him all along."

"I have to avenge my people's deaths." She stole a glance to the mage, saw him making his way across the rumbling mountain to get back to her. He was just as determined to kill her as she was to kill him. She gripped the dagger tighter in her fist.

"Laerwen, you're injured. And the volcano could blow. I won't leave you." And then he looked to the sky. "Nero!"

She wanted to shout at him, tell him no, she wasn't going. She wanted that mage dead. She wanted to make sure he gone and would never come back again to hurt her or any of her people. But as she stood there, she realized she had become like Lorcann. She had allowed her hate and vengeance and thoughts about hell-bent revenge cloud her mind and keep her from what truly mattered—Andahar and living in peace. Aye, Lorcann would be dead not by her hand. But so long as he was, what did the *how* of it matter? Andahar was right. She should let Nero or Aura burn the mage to a crips.

"Come on, Laerwen." He waved her toward him with urgency.

It was then she released her anger and hatred and dropped her dagger, letting it clatter at her feet. She reached for his hand, their fingers almost touching. But as she did, Lorcann grabbed her from behind, placing the blade at her throat again. His labored breathing was in her ear, the moist heat fanning her skin and turning her stomach.

"This time, we won't be separated."

At least with her captured, neither of the dragons would attack. Lorcann backed away heading now for the bigger opening.

"We're going to visit the fires now," Lorcann said. "You be a good king and stay here."

Andahar's face pinched with fury was the last thing she saw as Lorcann stepped off the rim.

By some miracle, Eldrin found a healer for Cormac. But the mage was still in a weakened state. Gweneth hadn't left his side the entire time. They found a place out of the fighting so the healer could attend to him. He spent several long minutes with the mage. He'd managed to stop the bleeding while Derron paced a hole in the ground behind him.

"We're running out of time." Derron didn't hide the urgency in his voice.

"Can he open the Barrier now?" Eldrin asked the sorceress.

"Cormac?" She looked to him with question in her eyes.

He sat on the edge of a rock, breathing deeply. As though he were trying to catch his breath.

"I will try."

"He's too weak." The woman put herself between Cormac and Eldrin. She folded her arms across her chest.

Derron hurried around her to stand next to Eldrin. "What do you mean he's too weak? We need that Barrier open."

"We didn't account for him being injured." Fire flashed in her eyes.

"Our men are dying," Eldrin said. "As are yours. I suggest you figure out how to get that Barrier open and now."

"I can do it." Cormac rose to his full height and stepped next to her, though he still looked ashen.

"Are you certain?" She placed a concerned hand on his shoulder. "If you're too weak—"

"Eldrin is right. Men are dying. I made a promise to the Fae and the Elves I would open the Barrier and that's what I'm going to do. Come, Gweneth." He held his hand out to her.

"I'll cover you," Eldrin said.

Cormac nodded. "You may want to step back. Once the Barrier is open, we will pull the Fomorians in. Try to get your people out of the way."

"I'll push back the troops," Derron said. "Just get that Barrier open as fast as you can."

Gweneth took Cormac's hand as Derron trotted away. The three of them walked several steps from the fire consuming the camp and the men fighting. Eldrin followed, killing anyone who attempted to step into their path and thwart their progress.

He only paused once to glance into the night sky to see the dragons flapping around the top of the volcano. He couldn't see his brother or Laerwen on the mountain. He sent a silent prayer to the gods to keep them safe.

Cormac and Gweneth turned to face each other, their hands clasped. They closed their eyes and chanted something. Words Eldrin didn't understand. They were not Elvish words nor were they Fomorian. It was a language he didn't know. As they chanted, the air around them crackled. Sparked. As though coming to life.

Several men tried to attack them but when they saw what was happening around the mage and the sorceress, they quickly retreated.

A white cloud of magic swirled around the two of them. Light flashed and sparked and another second later, the wind kicked up. It was so fierce, it blew from them and puffed out over the land, extinguishing the fires as though they were nothing more than a candle flame.

Magic hit Eldrin like a fist punching him in the gut. The force of it knocked him back and he fell to the ground. He heard shouts and screams. Behind him, the wind gained strength and power.

When he glanced over his shoulder, he could no longer see Cormac and the woman in the cloud of magic. Derron was suddenly at his side, shouting something to him he couldn't hear. He grabbed him by the arm and hauled him to his feet, made a motion to follow him.

They took off at a run away from the couple. The ground rumbled and overhead they could hear the squawk of a dragon. Eldrin glanced up but could still see nothing in the darkness. Nothing but the shape of Nero as he flew in circles over the top of the volcano. As though he was agitated and couldn't get to someone or something.

Then a resounding crack sounded throughout the land. The earth rumbled with such violence they all collided with the ground. Eldrin rolled to his side and looked back. There seemed to be a rip in the air and an opening widening to show the other side—the Unseelie realm.

And then the suction started. It was as though something had gripped him by his ankles and pulled. He clawed at the ground, trying to stop but it was really no use. He was being dragged toward the opening, toward the Unseelie realm. He was going with the others—mostly Fomorians but some Elves and some Fae, too—those who couldn't get out of the way and who were unfortunate enough to be pulled into the vortex.

Derron collided with him. They banged heads and immediately Eldrin groaned and saw stars. Pain lanced through his head, down his neck and shoulders. But Derron's weight was able to stop Eldrin from heading toward the opening. He latched onto him and as Eldrin looked up, he could see the Fae king had shoved his sword into the earth. His hand clamped around the hilt in a death grip. His other hand had hold of Eldrin's upper arm, his fingers biting into his flesh and bone. Eldrin had lost his sword and used both hands to grab onto Derron.

"Don't let go," he mouthed.

As the words escaped his mouth, an explosion rocked the entire realm. Eldrin looked up, saw the smoke spiral out of the top of the volcano. And another moment later, molten rock spewed upward.

"The volcano—" Eldrin started.

"I see it!" Derron shouted back.

But they couldn't move. And they were right in the path of the volcano.

The only thing Eldrin could think of at that moment was that his brother and the queen of the Hin'dar Rhule were on top of that mountain. He had no way to get to either of them.

Suddenly there was silence. Eldrin dropped to the ground as Derron released him. He huddled there a long moment, trying to get his bearings. Finally, he managed to look up and see the Barrier had been closed. Dead bodies littered the ground. There were a few Elves and Fae that were left alive. And no Fomorian in sight.

Cormac had done it.

Eldrin saw him curled against the ground, the sorceress crouched next to him. Derron yanked his sword out of the ground and started for the two of them. Eldrin peeled himself off the ground stumbled after him.

When they arrived she looked up at them. Tears glistened on her cheeks.

"It was too much for him," she said. "We couldn't make it through after everyone else."

"Is he dead?" Derron asked.

"Not yet. But he's very weak."

"We'll find the healer again," Eldrin said.

"It may be too late for that," Derron said. "The volcano is starting to erupt."

To press his point, the ground rumbled again and the top of the mountain spit more lava. It fell toward the ground, sizzling against the earth not far from them. They all flinched.

Those who had been left alive retreated. Overhead, he could see the moon dragons head down from the sky and pick up the survivors. Lady Talaiel must have known the Barrier was open and sent them as soon as she saw the volcano begin to erupt.

"What's happening? I thought the volcano wasn't supposed to erupt until the eclipse." Eldrin turned his gaze on the sorceress.

Her eyes were fixed on the mountain. "Our magic must have affected it."

"Powerful enough to cause volcano to erupt?" Derron asked.

"Aye. Powerful enough."

"We have to get out of here," Eldrin said. But what about Andahar and Laerwen? They were still on the mountain. He couldn't leave them there.

"I've already called the dragons," Derron said, his gaze fixed on the night sky.

Ambrielle and Luna swept down toward them and landed. They scrambled toward the dragons. Derron climbed on the back of Luna. Eldrin motioned for Cormac and Gweneth to take Ambrielle.

Eldrin had to see if his brother was all right. He had to find them on top of the mountain. He called for Aura and a moment later, she appeared out of the smoke and shadows and landed near him.

"What do you think you're doing?" Derron called.

"Take them to safety. I've got go find Andahar and Laerwen. They're still on the mountain."

Derron stared in disbelief.

"I can't leave them there," Eldrin said. He shooed them away. "Go."

Reluctantly, Derron gripped the reins. As the others headed away from the former Fomorian camp, Eldrin headed to the top of the mountain.

Into the fire.

As Lorcann backed away from Andahar and stepped off the rim, the mountain rumbled beneath their feet with a violent shake. A few feet away, the first spewing of lava shot into the air, arced and then cascaded down over the edge of the mountain.

Laerwen experienced the first flurries of fear. She had never been this close to one of the volcanoes when it threatened to erupt. Andahar was probably gone by now, though he said he wouldn't leave her. Would he? She hoped he saved himself at the very least.

She still pressed her injured wrist against her chest as Lorcann dragged her toward the opening. The yawning chasm grew wider as they approached and she could see more lava spewing upward. Her skin could withstand the heat but not for long. And that was what Lorcann wanted.

He grabbed her arm with one hand, keeping a dagger trained on her with the other. As they neared the opening, the fumes become more and more suffocating. She tried to hold her breath but she was already lightheaded. Her stomach cramped and she coughed several times.

The fumes got to Lorcann too. He coughed and sputtered, trying to gasp for air. But it was tainted with the stench of sulfur.

"Come meet your doom, your majesty." His words were followed by another coughing fit, one he had a hard time coming back from.

He loosened his grip on her arm as another rumble rocked the mountain beneath their feet. She took the moment to kick his legs out from under him. He collapsed in a heap, still trying to breathe. Still trying to stop the coughing.

She kicked him in the ribs. He swore at her, though she couldn't hear exactly what filthy words he spewed at her. His dagger had clattered from his hands. Now the mountain was really rumbling and it was hard to maintain footing. She almost lost her balance but managed to stay on her feet by placing them shoulder-width apart.

Lorcann scrambled for his dagger, trying hard to find it. She stomped on one of his hands and he screamed.

"That's for my parents, you son of a bitch."

When he looked up at her, she could see the fear in his eyes. For the first time, he actually looked as though he were terrified of her. Which did nothing but give her more courage.

As much as she wanted to kill him, she needed this situation to be over. Panic seized her and she knew she had to get off the mountain before it was too late. Before it really did erupt.

With a surge of adrenaline, she kicked him again. This time the toe of her boot connected with his cheekbone. She'd forgotten she held her own dagger. He scrambled backward to get away from her but she lunged, taking the moment to plunge the dagger right into the Fomorian's heart.

They were eye to eye for a breath. His eyes widened in first shock and then fury as he realized what she'd done. She left the knife in his heart and shoved away from him, getting back to her feet.

"And that's for Randir."

She spit on him in one final act of defiance.

Andahar landed next to her. Startled, she looked up, saw he had leapt from the hovering Nero. Relief sputtered through her. Relief that he hadn't left her after all. He grabbed onto her, pulled her to him and wrapped an arm around her shoulders.

"Stubborn woman," he muttered.

Behind them, the volcano exploded with another burst. Looking back, she saw the magma emitting from the growing chasm along with the thick white smoke. And Lorcann's body was completely lifeless.

But Andahar wasn't waiting around to make sure the mage was dead. He dragged her toward the dragon who had landed nearby. They scrambled onto the beast's back as he lifted into the night sky. It was then she saw Eldrin riding Aura, heading right for them. She coughed with the noxious fumes and tears stung her eyes.

Tears of relief and joy.

Despite everything they had been through, Andahar had still come for her. He hadn't abandoned her. Her mind whirled with all the things left unsaid between them. She would, eventually, have to face that. And she also knew that she had been a fool. She had faced death and nearly lost her life on the top of the volcano. She could have lost her husband, too.

Andahar was still that. She hadn't lost him.

Nero and Aura flew as fast as they could away from the area. Even she knew the dangers. That they had to get away. But she had to see it through with Lorcann and she was glad now she had. The mage who had murdered her family was dead.

It was then she noticed the land was completely devoid of anyone else. As though they had been evacuated. She caught sight of the moon dragons winging their way through the night sky, the moonlight glinting off their iridescent wings.

An explosion made her turn to look, to see the molten rock burst from the top of the mountain.

She turned away. She could no longer watch as the volcano destroyed her realm. And it would. She knew. There would be nothing left of the land once the fury had ceased.

Laerwen leaned her head back on Andahar's shoulder as he wrapped an arm around her and held her. All the energy fizzled out of her. Without the adrenaline flowing through her, she no longer had the strength to keep her eyes open or to even think of anything else. The last thing she remembered was her husband's warm breath over her ear as he kissed her.

Chapter 18

Laerwen woke in her own bed. Or at least she thought it was her own bed. She blinked, staring up at the ceiling with the wood rafters. She never remembered her room having wood rafters. It took several minutes for her disorientation to subside and for her to remember exactly where she was. She knew she was in large bed snuggled under layers of blankets but she had no idea where.

She turned her head. She finally realized she was back in her bedchamber in the Woodlands. Not the Hin'dar Rhule. The room was a welcome sight.

Yet as she comprehended where she was not, sorrow pressed against her. The room she remembered—the one she grew up in—was no more. The palace had been destroyed and whatever was left of her realm was surely gone as well. She wanted to see it. She needed to see it to give her peace of mind and mayhap closure.

Her last moments on the volcano came back to her in a rush. She had to squeeze her eyes shut to block out the memories. How Lorcann had dragged her toward the widening fissure. How she had stabbed him. How the volcano had erupted moments after Andahar and Nero rescued her from the top. From certain death. He had held her close to him as they flew away. Being in his arms gave her that security she always cherished. And yet sadness mushroomed through her that her homeland was gone.

Andahar.

Where was he? She scooted to an upright position, pain flaring through her arm and hand. Glancing down, she saw her wrist tightly bound in gauze. And then she remembered that too. When Lorcann slapped her wrist with his sword, making her drop her own. Cutting her. She remembered the way the sticky blood seeped through her tunic, drenching it. She must have lost a lot of blood.

But she had forgotten the pain. Revenge had blinded her, made her forget the discomfort. She took comfort knowing Lorcann was dead, incinerated in the molten rock.

A knock on the door preceded it creaking open. Andahar stepped inside, held open the door for a servant who placed a tray of food and drink on a nearby table. Her heart pounded wildly at the sight of him.

Gods, he looked handsome. He was dressed in a crushed velvet tunic in a deep azure with a high collar trimmed in gold. Gold buttons. His sword swinging at his side. Black pants, boots polished to a high shine. His silvery hair brushed the collar of his tunic. Those piercing green eyes met hers, held her gaze and never looked away as the servant girl bustled from the room.

"Good morrow." His voice was soft in the quiet of the room.

She wanted to swoon. Instead, she blushed. "Good morrow."

He walked to the bed and perched on the edge. "Glad to see you awake. I was worried about you."

"I'm awake."

His gaze landed on her wrist. He reached for it, gently pulled it to him and turned it over in his grasp to examine the bandage. "The healer says you are mending well. Do you have any discomfort?"

"It hurts a little," she admitted.

His gaze met hers again. "I'm glad you're all right. You gave me a scare."

"What happened? The last thing I remember is passing out as Nero flew away."

He nodded. "You did pass out. Lady Talaiel and King Derron managed to get what survivors there were away from the volcano. We would never have made it back here had it not been for them." He clasped her hand in his. "I had Nero fly here to have Brom tend you."

"Andahar...I'm so sorry..."

"For nearly getting yourself killed? You should be."

She couldn't meet his gaze. She knew he was angry and he had a right to be.

"No revenge is worth dying for," he said softly.

"I know but all I could think about was vengeance for my realm, my people, my parents. It was wrong of me. I know that now and, Andahar, I'm so sorry. I'm sorry I put everyone in danger. I shouldn't have." Her voice cracked and she couldn't stop the well of tears. She had held her emotions in check far too long. "What of the rest of my people?"

He squeezed her hand, as if steeling her against the news he was about to deliver. "There are a few Fire Elves left. They made it back here to the Woodlands."

She lifted her eyes, met his gaze. He'd softened. No longer did he have the creased forehead of anger. Or the lips thinned in irritation. "That's good. I'm glad. What of Hiram?"

"He's been beside himself since you returned. He'll be glad to know you've awakened."

Dear Hiram. How she missed him.

"I'll send him to you if you'd like," he continued.

"Aye, I would. And the Hin'dar Rhule?"

He looked away and she knew the answer. "The volcano did a lot of damage."

Tears burned the backs of her eyes as she nodded. "I'll want to see it for myself."

"I knew you'd say that. I can take you back."

"When?"

"Soon. When you're healthy. Nero seems to be hanging around lately. I think he must like you."

"What of Aura and the others?"

He shrugged. "They returned to wherever they came from. I suppose they live somewhere with the Fae and didn't wish to be parted from them. Derron and Elyne have returned to their kingdom."

"And the Fomorians? What of them?" It was the first she'd thought to ask him of the wretched race that had destroyed her people.

"Cormac came through. He and his sorceress sent them through the Barrier into the Unseelie realm."

Grim satisfaction seeped through her. She was glad they were gone. All of them.

"Cormac, though, he hasn't fared so well. He was injured during the fighting."

"Where is he now?"

"Here. Recovering. I allowed him to stay because he managed to hold up his end of the bargain. We are rid of the Fomorians."

"But he didn't make it through?"

"He was weakened from being attacked. His sorceress thinks they can go to the Unseelie realm once he's recovered."

"I see." She was ready to be rid of all things Fomorian. Even

Cormac. "How long have I been out?"

"Several days."

"Days?" she repeated, surprised to hear it. She'd been in this bed for days and she hadn't even known it?

"You're probably famished." He grinned, rose and walked over to the tray. He poured a tankard of water which made her suddenly realize how bloody thirsty she was. When he brought it to her, she took a deep draw on the cool liquid.

"Thank you."

"And thirsty, too, I take it." He smiled again, though the smile didn't seem to reach his eyes this time.

An uncomfortable silence settled between them. She knew what he was thinking. She was thinking it too. When were they going to talk about their fight? The thing that came between them just before battle? He knew she regretted her vows. But facing Lorcann, seeing the volcano erupt had changed something inside her.

She reached for him, placed her hand over his. "Andahar—"

"You don't have to explain anything to me, Laerwen."

"But I want to."

"But it's not necessary. You did what you had to do. What you felt you had to do. I may not be able to understand that but I can respect it. I wish you had confided in me before, though."

There was no mistaking the pain in his voice, how hurt he sounded. Hurt she had put there. Hurt she could probably never take away. Mayhap, though, she could make up for it.

"I'm sorry. I thought it was something I had to do alone. You seemed so…determined to keep me out of harm's way. When you changed the plans, when you decided to go with the surprise attack, I knew I had to alter my plan too. That's why I decided to take Aura and find Lorcann myself."

Andahar clasped her hands between both if his. "I know you've thought you were alone since the attack on the Hin'dar Rhule. But Laerwen, you have never been alone. You've always had me."

Damn him. In four words, he made the guilt swarm to the surface.

She had always had him. And she was too blind to see it. And now it could be too late for them. She blinked back the tears that wanted to come, trying to remain strong. The last thing she wanted to do was fall apart here in front of him.

He released her hands and stood. "I'll leave you to eat and rest. When you feel up to it, I can have a bath brought up for you."

Before she could reply, he walked to the door and left.

As the door closed behind him, she could no longer hold the tears at bay. She put her face in her hands and wept.

Andahar walked briskly down the corridor away from Laerwen's bedchamber. The only sound was that of his boots on the wood floor as he made his way back to his own solitude.

He slammed the door behind him, leaned against the door and blew out a heated breath. When she had passed out in his arms on the back of Nero, he had feared the worst. She had been so pale, so lifeless, he was sure he'd lost her.

He'd kept a vigil by her side. Refusing to leave. Refusing to sleep. Refusing to eat. He would not rest until he knew she was going to live. Hiram had hovered, demanding to be there when she woke but Andahar had sent him away, making sure he stayed away until she was ready to see him. In truth, he wanted to be the one she awoke to and, as it turned out, she awoke alone. He would never forgive himself for that.

Brom had worked miracles. Her wrist was healing. Color had returned to her cheeks. For the first time in days, she looked alive and well.

Relief had sputtered through him when he saw her sitting up in bed. He tried hard not to make eye contact with her at first but he saw her expression. That look of hope and something else—love. Her cheeks flushed pink when he entered the room with the servant girl. She had sucked her bottom lip between her teeth— though she hadn't realized it—and looked delighted to see him.

Gods, he loved her. How could he ever get it through her thick skull that he was madly, passionately, forever in love with her? The woman drove him mad but he could never help his feelings for her.

A sharp knock on the door startled him out of his thoughts. He straightened his tunic and pulled open the door. His brother stood on the other side.

"Cormac is ready to leave," he announced.

"He must be feeling better then. Tell him safe travels."

Andahar started to close the door but Eldrin stuck out his foot and stopped it.

"He wishes to speak with you."

"Why?"

"How should I know? Mayhap to tell you goodbye. He's waiting on the ground for you. At the foot of the stairs."

The king heaved a sigh. "Fine then. I'll see him."

He followed Eldrin from his chamber, through the corridors, down the winding staircase. Cormac and his sorceress waited patiently for him to arrive. Eldrin halted next to his brother, his hand on the hilt of his sword as if ready to spring into action should the need arise.

Andahar had to admit the mage looked much better too since they returned to the Woodlands. Gweneth had fretted over him for days, worrying that he would die and then where would that leave her? She, like Andahar with Laerwen, had stayed by Cormac's side, refusing to move until he was mended.

"King Andahar," Cormac greeted. He stuck out his hand. "The time has come for me to bid you farewell."

Andahar shook his hand. "Best of luck to you in the Unseelie realm. How will you get there?"

"My lady sorceress has devised a way for us to get through the Barrier."

She stepped up next to him, slipped her arm around his waist. "We'll be leaving the Woodlands, though, before I open the portal. It's safer for everyone."

"I thank you," Andahar said with a nod. He recalled seeing the horrific destruction from the air as he tried to get to Laerwen. There hadn't been anything he could do to stop it from the air. "You aren't going to flash there?"

"I'm afraid I've lost that ability since the opening of the Barrier," Cormac said. "In fact, I've noticed some of my magic has weakened."

"It took extraordinary power to do what we did, Cormac," Gweneth said. "You will fully recover in time."

He turned his attention back to Andahar. "I wish you good luck, health and happiness with the lovely queen of the Hin'dar Rhule," Cormac said. "Does she know yet?"

He knew the mage referred to the total destruction of the realm. He nodded slowly. "I told her. But she doesn't yet understand the scale of the disaster."

"You've not told her of the other volcanoes?"

"No. She only knows the one erupted. Not all six in the realm."

"Will you rebuild then?" Cormac asked.

"I will leave that to Laerwen to decide. I wish you all the best in the Unseelie realm as the Dark King."

"It will surely be a new adventure for me." He looked at Gweneth and smiled. "For us."

They bid them a final farewell and left the Woodlands. It wouldn't be long before they would be out the gates.

"How do you think Laerwen will react when she learns the truth?" Eldrin asked, his eyes still on the retreating Fomorian and his sorceress.

"She'll be devastated."

"When do you plan to tell her?"

"I don't," Andahar said.

He had sworn Hiram, her advisor and the one closest to her, to secrecy that he wouldn't tell her. That he was to be the one to tell her when the time was right. When Hiram had demanded why, he had to tell him the truth. That he was her husband and as such, he would be the one to break the news to her.

The man had looked at him as though he'd grown a second head. And yet, even though Andahar had admitted to him of their secret vows, he had seemed happy for them. Almost relieved.

"She wants to see it for herself. I'll take her as soon as she's able," Andahar said.

"You love her, don't you?"

He glanced at his brother. "Is it that obvious?"

"It has been since the first day she arrived here in the Woodlands." Eldrin clapped him on the shoulder. "Take good care of her, brother. As I'm sure you will. My lady and I are returning to the Skye Realm this afternoon. We have business there."

Andahar nodded and watched as Eldrin headed for the winding stairs.

"Eldrin…what would you think if I told you Laerwen and I were already wedded?"

It seemed to be a day for revealing secrets.

Eldrin halted mid-step and looked at him over his shoulder, one eyebrow raised and a smirk on his face. "I'd say felicitations are in order."

The ash clouds could be seen for miles. It hurt Laerwen's heart. And the longer the clouds lingered, the longer it would be before she could return to her beloved home. It had taken nearly a fortnight for the air to clear. By that time, she had healed and allowed Andahar to take care of her. He brought her fruit, cheese and bread. He doted on her. But yet their relationship still had not returned to what it was—warm and easy and comfortable.

By mid-afternoon days after the eruption, Laerwen summoned servants to bring her a tub full of warm water. One of the girls stayed behind to help her bathe and dress. She had decided today would be the day she returned to the Hin'dar Rhule.

Instead of donning her normal garb, she opted for a gown from his realm. She had decided somewhere after breaking her fast she would make it up to Andahar. She was going to prove to him her feelings. That she may have regretted their vows at one time but now she knew she couldn't live without him. She had to let him know her feelings were true and real. The only way to do that was to show him.

So she chose a gown the color of the sunset. She knew it would go well with her coloring, her hair and her eyes. He had said once her eyes were the color of whiskey.

Whiskey was definitely something she could use about now.

The servant girl helped comb out her hair. She wore it long and loose, letting the waves spill down her back. Even though weakness pressed through her, she hoped she could convince Andahar to take her to her realm. She was desperate to see it.

As the girl left, Hiram paused in the doorway, peering inside. Elation bloomed through her at the sight of him. He stood in the doorway and started at her wide-eyed.

"Good afternoon, Hiram. How do you like it?" She did a little twirl to show off the gown.

He stepped into the room, smiling. "It's as lovely as you are. I'm glad to see you looking much better, your majesty. How do you fare?"

"My wrist only aches occasionally now."

"Good. Good. Glad to hear that."

"I'm anxious to return home and begin rebuilding."

Worry creased his brow and he pulled his bottom lip between

his teeth. "Aye, of course. But shouldn't you rest here first? You need to be in top condition before we travel back to the Hin'dar Rhule, your majesty."

"What's with the 'your majesty' stuff?" she asked. "You've never called me that before."

He blinked, taken aback. "Isn't that your rightful title?"

She blew out a breath. "Aye, it is. I'm sorry. I suppose I'm a little on edge still after everything that happened."

"Andahar told me what you did. That you killed the mage and that you nearly lost your life on the volcano." His expression turned stern, his tone scolding. "You shouldn't have done that. What if you had died?"

Ah, so this is why he paid her a visit. It'd taken him this long to chastise her for her actions. She couldn't blame him. She deserved it.

"But I didn't. And the Fire Elves still have a leader."

"Good thing too."

She thought of Andahar and their wedding vows and knew she had to tell Hiram. "And there is something else I need to tell you. I am not the only ruler of the Fire Elves."

He raised a brow. "Oh?"

"You see….Andahar and I…we…we wed in secret."

"Did you?" He didn't try to hide his surprise or the smile that turned up the corners of his mouth. "When?"

"Before we left for the Hin'dar Rhule." She turned away from him, her hands clasped as she tried not to fidget. "I hope you're not angry."

"Laerwen, how I could I be angry with you? When you so clearly have found your one true love." He stepped next to her, turned her to face him. "I'm terribly happy for you. For both of you."

"You are?"

"Aye. Why wouldn't I be?"

"Because he's not a Fire Elf."

"Should that matter so much?"

"No, I suppose not."

"Does he make you happy? Do you love him?"

"Aye. He does. I do."

"Then that, my dear, is all that matters. Truly." He sounded as though he meant it.

"Oh, Hiram. I can't tell you what that means to me."

"I think I know." He smiled, kissed her cheek. "Now if you'll excuse me, I must prepare for our return to the Hin'dar Rhule. I'll see you later?"

"Aye."

As he left, she knew she had to find Andahar and tell him her true feelings.

She stepped out of her bedchamber and paused. Heading down the corridor was Andahar's sister, Princess Allanna. Usually she saw her with her husband. It was a rare thing to see the two separated from one another. They were always together.

"Queen Laerwen." Allanna dipped a quick curtsy. "Are you feeling better?"

"I am."

"We were all so worried about you. Especially the king."

"He was?" she asked.

"Oh aye. Where are you headed? Mayhap we can walk together."

"I was actually looking for the king."

"He would be in his private chamber off the throne room this time of day," she said. "Why don't I walk with you?"

The girl hooked her arm in Laerwen's and led her down the corridor.

"We feared the worst when Andahar returned with you. All that blood…" She shuddered with the memory. "Your tunic was soaked through. He thought you'd been injured elsewhere but was relieved to see it was only your wrist."

"Aye, only my wrist." Laerwen nodded agreement. But the girl continued.

"He was so worried about you he would only allow the healer inside the chamber with you. He wouldn't allow anyone else inside."

"I don't understand."

"He stayed by your side the entire time. To make sure you would be all right. We begged him to get some rest or to even eat, but he wouldn't. He refused."

"He refused?" she repeated. Her heart pounded.

"He didn't leave your side until the morning when you finally awoke. It was the first time he'd changed his clothes. He wanted to bring you food. You'd been stirring. Talking in your sleep. He thought mayhap you'd wake soon. And you did!" She beamed and squeezed her arm.

"I talked in my sleep."

"You did. Apparently you were having nightmares. Reliving the horrors with that awful mage on the mountaintop. I'm glad you're all right."

She was too. She didn't recall any dreams or nightmares, but it could be buried so deep in her subconscious she didn't want to remember.

"I had those too," Allanna said quietly, not looking at her.

Laerwen remembered Andahar had mentioned his sister and her nightmares. She'd had an ordeal, too, with Marath. She would have plunged to her death off the rope bridge if it hadn't been for Eldrin and Sir Drake. Laerwen wrapped an arm around the princess and squeezed.

"You and I have something in common, then," Laerwen said. "Our loathing of Fomorians." The princess giggled. "Could I tell you a secret?"

"Aye, of course."

"Would you be terribly saddened to know your brother and I are wed?"

Allanna froze and turned to her, her eyes wide. "You are?"

"We are."

The girl clasped her hands. "I'm so happy to hear that."

"Truly?"

She nodded. "Truly." She hugged her hard. "I have another sister." When she pulled away, she said, "Let's get you to the king."

The princess took her hand and led her through the empty throne room to his private chamber. She knocked quickly before shoving open the door. Andahar stood when they entered.

"Your visitor, your majesty," Allanna said. Then curtsied with a flourish and a wide grin before she backed out of the room and closed the door.

He looked Laerwen over with an appreciative gaze. "I didn't think you'd be up yet."

So many things went through her mind. She wanted to tell him she missed him, that she was a bloody fool for pushing him away. That she loved him. That she didn't regret their vows. That she wanted to spend eternity with him. But that's not what she said at all.

"I wonder if we could visit the Hin'dar Rhule?"

His brows drew together. "Today?"

She nodded. "Today, if you please."

His lips thinned. "Are you feeling up to traveling?"

"Aye. I've regained much of my strength these last few weeks."

He nodded slowly. "All right. I'll call Nero. We'll meet him near the loch."

He hadn't argued with her. He must have known how determined she was and that she would have demanded to go with or without him. Her heart beat with excitement and just a little fear. She had no idea what she would see when they returned.

She followed him from his private chamber, down the winding stairs and to the edge of the loch. She noticed the thick grayish clouds filling the sky. A flicker of warning fear went through her.

They waited in strained silence until the great black dragon came and landed nearby. Andahar helped her climb on his back and settled behind her, holding her close. His warmth pressed into her, giving her comfort. But nothing could still her wildly beating heart.

With a silent command, Nero took flight and headed west.

The farther west they flew, the niggling fear grew stronger. She knew, deep down, something was horribly wrong. That something had happened in her realm.

Nero dropped down toward the land and that's when she saw it. From the air, she could see the peaks of all six of the volcanoes. And from the peaks of all six of the volcanoes, the tops were caved in and gone, indicating they had all erupted. She could imagine the thick columns of gray-white smoke that must have filled the air. She saw the ash clouds in the Woodlands. She had expected and feared the worst, but nothing could prepare her for this utter devastation.

Her heart broke.

She turned her head so Andahar could hear her. "I want to land."

"Laewren, I don't think—"

"Nero, land somewhere safe."

He stiffened behind her and she knew she'd made him angry. But she had to see the destruction from the ground. She had to take one long last look at the realm before she gave up the hope she could rebuild, that her people would once again thrive here.

Nero followed her command and landed where the encampment had once stood. As soon as he alighted, she slid to the ground. And stood staring at the volcano in the distance. The one that had nearly killed her. The one that had taken Lorcann's life.

She heard Andahar drop to the ground behind her. But he made no other move. He stood there, waiting.

"You knew, didn't you?" she asked.

"I did."

"And you didn't want to tell me."

"No."

"You knew I'd ask to see the Hin'dar Rhule for myself. You knew I'd have to see. To know. That's why you didn't argue with me when I asked to come here today."

"Aye."

The only sound was that of the wind blowing. She scanned the land, looking at the earth covered in ash and hardened molten rock. It looked gray and sad and nothing had survived.

The desolation was like a knife in the gut.

But she didn't cry. She'd shed enough tears.

"We can still rebuild," Andahar said.

She knew that's what she wanted to hear. Her eyes closed for a moment before she opened them and turned to face him.

"No, Andahar. I don't wish to rebuild. Nothing and no one can survive here any longer."

"What will you do then?"

"The Fire Elves may not have a home in the Hin'dar Rhule anymore. But we are a strong people. We will find a new place to live and thrive." She took a tentative step toward him, placed her hands on his chest. "I hope that place is in the Woodlands."

"Your people are always welcome there, Laerwen. That's never changed. No matter what happens between us."

"And about us…" She stood on tiptoe, brushed her lips against his. "I love you. You were right—I've always had you. I was a fool to think otherwise."

His arms slid around her waist as he pulled her to him. "You no longer regret our vows?"

"No, I don't. I even have Hiram's blessing."

"You told him then?"

She nodded.

His grin was mischievous. "I already told him. It was the only way to keep him out of your room until you recovered."

"You took care of me."

"I never left your side. Except that morning to get your food."

She melted. "I'm sorry I lied to you. Can you forgive me?"

"If you promise never to do it again."

"I promise."

She threw her arms around his neck and hugged him hard, the joy filling her. "I should also tell you I mentioned our vows to your sister."

"How sneaky of you. Did my sister approve?"

"She was quite happy with the news."

His mouth covered hers in an unexpected kiss. She let him kiss her as though they had never kissed before. As though it might be the first and last time. She sighed with contentment. When they broke, her fingers fluttered through his hair. She couldn't imagine her life without him.

"I may have lost everything, Andahar, but I never lost you."

"And you never will."

Realm of Honor Cast of Characters

The Humans
Sir Finian "Finn" McCullough: Scottish knight

Maggie Chase McCullough: Finn's wife

Sir Drake Attenborough: English knight and jousting hero

Henry Chase: Maggie's father

The Fae
Princess Elyne: crown princess of the Fae Otherworld

Lord Derron: Knight of the Realm, Protector of the Otherworld

Queen Maeve: ruler of the Otherworld and the Seelie Court

Lord Roderick: member of the High Council

Lord Aldun: member of the High Council

Lord Vaughan: member of the High Council

Seamus: healer for the Fae

King Adhamh: the queen's husband who was murdered

Morrigan: Goddess of War

Lord/Dark King Kieran: dark elf bent on human and Otherworld domination

Lord Gawaine: Queen Maeve's high councilor

Dark King Fergus mac Delbaith: dark king of the Unseelie court

Lord Pwyll: Guardian of the Stone of Destiny

Lord Malcolm: Guardian of the Sword of Light and Derron's father

Lord Llewelyn: Guardian of the Club of Dagda

Lord Udrich: Guardian of the Spear of Lugh

The Elves

King Urdithane emar'Rudul: ruler of the Wood Elves

Andahar emar'Rudul: crown prince of the Woodlands Elven throne

Leopold: Wood Elves royal advisor

Eldrin emar'Rudul: brother to Andahar, Elven ranger

Allanna emar'Rudul: sister to Andahar and Elven Princess

Lord Navin emar'Rudul: brother to Andahar, Woodlands Gatekeeper

Lord-Regent Marath: Wood Elves liege lord

Lord Randir: Fire Elf and Laerwen's betrothed

Laerwen emer'Aranhil Bloodfire: Fire Elf and Princess of the Hin'dar Rhule

Hiram: Laerwen's royal advisor

Lady Talaiel: ruler of the Skye Elves

Turin: healer for the Skye Elves

Brom: healer for the Wood Elves

Lord Malack: one of the noble Wood Elves

Queen Lucinda and King Aleron: ruler of the Fire Elves

The Fomorians

Cormac: Fomorian mage forced to help Kieran

Lorcann: Fomorian mage

The Dragons

Ambrielle: the emerald dragon

Aura: the azure dragon

Luna: the silver dragon

Nero: the black dragon

Moon dragons: silver dragons of the Skye Elves

The Realms

Fae Otherworld: home of the Fae, includes Seelie and Unseelie Courts

Woodlands: a humid forest region and home of the Wood Elves
Hin'dar Rhule: dry, arid volcanic region and home of the Fire Elves
Skye Realm in the clouds: home of the Skye Elves and the moon dragons

Human Realm: home for Maggie and Finn

Underworld: where Morrigan was banished

The Races

The Fae: also known as Faeries, a race of magical beings who can alter time and travel from their realm to the human realm.

Fire Elves: Elves who live in the volcanic realm known as the Hin'dar Rhule. Their bodies can withstand the hottest heat of the fires, but the lava is still deadly to them. They seek help from the Wood Elves when the Fomorians destroy their home.

Fomorians: an ancient race of vile creatures who wreak havoc. They were banished to a watery prison but one powerful Fomorian mage managed to break out and free his people so they could rampage once more.

Skye Elves: a reclusive Elven race living among the clouds with their moon dragons. The legend of the Skye Elves says one is as strong as ten men and they are undefeatable in battle.

Wood Elves: Elves who live in the trees of the Woodlands and who had a long-standing Treaty of Separation with the Fae, dividing the two races. The Treaty has since been abolished, uniting the two and allowing them to work together to defeat the evil in the realm.

ALSO BY MICHELLE MILES

Age of Wizards
In the Tower of the Wizard King
On the Hunt for the Wizard King

Realm of Honor
One Knight Only
Only for a Knight
A Knight to Remember
A Knight Like No Other
Shadows of the Knight

Dream Walker
Call of the Dark
Blood and Bone

A Ransom & Fortune Adventure
Highland Fling
Dead of Winter
The Citadel
Lord of the Underworld

Dragon Protectors
Desiring the Dragon Lord
Seducing the Dragon Knight
Tempting Her Dragon Bodyguard

Guardians of Atlantis
Tempting Eden
Seducing Eve
Ravishing Helene
Guardians of Atlantis Box Set

Coffee House Chronicles
Talk Dirty to Me
Nice Girls Do
Have Yourself a Merry Little Latte
Take Me I'm Yours
Sex, Lust & Martinis

Forever Yours
A Little Taste of Heaven

Shorts and Anthologies
Free on Prolific Works (formerly Instafreebie)
A Dance Among the Faeries, Short Story
Eorwulf, Short Story
The Soul of Sharah, Short Story
Sinfully Sweet, Short Story
Flights of Fantasy: A Collection of Short Stories

Watch for more at www.michellemiles.net

Did you love *Shadows of the Knight?* Pick up the first book in Michelle Miles' epic fantasy Age of Wizards series, *In the Tower of the Wizard King,* on sale now in ebook, paperback, and audio at your favorite retailer.

In the Age of Wizards, Time is a commodity more valuable than gold.

Her magic is dormant.

When Aoife (EE-fa) Burke rushes home after the unexpected death of her father, she discovers her mother has vanished amidst inexplicable circumstances. She returns to her childhood home to search for clues of her mother's whereabouts but another shock awaits her. Sean O'Connell, the object of her girlhood crush, has purchased the family home. She senses Sean is hiding something from her, refuses to let her inside and does everything he can to keep her out. A determined Aoife breaks inside and stumbles upon an antique trunk in the attic. When she opens it, instead of the normal musty clothes and ancient letters, she finds a stairway leading into darkness. It calls to her and she cannot resist stepping into the trunk and onto that first stair where it leads her to magical truths her mother never wanted her to discover.

His magic is dangerous.

Sean O'Connell has been assigned by the Inter-dimensional Portal Protection Agency to keep Aoife and her mother out of Faery. But when she breaks into the house and disappears through the portal in the trunk—like her mother—he has no choice but to follow her, even though stepping into Faery will force him to face his past. Keeping her safe and out of the hands of the Wizard King also becomes a fight to save Aoife's life from her own mother, who has discovered a time portal in Faery leading her back in time to alter her past mistakes, putting Aoife's life in peril. Sean is willing to do anything to make sure she's safe. Even if it means he has to tap into his dangerous magic to do it.

About the Author

Michelle Miles believes in fairy tales, true love and magic. She is the award-winning author of the epic fantasy, IN THE TOWER OF THE WIZARD KING, as well as the fantasy romance series, REALM OF HONOR, featuring knights and their ladies fair, and the paranormal dragon-shifter romance series, DRAGON PROTECTORS.

In her spare time, she enjoys listening to music, reading, cross-stitching and watching movies. Even though she's a native Texan, she loves castles, dragons, fairies and elves and is an avid Game of Thrones fan. She can be found online at Facebook, Twitter, Instagram, Pinterest, and Goodreads.